I0668442

WHAT SPOOKERY IS THAT?

SAM CHEEVER

ELECTRIC PROSE PUBLICATIONS

ABOUT ROME

Crafting worlds is crazy good fun. Authors love to make stuff up. Sometimes locations that are created for books seem like real places, even though they're not. That's actually good, because it means the author has done her job well. My fictional town of Rome, Indiana is not based on a real place. I've created a location that lives in my mind—one that fits the stories I wanted to tell. Hopefully you have enjoyed the picturesque town of Rome with all its paranormal challenges. I'm thankful for the opportunity to share this fictional town and its inhabitants with you.

xo

Sam Cheever

PRAISE FOR SAM CHEEVER

"You have that essential Je ne sais quoi that it takes to tell a story so mesmerizing you cannot stop reading once started. You are not telling stories to your readers...you are taking them with you on your adventures so that the experience can be shared by all as it happens and not simply replayed like a memory on the page of a diary! You are indeed gifted and it is my pleasure to read your books!"

Valerie Irwin

❧

I'm trying to find my missing Council member, which might involve visiting the spectral plane. Something that I'm strangely not looking forward to. (sarc) The last thing I need is this...this mess. Achieving my full powers feels like mega-menopause, hot flashes and all. Unfortunately, these flashes can actually burn.

Something's changing. Something big. I'm finally achieving the last stage of my Lares power. I realize the transformation is going to be hard. It's going to be painful and confusing. I know all of this because my advocate, the world's crankiest moon hound and consummate know-it-all was elated to inform me about it. What I didn't know was that I'd be trying to save one of my council members and beat off a demon invasion in the middle of the whole mess. Unfortunately, this is all starting to remind me of my initiation into the Lares gig. I barely survived that transition. I'm not so sure I'm going to survive this one.

STAY IN TOUCH

Sam doesn't give away a lot of books. But she values her readers and, to show it, she's gifting you a copy of a fun book just for signing up for her newsletter!

SIGN UP HERE!
https://samcheever.com/newsletter/

THE LARES MUST HER COUNCIL KEEP

When every soul is drawn to see, a place where only death decrees, then life becomes a distant thought, and each torn heart once pleasure wrought, the devil rises on its heels, and every soul its future yields.

A Full Blue Moon Does Magic Hold
Its Rays Ensure Adventure Bold
The Lares Must Her Council Keep
An Unknown Friend, an Intrigue Deep
The Dead Will Roar in Helpless Rage
To Feel the Touch of a Fleshly Sage.
The Lion Bellows and Bares its Claws
The Celestial Spy its Ire Draws
A Supplicant, Her Pain Must Bear
A Bargain Struck, a Price Most Fair
The Lares' Friends are Worse Than Foes
With Weapons Thrown the Tension Grows
A Friend Whose Family Needs Her Aid
A Dastardly Foe His Presence Made
Prisoners of the Beast Afraid

An Unpalatable Plan, a Favor Given
Unlikely Allies, Bargains Driven
Regrets and Revelations Sour
Our Friends Approach Their Darkest Hour
A Warning Comes, its Visions Dire
Regrets Renew the Lares Ire
A Tiny Fiend, a Mystery Brings
Our Heroes Plan, a Loved One Sings
A Demon's Threats Strike the Child Most Dear
The Loss of Heart, the Lares' Fear
A Battle Comes, a Killing Ground
And in the Fight Clarity is Found

1

A FULL BLUE MOON DOES MAGIC HOLD

The moon was blue. It hung over us like a threat, so big and so close I imagined I could feel the touch of its rays against my skin.

My hot, sweaty skin.

Ten feet away, Wanda and Caleigh, otherwise known as the crone, had their heads bent over a grimoire they'd opened in the thick, overlong grass of the graveyard. I'd been informed by my groundskeeper, the gnome, that the grass would go into shock and falter if he cut it so late in the season.

I didn't know about any of that. I just wished it wasn't drenching my sneakers. Blowing air through my lips, I felt instantly shamed. I was a sweaty, cranky mess. I knew my mood was bad, but didn't seem able to do anything about it. I was facing the last stage in becoming a full-fledged Lares, a guardian protector for Rome, Indiana. The process encompassed four levels of acclimation: Understanding, Acceptance, Outreach, and Response. I was working my way through *Response*, and, as far as I could tell, it seemed way too much like menopause.

Just delightful.

I tugged the damp t-shirt away from my chest and sighed as a wisp of cool air slipped beneath it. Impatience rippled under my skin. I bit it back, knowing its source. I'd been impossible to live with for a month. Maybe longer. Really, since my friend and council member, Trish had left us to manage the fairy realm.

With Reverend Dodson also missing, I was feeling out of sorts and scattered.

That was what I blamed it on, at least. But I had a notion that wasn't really the cause.

I had bigger problems.

Wanda broke away from the crone and ambled toward me, her long legs eating up the distance between us and her hands shoved into the pockets of her fashionably ratty jeans. I took a moment to enjoy watching her move. She'd grown a couple of inches since she'd moved in with me. Filled out a little. And her dark brown eyes sparkled with humor and pleasure more often than not. She reminded me of a colt whose legs had grown too fast and she wasn't always sure what to do with them.

I smiled at the thought.

A large black cat trotted after my kid, long tail lazily fanning the air. Wraith fixed me with round, yellow eyes and licked his chops as if wondering if I'd taste like chicken.

The teen stopped in front of me, tucked a heavy strand of straight black hair behind one pierced ear, and frowned. "Aggy, it's sixty degrees out here. Are you sure you don't want your coat?"

I shook my head. The temperature of the air might be sixty degrees, but I might as well be standing on the crust of a volcano judging by my internal temperature. "I'm fine, sweetie. Did you figure it out?"

She narrowed her gaze for a beat. "Are you feeling all right?"

My entire body went rigid with irritation. I tried to hide it, hoping Wanda wouldn't notice. Everybody kept asking me that question and I was getting sick of answering it.

Taking a long slow breath, I forced a smile. "I'm okay." When she started to frown, I reached out and touched the sleeve of her coat. "I promise."

She expelled air. "Okay. Well. We think we know where he has to be." Her gaze slid toward the woods and her frown deepened.

At the back of the wide lawn, galloping from the woods at full speed, the White Mare thundered toward us. Normally, the sight would alarm me. It usually meant trouble. But I knew from my own experience that the magical horse was simply reacting to the magical influences caused by the thinning veil.

The blue moon. I'd been told by the white-haired woman crouched a few feet away that the veil was at its absolute thinnest during a blue moon. I could feel the truth in her statement. Magic danced along my skin, pulling up gooseflesh in its wake.

The crone was wearing faded stretch jeans, bright red sneakers, and a tee-shirt that read "Dachshunds Aren't Dogs. They're Necessities. Like Potato Chips and Wine."

That sentiment wasn't wrong. My own little necessity was in the house romping with the crone's two sweet girls. I could hear their happy yips as they played.

"How much time do we have?" I asked the teen.

Wanda turned around and bellowed. "Caleigh? What's the timeline?"

I tensed every time the girl called the crone by her given name. Something told me the powerful witch slash magical historian didn't allow such intimacies easily or often. But the crone simply pushed herself out of a crouch and started toward us, her gnarled fingers wiggling as if she were mentally doing a math problem.

Or a spell. At five feet six inches tall, the crone was my height and slightly stooped from her unknown but decidedly advanced age. Her abundance of white hair blasted straight up from her scalp, rolled into a soft lift at the crown, and then plummeted straight down to skim the tops of her flat butt cheeks. Her eyes were her best feature. They were a beautiful ocean blue, touched with green and silver specks that made them always seem to dance with humor.

"Eight hours," she finally said. "In and out. If you're not out by then, you're stayin' there."

Ignoring Wanda's worried gaze, I asked, "Where exactly am I going?" I really didn't want to know...but I needed to.

To say I wasn't excited about ducking into the spirit realm to rescue my missing ghostly council member would be a massive understatement. I'd grown accustomed to the ghosts who haunted the little church graveyard and had considered Reverend Dodson a friend. But my advisor, the ever-snotty moon-hound shifter, Sir Ferral of the Guardian Assembly, a.k.a. my advocate, informed me that the spirits in the spiritual realm were generally a nasty bunch. It appeared the closer they got to the heart of spookdom, the meaner a spirit became. He'd also delighted in informing me that the kind and benevolent Reverend Dodson might not even know who I was if he'd gone too deep, which would make him a solid "them" in the "us vs them" column.

Swear.

Since it was Ferral's job to keep me informed and up-to-date on all the weird stuff my new role as Lares guardian for the tiny town of Rome, Indiana threw at me, I trusted him.

He was generally an arrogant as...um...jerk, but he did know his stuff.

"I don't suppose you can tell by all that..." I swirled a finger in the general direction of the open grimoire. "...magic stuff, where the Rev is and if he's gone mutant on us?"

The crone glared at me from her mostly unlined face. The only signs of age on her face were a sunburst of "laugh lines" at the corners of her eyes, badly misnamed in her case, and the area around her mouth, which was heavily lined, probably because she had a bad habit of pursing her lips as she was currently doing, making her mouth resemble an anus. I squelched a smile at the thought. "I'm not a magical GPS, Lares. Nor am I a mystical mood ring."

Wanda snorted before catching a look from me that turned her expression neutral.

"What I *can* tell you is that you're going to be fighting for your life in there." She frowned, a smidgeon of warmth taking some of the coolness from her blue eyes. "Are you sure you want to go in there alone, girl? There's a reason you have a council, you know."

Wanda nodded enthusiastically. "Let me go with you," she said, her tight expression revealing the full extent of her concern.

I shook my head. "I need to go it alone," I said, my gut twisting at the thought.

"Who says?" barked the crone, sounding like an angry kid on the playground. "Is it written in the stars?"

I narrowed my eyes at her mockery. Even if I'd wanted to, I couldn't tell her why I felt an immutable need to enter the spiritual realm alone. I couldn't tell her because I didn't understand it myself. So, instead of responding to her question, I asked a new one of my own. "When do I need to go in?"

The crone held my gaze for a long moment. I got the sense she was considering pressing for a response to her question, but she broke eye contact before I did—go me—and shook her head. "Before the moon falls from the sky."

Then she turned on her heels and headed for the White Mare, who was waiting patiently for her near the house. The crone gave a shrill whistle and the door to my house swung open, seemingly without any help. Two little female dachshunds ran barking out of the house, my little darling, Monty, hot on their heels.

"Oh no you don't," I said, reaching out to snag him as he ran past. "The girls are going home, and you're staying here."

He barked enthusiastically in my arms, his happy brown gaze following them into the forest bordering my property. As they disappeared from sight, he sagged, whining unhappily.

I kissed him between his sad eyes. "Sorry, little man. We'll have another play date soon."

He lay his glossy head on my shoulder and sighed.

Wanda giggled. "You've broken him."

I grinned, bumping her shoulder as we fell into step, heading for the house. High above us, a dark shape fluttered against the night sky and yellow eyes shone through the darkness. I settled Monty's feet into the grass and he took off running toward the house, racing Wanda.

Watching them go, I smiled.

The spirit realm is restless.

I glanced up at the bat, which darted to and fro, chasing bugs that should have already been gone at that time of year. "I'm going in soon."

When?

"Early tomorrow morning."

The bat fluttered up to the belfry high above my head. I glanced up as moonlight painted a ribbon of light across its midnight-hued wings.

He's deep into the spiritual realm, Batty told me. *It's not going to be easy to get him out.*

I opened my mouth to respond as agony tightened through my middle, and I doubled over, a scream throbbing in my throat.

Wings fluttered overhead and a raven cawed three times. A beat later, the door to the house slammed open and I heard Wanda calling my name.

Footsteps pounded toward me. Wanda's small hands, nails painted bright pink, grabbed my shoulders and eased me backward onto the grass. I sat down hard as another wave of misery clawed through me. Riding the wave were hundreds of voices, pleading for help, for advice, or just to be heard. It was overwhelming, impossible, and I fought to shut it down because it felt like the pleas were tearing me apart.

Soft hands pushed strands of silver-tipped black hair off my face and told me to take slow, careful breaths.

The jagged claws of pain eased slowly away and I was finally able to breathe.

A raven cawed again, closer than before. The big black bird dropped to the grass beside me and began to pace, its wings lifting and lowering with apparent stress. "Pee!" the raven announced enthusiastically.

I laughed, wincing as my stomach tightened around the pain. "Yeah, I almost peed myself too."

The raven ducked its head a few times and then, with a final caw, took to the air and flew away.

Wanda sat down next to me. "Is it getting better?"

I nodded, one hand rubbing my stomach where the pain had been.

"Aggy, you can't go into the spiritual realm by yourself. What if you have an attack and nobody's there to help you?"

The "attack" she referred to was a side-effect of my body reaching for the final level of power inherent in my Lares magic. As my advocate, Ferral, had explained, the last phase included an elevated ability to mentally communicate as well as the ability to fix things without physically being present. The transformation required a full physiological overhaul that was extensive and painful.

I'd reached the third level several months earlier, but ascending to the last one had been slow in coming.

Judging by the pain of reaching it, I'd be okay if it took its sweet time. Or never came at all.

"I'm going to talk to Ferral about someone coming with you."

I shook my head. "No."

Wanda frowned, clearly annoyed that I wouldn't listen to reason...her reason, which, as a teen, she believed was the only reason there should be. I knew she didn't understand why I'd been digging in my heels. But I couldn't explain the feeling that I wouldn't need anybody to come with me. That I'd have everything I needed to accomplish my task when I crossed into spirit realm.

Besides, I had a burning need to prove myself worthy of attaining the fourth level of magic. Since taking over the Lares job, I'd been plagued by feelings of inadequacy and self-doubt. I couldn't shake the feeling that the magic had been given to the wrong person. Despite the fact that my own father, who for all intents and purposes had abandoned me when I was fifteen, was also a Lares, I couldn't get past the fact that I hadn't even known magic existed until I was already ankle deep in my seating, the hellish process I'd gone through to become Lares.

Andrew Lenore had left my mother and me behind to pursue his own guardianship. The scars of that rejection still stung, even thirty years later.

A new tightness began to build in my gut. Seconds before the wave of jagged pain hit me again, cold, oily sweat broke out on my forehead and trickled between my shoulder blades.

I took a deep breath and clenched my teeth against the building pain.

I had no idea how I was going to rescue Reverend Dodson from the spiritual realm in my current condition.

But somehow, I had to do it.

2

ITS RAYS ENSURE ADVENTURE BOLD

Delicious, soothing hot water sluiced over me. I smiled at the sound of Monty barking in the distance. My little man was twenty-five pounds, covered in silky black fur that flared away from his legs like the boots pirates used to wear and curled over his soft, floppy ears. Monty was a standard-sized black and tan dachshund. He had the charm, cleverness, energy, and unflagging drive to eat that were inherent in every doxie.

It was the eating thing that kept me on my toes.

The barking likely meant that Monty was begging for food, and I'd bet my left big toe he was succeeding. I sighed. According to the vet, he should be two or three pounds lighter. But I was never going to get those pounds off him because he charmed everyone in his sphere into feeding him tasty tidbits all day long.

I'd left Wanda and my adopted mother slash ex-mother-in-law, Mavis Adyms in the kitchen, cooking up a midnight mystery meal that smelled amazing.

As I stepped out of my new shower onto the thin rug I'd stretched over the naked plywood floor, a deep, sonorous tone filled the little church I called home. The doorbell, a gift from my sister, sounded like the gonging of a church bell, a fact that made me smile each time it rang.

And speaking of my sister. A confident female voice called out as Bev announced her arrival in my room. I barely got the towel wrapped around my dripping body before she stuck her blonde, ponytailed head through the door, looking around. "Hey, nice shower. Any chance you're going to add walls and a floor some day?"

I gave her a look. "I have walls."

She grimaced at the unpainted drywall. "If you can call them that." Despite the criticism, her gray eyes sparkled.

I shivered. "Can we maybe table the construction discussion until I'm dressed?"

Bev grinned. "Okay, but don't dally. Mom says you need to eat before you leave."

I arched a soggy black brow and shooed her out with a flap of my hand. "I'll be out in a minute." Talking about my partially baked master bathroom and bedroom project was a sore subject for me. My friend and council member, Trish, had been doing the work. It had been somewhat sidelined when I'd brought my ward Wanda into the house because she'd needed a bedroom and that had been more important. Then a Trickster had moved into Rome and the other half of my remodel, my candle shop, had been put on hold in favor of letting our favorite brownie Tilly, bake and sell delectable treats in the space.

Having a magically delicious bakery in my home clearly had benefits, but losing my contractor to her duties as an Ancient Warrior Fairy queen of the unseelie branch had been hard on both a personal and professional level. Unfortunately, the first fairy queen had needed to be dethroned, and Trish had been the only one willing to temporarily take the throne so that her people could return the land of Fairy to its former glory. I fully supported what Trish was trying to do. I'd helped her do it, in fact, but I'd yet to find a decent contractor to replace her, and my projects were suffering as a result.

I brushed my wet, straight black hair, eyeing the silver ends curling at my shoulders and thinking it might be time to get rid of them. I was getting tired of the same style. Maybe something shorter...bouncier. At forty-five years old, I'd been wondering if my long hair made me look like I was trying to be younger than I was.

"Food's ready!" Mavis yelled down the hallway as I pulled on my battle leathers and boots. I sighed as I tugged the heavy, constrictive clothing on, wishing I could pull on yoga pants and a sweatshirt instead. I brushed out my wet hair and stared at myself in the mirror for a moment, noting the dark circles that had moved in under my hazel eyes as the *Response* level pounded the snot out of me physically and spiritually.

Taking a deep breath, I slowly released it, willing myself to rise to the occasion. At least my stomach had stopped screaming at me, and I'd stopped sweating.

Hopefully I could get into and out of the spiritual realm before my body turned against me again.

As I stepped out into the hallway, the sound of oversized wings filled my ears. I jolted to a stop, looking up at the ceiling. My favorite angel had arrived.

Behind me, the front door opened and slammed shut. I bit back an alarmed squeal and whipped around to yell at the advocate. Because nobody but Ferral slammed a door unnecessarily like that. I nearly screamed for help when I saw him.

Something was horribly wrong. He was smiling!

I narrowed my gaze. "What's wrong?"

My advocate strode toward me, the smile still firmly in place. "Nothing's wrong. Why do you ask?"

I twirled a finger in front of his face. "I think your facial muscles are broken. Your lips are curving upward in the corners. Have you been spelled?"

Adding to my alarm, Ferral laughed. I took two steps back and my staff, which had been sleeping in my room until I needed it, smacked into my palm. "Who are you and what have you done with my cranky advocate?"

Ferral's dark silver gaze sparkled with mirth. I looked him over, noting that his wavy blond hair had been pulled back into a ponytail at the nape of his neck. The style emphasized his strong jaw and sharp features, making him look even more handsome than usual. Or maybe it was the new light in his eyes.

He held my gaze for a beat and then shook his head. Reaching into the pocket of his leather jacket, he pulled out a well-creased envelope, offering it to me.

"Ah," I said, understanding blooming. "This is your resignation letter. That's why you look so cheerful."

Ferral rolled his eyes, an affectation he'd picked up from Wanda. He'd never perfect the action like my favorite teen had, but he carried it off better than expected.

The moon-hound shifter was ancient, with centuries of trends and postures beneath his belt. But until he'd met my magical historian, he'd seemed steeped in ancient manners and stuffiness. It said something about the strength of Wanda's personality that he mimicked her expressions even a little bit.

Though the mockery of the eye roll seemed perfectly suited to his air of constant and persevering disgust where I was concerned.

"No such luck for you, I'm afraid." Ferral nodded toward the envelope in my hand. "That, Madam Lares, is recompense for your first year of service."

I stared at him. A shocked look weighing my features down. "Recompense?" I knew what the word meant. At least, I thought I did. "They're finally paying me?"

They being the Council of Guardians. The overseeing body for all earthbound Lares. I'd known I was supposed to be compensated for my work as guardian Lares for Rome, Indiana. But as the months had spun past with no word and no "recompense" I'd given up hope of ever seeing it.

In the meantime, my savings had been depleting at an alarming rate and I'd been unable to pay any of my council for their invaluable work. A situation that made me very unhappy.

I valued my people. Two of them, Mavis and Bev, I'd considered family since I'd been basically orphaned at the age of fifteen.

As I tore the envelope open, I didn't expect much. But, whatever it was, I'd divvy it up between my council. They'd more than earned it, and I was getting good at making ends meet without it.

Soft footsteps came up behind me. I felt a warm presence a beat before soft arms wrapped around me in a side hug, enveloping me in a sweet rose scent. "You need to eat something before you go, honey," Mavis said, her voice soft. "You'll need your strength."

I leaned into her, nodding. "I'm coming. Ferral brought me something I need to see..."

All the air whooshed out of my lungs as I removed a check from the envelope. I stared at it for a beat before the number of zeros sank in. It was ten times what I'd expected. "There has to be some mistake."

"No mistake," Ferral said gleefully. "We've earned every penny."

I gasped in delayed reaction, my legs going wobbly.

Heavy footsteps pounded my way and a strong set of arms caught me as I wobbled.

Lungren Maker's delicious scent washed over me. I looked up into an angelic countenance, with molten brown eyes, glossy mahogany hair that fell around his strong chin in soft waves. My own personal angel made as if to hoist me into his arms but I stopped him with a shake of my head. I looked up into his molten brown gaze and went all gooey inside. For a beat, I forgot what had thrown me off my feet.

Gren nodded at the piece of paper in my hands, frowning. "Trouble?"

I tore my gaze from his, dazed as I looked down at the check. An enormous number—for me at least—stared back at me. "Not trouble. No." I said, my voice filled with wonder. "Good news." I finally found a smile as it sank in. "We got paid."

He held my gaze a moment longer, uncertainty in his expression, and then matched my smile. "It's about time they paid you," he said. "You've more than earned it."

And I had. It had been a rough eight months and I still had many challenges ahead. I didn't respond, only nodded, because I was afraid if I tried to speak I'd start crying.

"Okay," Mavis said. "I hate to rush you, but Wanda told me you're on a timeline..."

Back to work. I bit back a sigh. Handing the check to Ferral, I said, "You'll pay everyone?"

He nodded, taking it from me. "I'll pay bills, refurbish your savings, and distribute back pay to everyone who can spend it."

He was referring to my friend in the belfry and the Rev.

Even Ray, had helped us more than a few times. None of them would be walking into the grocery to buy chips and dip. I'd find another way to pay my non-living and non-human council members for their invaluable services.

I nodded. "Good. Thanks." Throwing an arm around Mavis' shoulders, I guided her toward the kitchen. At five feet seven, my sixty-two-year-old adopted mother was taller than I was by an inch, but her slender form made me feel much bigger. "Now tell me what that delicious smell is."

"Beef Stroganoff," she said with a wide grin. "An Adyms family recipe."

I snorted. "You've been waiting all this time to say Adyms family haven't you?"

Mavis released the laugh she'd been holding back. "I have. But I promise there's no eye of newt in this dish. Just beef, sour cream, and a little tomato paste."

"Sounds delicious," I said, giving her a hug. "And it smells even better. If you tell me you have a warm loaf of Tilly's whole grain and seed bread to go with it, I'll love you forever."

She tightened the arm she'd dropped around my waist. "You already love me. And who can blame you?"

I laughed.

Bev was putting bowls of stroganoff on the table when we entered the brightly-lit kitchen. Wanda dropped a basket of something wrapped in cloth in the center and the yeasty scent of warm bread wafted my way. Gren stepped past me, enclosing my arm in a brief, possessive grip as he headed toward the refrigerator. "Wine?"

I nodded, then reconsidered. I would be fighting for my life in a short while. Did I really want to do that with a soft wine buzz? Yep. Absolutely. "I'll have half a glass of the Riesling," I told him. "Thanks."

"Sit, honey," my adopted mom encouraged. "Eat. You'll need your strength."

I sat, taking the wine Gren handed me. Rather than sitting down at the table, he stood behind me, his warmth a wall of reassurance I wanted to lean into. I looked down at the savory dish in front of me. It looked delicious, but the smell that had drawn me in earlier no longer appealed. My stomach twisted with fear and dread for what I was about to do.

The rich, bold tones of a church bell filled the church and the front door opened, the change in air pressure tugging the curtains hanging over the window above the sink. A beat later, the front door closed and a familiar step, made heavy by steel-toed boots, clomped toward us.

Luke walked into the kitchen, flinching slightly when he saw us all staring at him. "Sorry," he said. "Am I late? Sorry."

A wolf shifter, Luke was pretty much what you'd expect in his human form. Though he wasn't exceptionally handsome, his grace and strength were very appealing, and his golden-brown eyes, though piercing when his emotions were high, brought out the golden highlights in his short-cropped brown hair. The perennial stubble on his lean cheeks seemed natural for a man who turned furry when the situation called for it.

"I had to feed Trish's canine crew before I came," he explained.

When Trish had decided to take the throne at Fairy, she'd asked her best friend Luke to keep her dogs for her. He'd moved into her small house rather than trying to keep them in his apartment. It had been a kind and selfless thing and I respected him for his sacrifice. I was also relieved, because if he hadn't stepped up, I'd have done it just so Trish didn't have to worry about her fur-babies. I would have loved having the dogs, but Monty was a handful all by himself. I wasn't sure I could handle any more.

Mavis patted his back. "You're just in time. Wash up and I'll get you a bowl of food."

Gren offered my resident wolf shifter a hand. "We haven't seen you in a while."

Taking Gren's hand, Luke's gaze slid guiltily toward me. "I'm sorry. It's just that, with Trish gone..." His voice trailed away. He looked so unhappy I felt a jolt of guilt. Of course he was suffering from the loss of his friend. I should have done a better job of keeping in touch with him.

I stood and walked over, forcing him to hold my gaze. "I'm guessing that having her gone has left a lot of work for you to keep up with."

He nodded. "It's been keeping me busy." He shifted uncomfortably. "But I can handle that. It's just that..."

"You miss her." I kept my voice soft. The others, seemingly realizing our conversation was private, had returned to conversation and activity as plates were filled and food devoured.

"I do. She's my friend. I'm also worried."

He didn't need to elaborate. I understood. Though Trish's decision to stay in Fairy had been her own, and a selfless choice to help her people, the situation was far from safe. There were many factions within Fairy that made intrigue and danger daily problems. "When I get back, you and I will go see her. Okay?"

A light filled his worried gaze. His lips twitched upward in the corners. "I'd like that."

I pulled him into an impulsive hug. "Me too. Now eat. There's plenty. As usual, Mavis made enough for an army."

"It's a good thing," my ward said, grinning. "Because that's what she's feeding. An army."

She wasn't wrong.

We ate, and chatted, and laughed. For a while, it almost felt like old times. I even managed to make a dent in the mound of food Mavis had given me. Unfortunately, every few minutes I'd remember that I needed to leave soon, and my stomach would twist with worry.

Finally, when Wanda gave me a look, I sipped the last drops of my wine and stood. Conversation ground to a stop, all eyes rising to mine. "I need to go..."

My goodbyes were dashed to a halt as the back door flew open and a small form buzzed through, magic boiling around her. "Aggy! Thank the goddess. I need your help."

3

THE LARES MUST HER COUNCIL KEEP

The tension shot skyward in the kitchen.

All eyes locked on the tiny warrior fairy and then slid to me. I stared at Trish, so shocked to see her in my kitchen, I was at a loss as to what to say.

Luke stepped around me and hurried across the room, stopping just short of Trish and staring at her with a shocked expression. "You're back."

Trish's tiny features showed an array of emotions. Pleasure at seeing him. Doubt. Worry. Then regret.

It was the final emotion that finally spurred me to action. I cleared my throat and Luke snapped a look my way. His expression closed down and he stepped back, shoving his hands into the pockets of his jeans.

I bowed my head. "Queen Trish. I hope all is well in Fairy."

Trish's expression showed frustration. "Ah!" she exclaimed. In a burst of light and fairy dust, she left her fairy form behind and was standing before me in her usual garb of aged jeans and a white tee shirt underneath a pink, black, and white flannel shirt. She held a silver backpack in one hand.

Trish lifted her arms to Luke, offering him a hug. He quickly accepted, squeezing her hard enough to lift her off her small feet. "I've missed you," Luke said, stepping back with a grin.

Trish laughed. "I've missed you too." She clasped his hand. Her gaze slid around the room. "All of you."

The back door slammed open again and a naked man covered in garden soil flew into the room, his stick and berries waving merrily for all to see.

A chorus of groans filled the room as the gnome stalked inside. Bev reached into the pantry and tugged out a pair of the moss shorts she'd made special for my grounds keeper. "Here. Don't scar the teenager for life."

I glanced at Wanda and found her hiding her eyes behind her hands.

Gren laughed softly and Mavis wrapped her arms around my kid in a motherly hug.

But Niele's heavy features were folded into a frown. He wasn't amused. My groundskeeper ran a beefy hand through his frizzy silver hair, his small black eyes filled with worry. "Madam Lares, the walls of the graveyard are illuminated in a silvery light. I think it's time for you to go."

I wanted to swear. I hadn't expected it for at least another hour!

I looked from Trish to Niele, torn. "Um. Trish...I..."

But Trish solved my problem. "Let's go," she said.

I blinked. "Uh..."

She reached out and grabbed my hand, giving me a tug toward the door. "Come on. I'll explain on the way."

Everyone followed us out the door. I was relieved to see that Niele had donned his moss britches. Wanda fell into step with us, explaining that the crone had told her the opening to the spiritual realm would only remain open for fifteen minutes once it appeared.

I had only moments to say my goodbyes.

Fear and regret clamped down on my lungs and I struggled to breathe. It took a moment before I realized Trish was talking. Forcing my thoughts away, I focused on her words.

"...got to get him back. Fae don't do well in that realm. I figure he's got about twenty-four hours before he fades completely away."

I jerked to a stop and looked into her eyes, seeing real fear in their vivid green depths. "Are you telling me someone from Fairy is in the spiritual realm?"

She nodded, blinking back her tears. "He was going to be my salvation, Aggy. He was going to save us all."

Well, that certainly sounded intriguing.

"You want me to look for him?" I asked, feeling the panic-induced clamp on my lungs tightening. I didn't know how I was going to find the Rev, let alone some unknown fairy I'd never met.

She shook her head, whipping the fine, blonde strands around her face. "I'm going with you. I need to find him." Displeasure must have shown in my expression because she hurried to add, "I know you're looking for Reverend Dodson. Maybe I can help you find him. Maybe we can help each other."

"Trish..."

She draped the backpack over a slender shoulder and threw herself into my arms, catching me off guard. If Gren hadn't been standing behind me, we would have both probably hit the ground. "Please, Aggy. The fact that you're going to Spirit seems fated. Without your help, I couldn't have found a way inside. That I have this chance is a miracle. Please let me come. Please help me save him."

I didn't know who the fairy was she was trying to save. I didn't understand why he was important. But I knew Trish. She was my friend. My council member. I couldn't bring myself to tell her no. I nodded and she hugged me again.

"Thank you." Her words came out in a sob and I squeezed her tight.

"You need to go, Madam Lares," Niele warned. "The light is fading."

My gaze whipped in that direction and I panicked.

"Woof!" I looked down at Monty and tears burned my eyes. My gaze found Wanda's. "Take care of him for me?" The meaning behind my request was implied. *If I don't come back.*

The teen understood. "Of course." She gave me a quick hug.

I snatched Monty off the ground, kissed him between his bright brown eyes, and handed him to Wanda so he wouldn't follow me into the graveyard.

Mavis and Bev were crying. I hugged them tight. "I'll see you soon," I promised, my own tears blurring my vision.

They nodded and stepped back, looking as worried as I felt.

A big, sexy body stepped in front of me. I looked up into Gren's intense brown gaze. Tears fell freely down my cheeks. I let myself get wrapped into his tight embrace and he placed his lips against my ear. "Take care, lovely Aggy. Don't make me come in there after you."

I gave a watery laugh and rose onto my tiptoes, pressing my lips against his. The kiss was sweet and warm, a promise I couldn't voice because fear and doubt kept the words locked inside me. With a soft sob I hoped no one heard, I broke the kiss and turned away. I started to run, seeing the weak silver illumination in front of me beginning to fade. Trish popped into her warrior form and flew ahead, glancing back every few seconds to see how close I was.

The light flickered when I was still several yards away. The illumination began sinking beneath the soil.

Panic encouraged me to pick up my speed, but it wouldn't be enough.

We were going to miss the window.

We weren't going to make it.

Trish stopped just outside the quickly disappearing illumination. "Hurry!" she yelled. I tried to run faster, but I'd reached my top speed. My heart throbbed in my chest. My breaths came out in gasps. Behind me, a dense throbbing sound pulsed the air. I wanted to look back, but knew it would lose me precious seconds.

The light ahead gave a long, slow flicker. So long I thought it was gone.

But then I noticed a slender glimmer of light just at the tip of the grass and prayed it would last until I...

Strong hands slipped beneath my arms. My feet left the ground As the seconds beat away my chance at success, massive wings throbbed above me and the distance between me and the graveyard quickly disappeared. Just before the light dissolved for good, Gren's wings gave a final powerful throb, Trish sped across the line with us, and the familiar world around me disappeared into a wash of muddy gray bleakness that ripped away every fiber of hope I'd been clutching that the spiritual realm wouldn't be so bad after all.

The grip under my arms disappeared and I fell. It was only a few feet to the ground, but I hadn't been expecting it and landed hard, the rocky ground a brutal cushion for my landing.

Trish cried out as she hit the ground, her slender form crashing down half on top of me.

"Umph," I grunted as she kicked me in the side with a heavy, scarred boot.

"Sorry." She rolled away, landing on her back and staring up into a boiling red sky. "Ugh."

I nodded, eyeing the maelstrom above as if it were lava preparing to roll over us.

For all I knew, it was.

Trish groaned again and I looked at her for the first time. I gasped. Blood gushed from a large wound in her head and she was holding one arm that was already turning purple beneath the sleeve of her tee. I shoved upright. "My goddess! Trish..." I reached for her arm but stopped when she flinched. "What happened? Why aren't you in your fairy form?"

She struggled to a seated position, the arm nestled protectively against her belly. "I don't know. As soon as we went through the barrier I lost my magic."

I had a terrifying thought. My eyes shot skyward. "Gren!"

Trish took in our yellow-gray surroundings. "I don't see him. Maybe he made it back out."

"Or maybe he didn't get sucked inside," I murmured, embracing the hope like a prayer.

Trish tried to shove to her feet and fell back, yelping as her injured arm was jostled.

"Here, let me help." I got to my feet and moved to grab her good arm. Between the two of us, we managed to get her on her feet, but she swayed violently once there, in danger of passing out. I wrapped an arm around her waist. "Do you need to sit down again?"

She shook her head and then grimaced, likely because the action jostled her throbbing head. "We need to move. The gateway will pass in a little under eight hours. We have to find them and get back here before then."

I wondered how she knew that but figured I'd ask later... after we got ourselves and the two men we were searching for out of there. But before we started...

I shrugged the small backpack off my shoulders and opened it. "Let me do some quick first aid before we go."

Trish started to argue but I held up a hand. "In your current condition all you'll do is slow us down." My coldly efficient tone rubbed me the wrong way. But I was right so I forced my lips to close, biting back the apology that wanted to escape.

Trish nodded. "Okay. Make it fast though."

As I set to work giving her pain meds, cleaning and bandaging her head wound as best I could, and fashioning a sling for her arm, Trish's gaze continually swept the area. Her vivid green gaze was brittle, intense.

"Are you looking for something specific?" I asked. I hated to admit it to myself, but she was making me nervous. Apparently, I hadn't been taking the danger seriously enough, considering her mood.

Her gaze swung to me, softening slightly. I must have looked like I was going to pee myself judging by the way she forced a smile. "Just memorizing this place. We'll need to mark our trail somehow so we can get back."

I rezipped my pack and gave her a tight smile. "With little pieces of peanut butter filled candy?"

She barked out a laugh. "It worked for ET."

With the laugh, the friend I knew returned. Trish lost a bit of the haunted look. I wondered what she'd been going through in Fairy. Nothing good, I speculated. I nodded toward the scrub trees that clung to a poor excuse for a life in the hard, dusty ground. "We can wrap small pieces of bandage on trees and bushes."

She nodded, eyeing my pack. "How much do you have in there?"

Not nearly enough, I thought. But I pushed the thought away. We'd make it work. "Worst case we can tear strips off our clothing."

"Great," Trish said with a flat laugh. "Luke will never let me live it down if I return in nothing but my boots."

I couldn't help it, I cringed at the thought. "We'll keep our bras and panties." The idea of leaving my granny panties hanging from a bush in the spiritual realm gave me indigestion. If I ended up having to do that, I was definitely going to have to live forever.

I was *not* returning to the ribbing *that* would earn me in the afterlife.

4

AN UNKNOWN FRIEND, AN INTRIGUE DEEP

I t was dark in the spiritual realm. We'd been walking for about a half hour and I'd been unable to see any identifying marks or delineations between areas. Ferral had told me it was a realm of interconnected, nested areas shaped vaguely like spreading puddles of water. Each area, according to my teen magical historian, had its own traps and challenges.

The crone had told me the Rev was located near a trap in the center of the realm, a noxious space filled with poisonous gases, plunged forever in darkness, and filled to the brim with frantic, desperate souls.

Lovely.

"How big is this place?" I asked Trish. "It doesn't seem possible we can get to the center and back in eight hours."

She shook her head. "We might not be able to. It's a best guess. There are no guarantees."

I definitely didn't like the sound of that. "Okay," I said, not happy. "That's not great."

"On the positive side, the spiritual realm isn't like the physical realm," she explained. "It doesn't take up space like you're thinking. It's amorphous and unformed like the spirits that inhabit it."

I tried to wrap my mind around that for a few minutes. I had more questions. But first... "Who is this guy you're trying to retrieve? Do you know where to find him?"

Trish didn't speak for a long moment. I glanced her way and was surprised to see a look of pure panic on her delicate features. Reaching out, I clasped her uninjured arm. "Hey. Talk to me. What's going on?"

Trish shook her head.

"I need to know what's going on, Trish. It will likely affect my retrieval of the Rev."

She sighed. "Hopefully, he's the future king of the fairies."

I jolted to a stop, my mouth hanging open. "Future...? Did you say king?"

I had so many questions. So. Many. Questions. I started with probably the least important for our journey but most important to me. "Does that mean you're going to marry him?"

A look of horror transformed Trish's face. I frowned, wondering why my question horrified her. A soft green glow suffused the warrior fairy and then faded, sputtering away. "Run!" she screamed.

I spun to see what she was looking at and felt my own eyes go wide. "Goddess!" I yelled, my feet rooted to the spot as a wall of swirling fog roiled toward us. The enormous wall reached from the hard, rocky dirt high into the sky, blocking everything in our path. Within its chaotic churn floated skeletal faces with wide, black gazes and lips spread in silent screams.

Trish tugged hard on my arm, her words lost beneath the ominous sound of cracking that followed the wall's passage toward us. That was the point when I realized every rock and every tree the wall touched became flash-frozen, breaking into dust beneath the entity's devastating touch.

If we didn't start moving, Trish and I would join the immortal chorus of pain and agony within that chaos.

I all but levitated off the ground, my feet kicking up dust and a sulfurous kind of smoke that clung to the soil, releasing its foul taint to the air with every footstep.

Something gave a hoarse cry and I looked up to see a skeletal-looking bird getting sucked into the maelstrom.

I dug in, my heart slamming against my ribs and my breathing harsh with effort. My muscles burned but didn't give out as adrenaline drove me forward.

The air turned blustery. An icy mist bathed my back. My legs burned with a new kind of danger.

The cracking sound came closer...loud and relentless.

Trish stumbled and nearly fell. I closed the space between us and grabbed her arm just as icy fire lit my calves. With a scream, I saw our only hope ahead, and shoved Trish into it, leaping in after her as the icy wall rolled over the spot where we'd been.

The ground fell away and I hit a hard, sulfurous-smelling protrusion before plunging downward, into pure, unrelenting darkness.

Trish's grunts as she crashed into the wall were the only warning I got before I slammed into it too. Agony flared across my arms, my legs and my skull as I bounced from rock, to rock, to rock.

I hit the ground and more of the sulfurous smoke I'd noticed outside wafted up around me in a choking fog. Coughing violently, I tried to expel it from my lungs.

I lay there panting, my chest heaving, as the ominous sound of cracking moved by overhead.

Trish's coughing was every bit as violent as mine. She also sounded as if she'd landed farther away from me than she should have. "You okay?" I asked her between my own bouts of coughing.

It took her a moment to respond. Finally, she cleared her throat. "Mostly. The good news is that I managed not to land on my injured arm," she said in a rough voice. "The bad news is that now both arms hurt."

I snorted out a laugh. "I think I broke my head."

Shuffling noises moved my way. I assumed it was Trish moving closer and forced myself to stay very still. She stopped when our knees touched. Apparently she was lying on her side too. "That was fun," she said.

I shook my head. "What was that thing?"

"I have no idea. But let's stay away from it."

"Good plan." I sat up, biting back a groan as my entire body throbbed in pain. I squinted into the blackness. "We need to move but I can't see anything."

Trish coughed again. "We could sure use Luke's night vision right about now."

Despite her inability to see me, I nodded. Luke was a wolf-shifter and his eyesight was nearly as good at night as it was during the day. However, that assumed there was even a modicum of light for him to glom onto.

The cavern into which we'd leaped appeared to be completely devoid of illumination.

I shivered violently, my teeth chattering. For a moment, I was afraid the icy wall had found us, but nothing in the underground cavern was freezing or cracking into bits, so that was good.

"It's always cold here," Trish said, sounding as if she knew that for a fact.

"Have you been here before?" I asked, hugging myself with my goose-pimpled arms.

Her shoulder moved against mine and I pictured her shaking her head. "I've been undergoing training on the realm for the last couple of weeks."

So had I, but it appeared my training had been less thorough than hers. Then it hit me what she was saying. "You've been planning on piggybacking on my trip."

She went very still. For a moment she didn't speak. Then, "I have. I'm sorry I didn't ask you, but things are... sensitive in Fairy right now."

"Does this guy you're hunting for have something to do with that sensitivity?"

A sigh filled the space between us. "His name is Nova. He's a prince of the seelie court."

My eyes went wide. "What's your connection to him?"

"I'm sure you know the two courts aren't generally on good terms..."

I started to nod, remembered, and then said, "That's what I thought."

"In general, we're not. But Nova was banished from seelie."

"Banished? Why?"

"That's not important right now. What is important is that he has won the favor of much of the unseelie court. He has agreed to be judged for the throne."

I thought about my part in Trish temporarily taking over the throne. It had required me to sponsor and vouch for her. With my blood and, I'd later learned, potentially my life. "Does he have a sponsor?"

Silence.

"Trish?"

She cleared her throat. A feeling of dread slid through me. "Tell me you didn't?"

"I had to. I need a replacement and he's perfect."

"Is he though?" I asked, worry sounding like anger in my voice. "How well do you know him? Well enough to risk your life in a sponsorship?"

"It's a risk I'm willing to take."

That wasn't exactly an answer to my question. I wished I could see her face. Maybe I could read something there that would help me understand. "How did he end up here?"

"That's a long story. We need to..."

"Trish." I used my Madam Lares tone and she stilled. Tension fairly vibrated through the darkness separating us. "I'm worried about you," I added softly.

She sighed again. "There's another who covets the throne."

I frowned. She'd only been on the throne for a month and she was already starting to sound as if she'd never left Fairy.

"...is vile and not to be trusted. She called the spirits to her and set them on Nova. It was the most disgusting display of her dark power. I cannot allow her to become queen."

I'd missed the culprit's name with my woolgathering, but it didn't matter anyway. "If you need to take her down, I'll support you."

The rustling of cloth told me she was shaking her head, shifting nervously. "I cannot. She has presented an intention to fight for the throne. My hands are tied."

"Can she beat Nova?"

Rather than answer my direct question, Trish said, "Nova was one of the elite guard in seelie."

Spoken like a true politician. "But he was thrown out of seelie. Why?"

"The king died and the queen remarried."

Though she hadn't answered my question directly... again...I got the gist of it without any details. The queen remarries. The new man is jealous of the queen's son. The queen's son is framed for some crime and removed as an obstacle. I shook my head, wondering how so many otherwise smart women allowed themselves to be manipulated by men. "He seems to have seriously bad luck with women."

I kept my tone light and Trish snorted. "Understatement."

"So..." I expelled air and pushed to my feet. "How are we going to navigate this cavern so we can get back to the task at hand?" I would leave fairy palace intrigue to Trish for the time being. I'd help her find this Nova guy if it didn't interfere with bringing back the Rev. And I'd bribe my warrior fairy with one of Tilly's chocolate-chocolate-chip muffins for more details when we got back to Rome.

"Without magic, I don't know," she said thoughtfully.

I reached for the stored magic at my core and found nothing. Flattening my hand, palm up before me, I said, "Illumine."

Nothing happened. Panic flared. Gren and Ferral had neglected to mention that I'd be without power to defend myself. That seemed like kind of a large oversight. "Me neither, apparently," I said.

Then I remembered the weapon I'd shoved into my pocket. I pulled it out and shook it once, hard. The staff expanded and hope soared. "Hold the fort," I said. "Maybe..."

Holding it in front of my face, I thought about what I needed.

Nothing.

I sighed. "Never mind. I don't suppose ghosts are vulnerable to big sticks with useless orbs on the end?"

She chuckled. Her clothing swished as she stood, her shoulder bumping my arm. Next to my five feet six inches, Trish's five feet four inches seemed small. But there was a lot of firepower in her small frame.

Usually.

"It's possible your staff will work outside this cavern. Some of the spectral realm's hidden places become saturated with the magic dampening power that permeates this place. But outside the hidden places, the ancient magic items sometimes work. If I'm not mistaken your staff is a couple of thousand years old."

Shocked by that information, I gripped the staff harder. "Do you have any non-magical weapons?" I asked the fairy.

"A couple of iron knives. Some salt."

Ah. Ghost hunting 101. I grinned.

We discussed our predicament and decided to try to find our way toward the spot where we'd jumped into the cavern. We shouldn't be too far from it. The problem was one of orientation. I had no idea which direction we'd rolled when we hit the bottom.

"Shouldn't there be some kind of light from above?" Trish asked.

We'd clasped hands and were walking slowly in one direction and then the other, looking for the spot.

"You'd think so."

A long, low moan throbbed on the air, so soft I thought I'd imagined it at first. When it happened again, a bit louder the second time, I realized it wasn't my imagination. "I don't like the sound of that," I whispered.

"Me neither. We need to get out of here."

My hand touched a firm surface and I grimaced, yanking it away. It was covered in a greasy substance that was so cold it burned. Like dry ice. "Ow, ow, ow!" I rubbed my palm against my leather pants and immediately regretted it as the burning somehow found my skin through the leather.

The moan sounded again, much closer and filled with rising tension.

We shuffled forward another step. I kept my hands to myself, not wanting to experience any more of the burning stuff. My palm throbbed with pain and it didn't seem to be getting any better. "Don't touch the wall," I warned Trish. "There's something on it that burns."

"I..."

A blustery breeze crept through the space, putrid with the stench of death. We jolted to a stop as it wove through us, coating us with its deathly stink. Trish's hand tightened on mine. She moved closer and spoke softly. "I don't know what this is, but I'm not getting a warm and fuzzy feeling from it."

I responded by squeezing her hand.

The ghostly wail vibrated the air around us. The putrid wind tripled in strength, battering us with its horrible stench. We fought not to be blown into the burning wall and ended up bracing each other and dropping to our knees. Hair whipped around our faces, stinging my cheeks and forcing me to close my eyes. But having my eyes closed was unnerving, though I wouldn't see anything even with my eyes open. The wind slammed into us, continually changing direction and swirling its violence in every direction. The wind slashed us with slivers of rock, threatened us with its choking dust. We barely managed to keep from being thrown to the ground but I wasn't sure that was a win.

Something. A presence that lifted the short hairs all over my body.

Stood behind me.

Its breath was the air that filled the cavern...icy and horrible.

A blustery touch found the back of my neck.

I yelped and jerked, nearly knocking Trish down.

"What?" the fairy asked, her voice squeaking with alarm.

"Something's right behind me."

She shifted closer. "Don't. Move," she whispered into my ear.

Ice clamped my arm and I jerked away with a yelp. All I wanted to do was dive into a corner and assume the fetal position.

Trish grunted as we stumbled sideways. "Aggy!"

"Sorry! It grabbed me."

A scream burst over us, wild and incensed. Wind buffeted, blowing us sideways without warning. One of my arms pressed against the wall. My scream of agony met the specter's scream and challenged it for volume. But it didn't come close in power.

Trish was nearly blown away from me in the maelstrom. I could feel the specter trying to wrench us apart. I could hear the words beneath its howl.

Not your place...not your place...not your place...

A grainy assault blasted me in the face and I inhaled sharply as the wind drove what I assumed was some of Trish's salt into my collection of wounds.

The wind died so abruptly we fell to the ground. The howls cut off shortly after.

I hit the ground on my back, pain digging into me from several places.

From the panting breaths a foot or so away, I assumed Trish lay nearby. "You okay?"

She groaned. "Okay is a strong word."

I nodded, licking my lips. "What was that thing?"

"I didn't recognize her."

I blinked. "Her? It was a woman? You could see her?"

"Vaguely. She was too chaotic for a good look. But I got the impression of long dark hair and glowing white eyes."

"That's not creepy at all."

Trish made a soft sound of agreement.

I blinked up at the space above me. Then blinked again. "Hey, Trish, does that spot right there look lighter to you?"

A pause and then, "It does."

I climbed slowly to my feet. "I think that's our exit."

5

THE DEAD WILL ROAR IN HELPLESS RAGE

I rubbed my arm as we walked. The salt Trish had thrown had been agony at first, but it had apparently pulled whatever poison the goo on the wall had burned into my flesh away. The flesh was pink, slightly swollen, but most of the pain I was rubbing was memory pain. "I hope you brought a lot of that salt," I said, my tone half teasing.

Trish snorted out a laugh. "We've been here what, maybe an hour, and we've already been attacked twice. I'm starting to think we should have worn iron jumpsuits."

I nodded my agreement. One hand slipping into the pocket of my leather pants out of habit. My fingers encountered...nothing. My eyes went wide and I jerked to a stop, patting myself up and down.

"What's wrong?" Trish asked.

"My staff!" I said, panic truly kicking in as I realized I'd dropped it. With a sinking feeling, I realized it was probably inside that goddess-forsaken cavern. "I have to go back." Even the thought painted ice down my spine and I wanted to cry. "I have to go back," I repeated, my voice breaking.

Trish grabbed my wrist to stop me. "You can't go back there, Aggy. We'll be lucky to get where we're going as it is. We can't waste another hour going back and risking another confrontation with that thing."

I knew she was right. But it was my staff. A physical pang cut through my belly as I thought of losing it for good. Never mind it was the only thing I had for protection. My father had given it to me when I'd achieved my seating. It was a powerful icon of my position. I needed it. "I have to..."

Trish shook her head. "Reverend Dodson is counting on you to save him."

I glared at her, knowing when I was being manipulated. But her expression held nothing but honesty. Her green eyes were dark with concern. "I know it's hard for you to walk away, Aggy. But we don't have a choice."

I looked away as my eyes burned with unshed tears. The tears made me angry and I straightened my shoulders, lifting my chin. I was acting like a child. I was a forty-five-year-old woman for goddess sake. A guardian Lares. I wasn't going to cry over the loss of a weapon.

But it felt like more than a weapon, a small voice whined inside my head. *It felt like a friend.*

The sound of a distant bell gonged inside my head. I jolted, my gaze sliding toward the horizon, where the unrelenting gray of the sky was stained with a pale-yellow glow.

Trish followed my line of sight and sucked air. "That's it," she told me. "That's the central partition." Her gaze whipped to me. "Your Lares magic is showing us where to go."

The message in her excited gaze was clear. She didn't think I needed my staff to do my job.

She was wrong. I did need it. On a very personal level. She was also right. I maybe didn't have to have it to accomplish our current task. But I felt its loss with every fiber of my being.

The bell gonged again. I jolted in surprise. I hadn't been expecting it.

"What's wrong?" Trish asked.

"I'm getting a warning." Someone was in trouble. I glanced around, figuring *that* someone was probably us.

The glowing, amber-gray sky ahead of us flared brighter for a beat and then darkened, a bone-rattling roar filling the night.

"What was that?" I asked Trish, my steps slowing.

When the fairy didn't respond, I skimmed her a look. "Trish?"

She shook her head. "All I've got is prophecy."

"Okay." My tone sounded hesitant, but I'd take any help I could get.

"The dead will roar in helpless rage, to feel the touch of a fleshly sage. The lion bellows and bares its claws, the celestial spy its ire draws."

"Well," I said in my most cheerful voice. "I don't know how celestial we are..."

Trish snorted out a laugh.

"But it sounds like they're not going to be happy to see us."

Another roar pulled our attention back to the problem at hand. "It sounds like something's happening over there. I guess we'd best go find out what it is." I'd barely taken a step before agony cut through my middle. "Ah!" I screamed, wrapping my arms around myself as wave after wave of slicing pain tore through me. Oily sweat broke out on my face, trickling down my back, and I realized I was panting like a puppy as I tried to survive the pain.

I was barely aware of Trish's concern. She bent over me,

her mouth moving and words I couldn't hear spilling from her lips. I didn't need to hear them, I could read the terror on her face. She touched my forehead and snatched her hand away as if she'd been burned.

So many voices. Sobbing. Desperate pleas. I suddenly felt as if the entire world needed my help. And I wasn't even able to help myself.

My body was on fire. Yet my teeth clanked together as ice formed in my core. My muscles tightened under a series of shivers, the contractions only exacerbating the torment in my gut. I tried to look up at Trish. I tried to speak...to tell her what was happening...but the world fell behind a charcoal curtain and I could no longer see her face. At first, I thought I'd passed out. But pictures flashed across my vision. Horrible pictures of pain and fear.

A winged man, leaning against scarred metal bars, his wings askew and blood trickling from his drooping head.

The Rev, covered in chains that buckled his knees.

A familiar form—eight feet tall, with dark gray skin and a triangular face sporting slitted nostrils—downcast eyes the color of flame.

Another man...hair as dark as midnight and a clear blue gaze. He stood a distance from the others...watching with a detachment that made me want to yell at him. Help them! I screamed. The words exploded across my mind...harsh and desperate.

But he only looked at me and slammed a fist against the bars between us.

I didn't understand. Where were they? The background was crypt-like, with rusty stone walls and the foul stanch of mold and mildew.

Broken voices screamed in pain and hopelessness.

On top of the agony in my middle and the horrifying visions

feeding my mind, a deep sense of time being short assailed me.
Something was happening and I was going to be too late.

Then, Reverend Dodson's head lifted. He looked directly at
me, his normally kind brown gaze filled with fear. Run, Madam
Lares, he said, his voice a tortured whisper I could barely hear.
Get out!

Like a bucket of icy water, his words yanked me out of
the visions and I fell backward onto my well-padded backside in the dirt.

My breaths heaving in my chest, I dropped to my back
and used the hem of my tee-shirt to dry my sweaty face.
"Curse, curse, swear, swear." I looked up at the fairy. "That
well and truly sucked."

Trish laid a small, lightly-calloused hand on my shoulder. "What just happened?"

I tried to slow my breathing, taking deep, slow breaths
and releasing them just as slowly until I could speak
without panting. "It's okay."

"That was far from okay, Aggy," Trish said, her vivid
green gaze narrowing. "You looked like you were in a lot of
pain. What happened?"

I shoved at the ground and, with Trish's help, managed
to reorient myself into a seated position. "My body has
chosen this perfectly horrendous time to realign for the last
level of my seating."

"Seriously?" Trish's voice sounded a bit screechy with
disbelief.

I knew how she felt. I felt the same way. "As serious as
bat guano in the kitchen."

She grimaced. "How often does that happen?"

I shrugged. "I'm working on training Batty but she likes
to let loose whenever she feels like it."

"Not the bat guano," Trish said, her lips quirking. "These attacks."

"Some days the attacks are almost nonstop. Others...like today, less often. I have no control and get no warning. It's tons of fun."

To my shocked surprise, Trish pulled me into a one-armed hug. "I wish I had my healing magic."

Sighing, I nodded. "Me too."

The dense throb of wings sounded above us. We both looked up but there was nothing there. We exchanged a frown.

"I'm hating this place," I said. "How about you?"

"Ditto," she agreed. "So how about we get this done and get the heck out of here?"

"Sounds like a plan."

As soon as the residual aches smoothed away and my muscles stopped shaking, we broke into a light jog. Between the ice-wall, the attack on the cavern, and my own magic's attack on me, I figured we'd lost over an hour. We had less than three hours to find the Rev and start the journey back to where we'd entered the realm.

That didn't include the time we would expend looking for Nova. I didn't even bother trying to fool myself that I wouldn't help Trish with that. It was obvious that finding him was very important to her. She'd been there for me many times in the past. She'd given away her freedom to live as she liked in order to save her people. If anyone deserved my help it was the warrior fairy. And she would have it. I only prayed it didn't destroy any chance I had of saving my friend and council member. Reverend Dodson had also been there for me countless times. I owed him. He wouldn't have even come into the spectral realm if I hadn't asked him to. It was my fault he was there. It was my responsibility to get him out.

Even if it meant getting temporarily stuck there myself.

I shoved away thoughts of home...of Wanda and Monty...of baked goods and chocolate. After all, they called it sacrifice for a reason.

We were about a quarter mile away from a clear delineation in the land which I took to be the boundary between the outer segment of the realm and the inner one when I heard the throbbing of wings again.

I'd learned since becoming Lares to be fearful of large predators diving at me from above. We'd been caught too many times in the compressed reaction zone a skyborne attack created. That was why I reacted so quickly to the sound. Lifting my gaze toward the sky, I reached for a weapon I no longer had...and blinked, my gaze narrowing. "Is that...?"

Trish gasped. "It's not possible."

We stared in awe at the powerful pulsing of enormous charcoal wings beneath the leaden sky. The form was nearly as familiar to me as my own. The thick, mahogany brown hair falling around the square jaw. The molten chocolate gaze, sparking with intensity. My mouth fell open and I pulled sulfur-tainted air into my suddenly clenching lungs. "Gren," I whispered, not believing my own eyes. "How?"

He glided smoothly from the sky, his feet landing effortlessly on the ground, and walked out of the flight as if he'd just been striding across the realm. I watched him with a hungry gaze, concern for him warring with much deeper feelings that twisted heat deep in my belly. I shook my head. It wasn't good...him being there. It was bad. Dangerous. And I was thrilled to see him.

But he stopped thirty feet away. Something about his

large form seemed off. It wavered slightly, fading as he lifted his hands. His lips moved but nothing came out.

Then it struck me. What was wrong. I wasn't looking at Gren. Not his physical form. I was looking at something not quite real.

My chest tightened and I suddenly found it hard to breathe. Was he a ghost? Goddess in a haunted house...was Gren...gone?

"Aggy?"

Trish's softly spoken query had me shaking my head. "I don't..." A sob tore the words away from me. Had Gren gotten caught in the spectral realm when he'd helped us reach the gateway? Had they killed him?

His lips moved again, slowly. The intensity of his attempt to communicate painted ice along my spine. But never so much as when I understood what he was trying to say to me.

Those luscious lips, which could create a trail of delicious heat along my throat and send need spiraling through my body with the slightest touch. Those same lips formed three words. Just three small words. Words that stole the last of the breath from my lungs.

Trap, Aggy. Run!

6

TO FEEL THE TOUCH OF A FLESHLY SAGE

I ran.

Right at Gren.

Behind me, Trish screamed my name. I ignored the desperate plea in her voice. Something was wrong with Gren.

His form swelled to an unnatural size for a beat, and then shrank away to a pinprick on the air before disappearing as I reached for him. I slammed to a stop and fell to the ground, panting as another wave of fire and agony burned through my middle. I lay writhing, oily sweat pouring out of me as I tried to fight the attack from my own traitorous body.

My legs flailed in misery as cramps wrenched the muscles taut. The sky above me thickened, turned to charcoal gray, and I prayed I was about to pass out. Because anything would be preferable to the torment of my change.

I reached for silence. Release. But it didn't come.

Instead, I heard voices, cries, screams. My agony mirrored someone else's pain. My fear was magnified tenfold by another's fear. I reached out and clasped a pale, cold hand, a pair of terrified blue eyes shining with unshed tears. Please, Lares. Save him."

Panic swelled inside me at my helpless state. Anger flared as the woman blinked away, only to be replaced by a small child, crying desperate tears as an adult he trusted walked away from him. A man knelt on soggy grass, head bowed and fists clenched as a woman screamed obscenities, cursing him for the weakness of booze and other debaucheries. The parade of victims swept on and on, each one tearing away a tiny piece of my soul.

I gritted my teeth and held on as waves of helpless frustration vibrated beneath my skin.

"Aggy!"

Hands shook my shoulders. A terrified voice screamed my name. For a moment, I thought it was another vision and I fought to be free of it. I struggled to shove it away.

"Aggy, you need to snap out of it." Trish's voice was husky, broken, as if she'd been screaming for a while.

My eyes snapped open and, finally, my muscles softened out of the clench they'd been locked into. I blinked up at her. My body was limp, exhausted.

"This is going to kill you, Aggy?" Trish said. "I don't know how you've survived it so far."

I licked my dry lips. "Piece of cake." I tried to sit up but my arms were like noodles.

Trish pushed me back down. "You need to rest. I thought you were dying. Nothing I did got through to you."

In the distance, an angry roar broke the silence. And I remembered why we were there. I clasped her hand, my grip damp and wimpy. "How long...?"

She frowned, her gaze lifting to the horizon. "If I had to guess, you were in that state for about an hour and a half."

Ninety minutes?!

I shook my head, denying her words. "That..." I swallowed, my throat dry. "That's not possible."

Trish grabbed my pack, which was laying on a nearby rock. I didn't remember taking it off. Maybe I hadn't. Maybe Trish had?

I scrubbed a hand over my sweaty face. "We need to move."

She held a bottle of water to my lips and I drank greedily. She offered me a protein bar and helped me sit up, leaning me against the rock. "Eat this but don't eat all of them." She smiled. "We might need them for later. Rest. I'm going to go ahead and scout out the situation. Maybe that will save us some time. I'll be back for you in about a half hour. Try to rest, Aggy. You won't be much good to anybody if you don't."

I nodded. "Don't put yourself in danger," I said, nibbling on the bar.

"I won't."

I took another bite and nearly fell over as I nodded off.

I woke briefly at the sound of Trish's footsteps running away. Forcing my eyes open, I took another bite of the bar.

Silence padded the area around me. It was too quiet. I was so tired. My eyes slid shut. And an obsidian emptiness claimed me.

I JOLTED AWAKE, blinking rapidly to focus my bleary vision. I was alone, in the same spot where Trish had left me. My neck was stiff and sore, my legs aching. I looked down at the protein bar still clutched in my hand. There was a little dirt on the end where it had landed when I'd fallen over, but I pulled that part off and finished it. Trish had been right, I needed my strength to do what I was about to do. Grabbing the bottle of water, I finished off what was left and put the bottle and the wrapper into my bag. Light flared from a small object at the bottom of the bag. I reached inside and pulled out the kitchen timer Mavis had magicked to be our portal timer. I grimaced when I saw that over three hours had passed since we'd left home.

I had less than an hour to gather up the Rev, Trish, and Nova and head back. We'd figured our trip home might be accomplished at a faster pace, given that we'd probably have something snapping at our heels on the way back. But, given the fact that we'd been attacked by that wall thing and then by the specter in the cavern, that was cutting it close. There were almost certainly more monsters where those had come from to waylay us. And then there were my physical issues. I frowned. The last one had nearly done me in. If I suffered another one like that...

Shoving to my feet, I refused to dwell on it. I had to do what I had to do. I'd deal with each problem as it came.

Grabbing the backpack, I took off running, following the sounds of cheering and the roaring of what sounded like a sizeable crowd. The idea of a cheering crowd on the spectral plane was weird beyond words. The fact that it appeared to be happening in the very area where we believed my councilman was didn't bode well for a successful conclusion to my quest.

When I'd cut the distance to the central segment by half, I caught sight of a shadow moving across the ground. It was strange to see a shadow in a place where there was no discernible light to create them. My instincts screaming at me to avoid it at all costs, I ducked behind a tall, prickly bush that was covered in black berry-like fruit.

The shadow grew taller as it came closer, and I pressed nearer to the bush.

My heart thumping, I slowed my breathing as the shadow fell over my hiding spot. The murky form loomed over me, its sulfurous scent souring the air. It hesitated as if searching and I held my breath. A very long moment later the shadowy creature moved away and I was able to breathe.

Releasing a relieved breath, I moved away from the bush and started running again, scanning the area above and around me for more of the shadow things. I figured they were probably some kind of sentinel, which, at the very least, would alert someone that I was coming. At worst... I shuddered. Having already experienced some of the worst the realm could offer, I wasn't excited to bump up against any more spectral monsters.

My senses twanged the moment I crossed from the outside sector to the internal one. The ground went from rocky and fine, throwing a silty cloud of dust into the air, to sharp and black, like charcoal. Magic slipped over my skin. At the first touch it felt gentle, inquisitive. But it ended with a bite.

I jerked under the quick pain and picked up my speed, my pulse pounding under a feeling that something bad was coming my way. As I ran toward a dome of yellow light arching into the sky ahead, the weighted feeling grew, chewing its way along my spine.

Sweat beaded on my upper lip and trickled down my back. The feeling of impending doom grew until my gaze was scanning constantly, keeping track of my surroundings as I moved. I became aware of a rising sibilance on the air... the constant shush, shush, shush of disembodied voices.

I jolted to a stop and spun in an effort to see where it was coming from.

A long, drawn out "S" sound slipped over me, drawing gooseflesh with its ghostly hiss. I gave a violent jerk and stumbled, hitting the ground hard.

Rolling, I slammed up against a crumbly sort of rock that reminded me of the ancient bones of skeletons in a history museum. The rock disintegrated at my touch, sending a choking dust into the air that coated my lungs and made them clench. I coughed until I gagged, feeling as if I'd never draw another full breath.

A thunderous roar filled the night. The dome of light rose high above me, shimmering under the force of the roaring crowd.

Above the yellow illumination, what looked like a thousand shadow creatures skimmed the clouds. They never stopped, a force of constant motion in search of something. Or someone.

The shush, shush, shush of sibilant voices danced around me. A chorus of whispered queries from the dead.

Out of the corner of my eye, something dark dropped precipitously to the ground. I jerked my gaze toward the spot, seeing only the darkness of a shadowed space.

Then another dropped.

And another.

Panic flared through me and I shoved to my feet.

Another shadow plunged downward. Another, and another.

Without thinking, I threw out my hand and called my staff to me.

The invisible crowd roared.

Just as I remembered my only weapon would not come, the shadows moved. Darkness closed around me. Black, oily magic sang on the air, biting and slicing against my skin. I knew it was there but I couldn't see it. I was reduced to jerking away from each strike as it hit. Helpless against their poisonous touch.

The space between me and the dome of light turned midnight black as more and more shadows fell into it. Like good soldiers, the specters coalesced and began to move in a uniform way.

Coming directly toward me.

I spun in a circle, looking desperately for a route to escape. But there was no path. They circled me completely.

In that moment I knew, with an icy certainty, that I was going to die.

7

THE LION BELLOWS AND BARES ITS CLAWS

I spun in circles, eyes wide and hands out as if I had any chance at all of battling a bunch of amorphous, non-physical entities bent on my destruction.

Swear, curse, double swear!

I was so cooked.

Shivering violently, I tried my hand at a bargain. "Hey, guys." I frowned. For all I knew, the shadows were gals. I mean, they weren't man or woman-shaped, with flaring skirts for the woman shadows and trousers and ball caps for the men. Like the figures on restroom doors. I didn't think being inadvertently sexist would endear me to the shadows closing in on me. "Or gals," I added quickly, my arms extended as I backed and circled, trying to keep my eyes on all of them at once.

"Mr. or Ms." I said inclusively. "Or Mx." I added. "Let's talk about this, okay? I'm not here to cause trouble. I'm just here to find my friends. If you'll just go on your merry way and leave me to it, I'll grab them and scurry out of here. Sound good?"

On they came, their ranks swelling until I found myself

at the center of a wide, circular void that was so black I thought it might never have seen the light. I tightened my muscles against another shudder, not wanting to broadcast my fear.

The dense wall of unending blackness seemed to pull the light and life from everything it touched.

"Look, I..." I wanted to scream and rail against the unfairness of it all. But I had no time for tantrums. I needed a plan. And, with the circle of endless dark mere inches away, I'd run out of time to form one. "I'm not trying to hurt anybody. I just want to get my friends and..."

A whisper of sound was all the warning I got. Instinctively, I threw up a hand and, to my everlasting relief, my staff slammed into my palm.

Bitter, biting cold enfolded my toes and bathed my back. I looked down to see that the shadows had found me. The places where they touched went immediately numb, hardening like ice. The frozen sensation was quickly followed by waves if exquisite agony.

I screamed as my flesh began to burn from the cold like it was on fire. Making myself as small as possible, I prayed for an end to the pain. Fire. Burning cold. Agony without end.

My strength being quickly sapped from frozen limbs, I forced my arm above my head and whispered a last, desperate prayer. "Illumine."

On my island of pain, the seconds ticked by. One. Two. Thr... Power shot from the staff, a massive nimbus of painfully bright light that bathed the army of shadows surrounding me in a tsunami of golden illumination.

I nearly fell over from its power, barely catching myself with a hand on the icy ground.

Screams filled the air and, for once, they weren't mine.

The shadows writhed away from the light, twisting in torment, and then were obliterated.

The distant dome of light flickered and died, leaving behind a chorus of pain-filled shrieks and calls for mercy.

The screams spurred me into action.

I ran.

Heart pounding from fear rather than effort, I followed the heart-breaking sound of pain and fear, knowing there was a good chance that I'd been the cause of it.

My foot crunched down on loose sand. I jolted to a stop, looking around at what appeared to be a stadium, its enormous form rising around me like the skeleton of a giant predator.

Silence vibrated on the air. Ominous, unnatural silence.

A low grumble broke the silence and I flushed with embarrassment, placing a hand over my gurgling belly.

Awkward.

Pushing onward, I tried to keep my footsteps light so as not to disturb the silence and bring the full force of the spectral realm down on my head.

A twinge tugged in my stomach.

Heat blossomed in my face, drawing beads of sweat from my pores.

I tensed, dread turning my steps leaden.

"Curse, swear, curse, swear, swear!" I growled. I had no time or energy for another *Response*-stimulated attack.

I stood rooted in place, one foot in front of the other and my hand clutching the staff so hard it creaked. My heart thudded beneath my ribs. Too hard. Too fast. Sweat coated my skin. Another twinge at my core had me gasping, bending slightly as it worked its way through me, turning my muscles to soft rubber.

A single voice found its way to my hearing. *Help me, Lares.*

I forgot my physical problem as pictures played through my mind. A young woman, struggling with the decision to end a beloved parent's agony. She wasn't sure she was strong enough. She didn't know if she was selfless enough.

I knew the woman. She worked at the customer service desk of the big box store in Rome. She had a kind smile and bright, happy eyes. Her mother had been gravely hurt in a car accident the week before. They'd been keeping the woman alive with machines. But she wasn't really living. *I don't think I can do it, Madam Lares. Please take this burden from me.*

You can do this, LeeAnn. I know you can.

The words had barely left my mind before another wave of pain ripped through me—stronger and more violent than the last.

Help me, please, Madam Lares...

I pulled air into my lungs and dropped to one knee. The biting pain of small, sharp rocks beneath my knee took my attention from the physiological attack and allowed me to focus on the woman. "LeeAnn," I gasped, doubling over.

Had she heard me? I just didn't know.

A loud, metallic click ripped my attention upward. Lights flashed on from half a dozen stadium lights high above me. The lights painted the rocky ground before a concrete structure that rose into the leaden sky. Rows of pocked and broken steps were painted in rust and dirt, the upper levels lost behind layers of charcoal clouds.

I stepped forward, my staff coming up in front of me. Gooseflesh rose all down my arms. The skin at the back of my neck prickled with awareness.

Someone or something watched me.

A growl throbbed across the empty ground. Unfortunately, it wasn't my stomach that time. Thirty yards away, in front of the central bank of seating, the sand dipped in a perfect paw shape. I swallowed hard, guessing by the size and depth of the print that I was dealing with something scarily large.

Like, small-car-sized large.

Another roar and the lights flickered, briefly revealing an enormous black lion whose eyes sparked with dancing flames.

"Just great," I said. "Curse!"

The lights flickered again and the lion threw back its enormous head, its roar engaging an answering, bone-deep terror.

My hand that was holding the staff was slimy with sweat and I had to tighten my grip to snap it out, lengthening the weapon.

Pawprints sank into the center of the arena, forming a single large circle over the middle space. When the lion roared again, the risers were suddenly filled with a crowd of ghostly watchers, cheering for the coming battle. My gut twisted at the thought of fighting the beast, alone and inadequately armed. Panic followed on the heels of that pain and I said a silent prayer that my body wouldn't choose that moment to attack me.

The lights flickered out, and darkness clung to the arena for the beat of a few seconds. I stared at the enormous lion, which was only fifteen yards away. Its back appeared to be nearly as tall as my shoulders.

The orb on the end of my staff flared to life, its energy painting the space around me with a fierce golden glow. Where the light touched the ground near the lion, its paw disappeared. A truly spectral beast, it appeared the lion was only visible in the darkness. In the light I had to presume it was more deadly because its movements couldn't be anticipated.

My instincts told me I needed light to see my enemy. But the rules of the spectral plane told me light would hobble me.

Just freaking perfect.

When the stadium lights flickered back on, I blinked in surprise. Trish stood twenty feet away, looking just as she had when I'd last seen her except for a few fresh bruises along her jaw and encircling her slender arm. The sling she'd worn over her injured arm was gone and she held that arm protectively across her middle. Thankfully, I saw no bites. "Trish? You okay?"

She didn't swing her gaze away from the beast standing in the center of the arena. "I've been better. Please tell me you know how to kill this thing?"

The lion made a chuffing sound and its long, muscular tail snapped the air. In that moment, it reminded me of an oversized domestic cat.

Unfortunately, its teeth and claws removed that ridiculous notion from my mind.

"No. But my staff seems to be working. Sort of." I realized the only thing it had done was light up the shadows. Technically, light wasn't a weapon. Except against creatures who embodied the shadows. I didn't think the beast in the arena counted as one of those creatures. "If it's spectral then a physical weapon won't work against it."

Trish moved slowly, tugging the straps of her pack off and pulling it around to her front. "I've still got salt and iron blades."

I frowned as the lion's form shivered and reappeared a few yards closer. "You might want to hurry."

The lights flickered on again and a man appeared across the arena. I took a step forward before I realized I didn't recognize him. It definitely wasn't the Rev. Of average height with broad shoulders, narrow hips and muscular legs, the man had short-cropped black hair and a face meant for an angel. Despite his angelic features, however, he didn't have a pair of wings. He was holding what looked like a wooden bat in one hand and his shoulders drooped as if he were weakened by his time on the spectral plane. "Nova?" I asked Trish, keeping my voice low.

She nodded, her gaze locked hungrily on him. I felt my own eyes widening as I realized what that look meant. Before I had a chance to think too deeply about it, the lights went out again. The soft swish of sand told me the lion had moved. I whipped my head around to watch him, lifting my staff in front of me.

The lights came on and movement on my other side had me turning. A cry escaped my lips as I saw Gren, kneeling in the sand. His head was bowed and one of his wings was hanging crooked. They'd hurt him.

I growled with rage and lifted my staff. "You have no right to harm my people," I yelled to the empty arena. I longed to go to Gren, but worried I'd only draw the lion to him. "I am a guardian Lares and I would speak to the entity in charge!"

The lion threw back its head and roared and the sky suddenly swirled with gauzy silver and white forms. I ducked as a particularly agitated spirit swooped toward me, its amorphous form painting the air with ice as it slipped away. More worrisome, the shadowy edges of the arena folded inward and became the shadowy sentinels I'd fought before.

The lion roared again and the spirits roiling the sky

became more frenetic, diving toward our heads and swooping toward our feet in an effort to take us down.

I swung at them with my staff, as I threw Trish a glance. "I'm going to Gren. He looks hurt."

She nodded, slashing the air with her iron blades. Spirits scattered under her determined assault, but there were too many of the things. As soon as she struck down three of them, five more dove on her.

I hesitated, worried she needed me more than Gren at the moment. The hesitation cost me my chance. A horn blared through the specter-drenched space and the lion roared, leaping forward.

Running directly toward me.

I jolted into a run, heading for the beast. My staff was stretched in front of me and my heart thudded against my ribs. Trish took off toward the lion at the same moment I did. The ghostly forms in the cheap seats cheered, their dead black eyes locked on the action below.

My rage at Gren's condition and worry for my ghostly councilman, who unfortunately—or fortunately?—didn't seem to be part of the show, whipped me into an enraged frenzy. I opened my mouth and emitted a feral scream as I flung myself toward the ghostly beast stalking toward me.

I launched off my leading foot and left the ground as I came within battle range of my feline opponent. Gripping my weapon in sweaty palms, I prepared for impact. The scream was still throbbing in my throat as I attacked. And then died with a choked cry as the arena lights snapped on, bathing us in harsh white light, and robbing us of the ability to see our deadly opponent's attack.

A heartbeat later, my staff flew skyward and two enormous paws slammed into me, taking me to the ground.

8
_____

THE CELESTIAL SPY ITS IRE DRAWS

Teeth snapped so near my nose I felt the heat of the thing's breath against my skin. Hot liquid splashed my cheek and the meaty stench of a carnivore's breath washed over me.

I tried to hold the beast away with one arm and swing my staff at it with the other. All I succeeded in doing was dropping my weapon, leaving myself with few options to keep my throat intact.

The lights flickered and I found myself looking up into the gaping maw of the enormous lion, whose weight and snapping teeth felt all too solid and real.

"Incoming!" Trish yelled and I closed my eyes as she threw a handful of coarse yellow salt at the beast. The over-sized feline reared back and rose to its full height, giving a mighty bellow before slashing at Trish with its finger-length claws.

I rolled to the side and snagged my staff, jumping to my feet. Swinging it toward the beast, I yelled, "Disapparate!"

The lion dove at Trish, nearly managing to grab her left

thigh in its snapping teeth. "Magic doesn't work, Aggy!" she screamed.

I didn't tell her about the light from earlier. Technically, light wasn't magic, but my summoning of it was. And speaking of shadows...

My back was suddenly bathed in burning cold. I arched away from it and screamed as the icy burn seared through me, leaving behind the sensation of having cleaved off huge sections of my flesh. Shadows dropped onto me from above and encircled me, closing in until I could barely draw breath through my frozen lungs.

"Illumine," I gasped out. I was on my back and had no recollection of falling. My body was a frozen block, the pain like being entombed inside dry ice.

The orb on the end of my staff flickered with golden light, nearly went out like a candle, and then flared illumination over the area surrounding us. The shadows nearest me dissipated. Before I could draw a relieved breath, a deadly paw swung in my direction and the staff was knocked from my grasp. As soon as I was no longer touching it the light went out.

The shadows fell. I folded myself into the fetal position and they covered my frigid form like a wintery blanket. My entire body went numb, my limbs locking and growing impossibly heavy as the shadows' blustery magic completed its lethal purpose.

Another roar sounded behind me, but it wasn't the lion. I thought I recognized the deep timbre of my angel's growl. A battle ensued above me, shadows dispersing into nothingness as they were ripped away.

The lion gave a muted cry and I rolled my eyes in that direction. The beast was on its side on the ground, two iron blades pinning it to the ground and salt peppering its black fur. The creature's limbs were unmoving and limp. Standing over it were Trish and the dark-haired man. They were grinning at each other.

"Aggy!" Warm hands ran over me, testing the flesh of my back and shoulders. "Can you move?"

I tried to respond but found the words wouldn't come. My mind was slightly muzzy, thoughts and speech beyond my capability.

"Is she okay?" Trish asked.

"I don't know."

Why did Gren sound so upset?

I frowned. Or, at least I thought I did. But my face didn't really move.

"The shadow guards were all over her when I got here." Tender hands grasped my shoulders and gently turned me to my back. "They had hold of her for too long." Gren nearly growled the words, his emotions raw.

I looked up into worried brown eyes and had a sudden urge to lift a hand and touch his gristly cheek. But my hand wouldn't move. I opened my mouth but the words wouldn't come.

He leaned over me, scooping me up and pulling me onto his lap. "Somehow we need to get her warm."

Trish stepped forward. "We can all wrap ourselves around her."

Gren shook his head. "Not here. The specters are gone now, but they'll be back."

"Let's take her outside the city," the dark-haired man said.

Gren stood with me and started running. I couldn't imagine anyone being strong enough to run while carrying me. I wasn't exactly a small woman. I frowned again without my face moving. Was I? I realized I didn't know. I couldn't see my body, but I didn't feel small. I actually felt kind of pudgy.

And old.

Why did I feel old. Old women didn't fight lions. Did they?

Wait. Did I really fight a lion?

I shook my head without shaking it. "Nah." I said. "I must have been dreaming."

My handsome brown-eyed savior looked down at me, a light filling his eyes. "You aren't dreaming. You've been hurt. But I need you to pull out of it, beautiful Aggy. Can you do that for me?"

Pull out of what? I asked myself, followed by an internal shrug.

"She's fighting through it," Trish said.

"We need to get somewhere and build a fire," the dark-haired man said. "Preferably a cave or something."

His mention of a cave stirred something deep inside me and I tensed. I reached out and clasped a well-muscled arm. "No!"

Sexy brown eyes slid to mine. "It's okay, lovely Aggy. We'll get you warm. You're going to be fine." He stopped running and lowered my feet to the ground. "How do you feel?"

My vision wavered, making my savior sway back and forth. My stomach roiled. "Please stop swaying," I ground out. "You're making me seasick."

The three of them shared a look.

"Um, Aggy?" Trish said. "You're the one who's swaying."

"Huh?" I rubbed my forehead. "I feel like a hundred and fifty pounds of frozen beef."

Trish grinned. "I told you not to eat all of the protein bars. A second on the lips, a decade on the hips."

I snorted. "I only ate one."

She pulled me into a hug, setting me to swaying again.

"I think the ground is moving."

"Something's surely moving," said the man whose name I wasn't remembering. I frowned. "You are?"

He gave me a shallow bow. "I am Nova, Prince of the seelie court. It is an honor to meet you, Madam Lares."

Trish frowned at him and he made an "Ah!" face. "My apologies. Unseelie court." His smile was only for Trish and, amazingly, her cheeks pinked underneath it.

"Aggy?"

I looked up into Gren's handsome face. "Hey."

His worried expression fell away under a sweet smile. "Hey." He pulled me into a hug that made my bones creak. He quickly released me when I groaned. "I thought we were going to lose you there for a minute."

I shuddered violently. "I think my insides are still frozen."

He nodded. "We need to get you warmed up." He lifted his head and looked around. "We need a cave."

"No!" Trish and I both said at once.

The men stared at us in surprise.

I shook my head. "Trust me, you do not want to go into any caves here. Do. Not."

Gren's mouth flattened out and a sparkle lit his eyes.

I narrowed my gaze. "Are you laughing at me?"

"No. In fact, I'm doing everything I can to keep from laughing."

"Uh huh." I pursed my lips to keep them from curving too. "I'm not lying about the cave."

"She's not," Trish agreed. "A cave is a bad idea."

"Okay. We'll just look for a sheltered spot where we can build a fire..."

I held up a hand to stop him, suppressing a shiver. "We

can't afford to waste the time. We need to get the Rev and get out of here. I'll warm up as soon as we start moving."

I looked around. "Do we know where he is? Was he being kept in the same place you were?"

Silence met my question. I looked from one face to the other of my three companions. Only Nova was able to look me in the eye. He simply shrugged. "I have no idea who that is."

"Trish?" My spidey senses were clanging at me. Something was wrong.

The warrior fairy stared at her dusty shoes. When I realized she wasn't going to respond, I glanced at Gren, raising a questioning brow.

"Aggy..." he started to say.

"What they don't want to tell you is that I am not coming home with you."

I whipped around with a cry of surprise.

Reverend Dodson stood several feet away from me, flanked by two guards who towered over him by a couple of feet.

I gave a squeal of delight that was definitely not Lares-like. I didn't care. Hurrying over, I reached a hand toward him, wishing I could pull the ghost into a hug. "You're okay. Thank the goddess. And just in time too. We need to go now. The portal won't stay open for long."

Dodson's smile was sad, but he didn't get a chance to respond.

One of the guards moved and Prince Nova lunged at them, a blade in each hand.

Trish threw out an arm, stopping him. "No. They're friends."

Nova gave her a disbelieving look. "Surely you jest?"

"No jesting here," I confirmed. "We have an agreement

with Princess Layla of the lost ones," I told him. "They are our friends and allies." My questioning gaze slid to the larger of the two lost ones and he shifted from one cloven-hooved foot to the other on bent legs. "But I have no idea why they're here."

Nova didn't look convinced but he stepped back, lowering but not sheathing his weapons.

"Madam Lares," the nine-foot-tall demon said with a bow. "Princess Layla sends her regards."

My lips compressed with irritation. "Matthew. Layla sent you here? Did she ask you to take my councilman prisoner?"

The smaller demon stepped forward and mimicked his friend's bow. "Madam Lares."

"Glenn," I said, fighting a grin. If someone had told me that devils and demons existed eight months ago I would have scoffed. If that same someone had told me that one of them would be named Glenn and another Matthew...I'd have fitted that unfortunate messenger for a white jacket with wrap-around sleeves.

"We wish only to help, guardian. Things have occurred that the Princess desires to speak with you about."

"What kinds of things?"

He looked to the Rev and my friend, unbelievably, patted him on one scaled charcoal arm. "In a nutshell," the Rev said. "Things have gone tits up on the spectral plane."

Trish giggled. "Reverend Dodson, is it okay for a man of the church to say *tits*?"

He frowned. "Teets?"

I made the mistake of catching Matthew's black gaze and barked out a laugh at the look of shock on his face. "Rev, I think you've been on this plane too long."

He shrugged, looking very corporeal in the land of the spirits. "It's chaotic here right now, Madam. I have no time for niceties or long explanations. "Long story short, the demons have invaded this world with the intention of finding a way to the human realm. Rumors are, they've found something that will allow them to do it. I must stay and stop them if possible."

"Why you?"

"Because I am here and capable, and I represent the Office of the Guardian of Rome, Indiana. It is my duty."

A deep sense of pride warred with disappointment and I opened my mouth to argue. "What about your reason for coming here? Did you find Wanda's mother?"

He sighed. "I did. And that is a conversation for another time, I'm afraid."

"No," I said, shaking my head. "Tell me. Wanda deserves to know…"

Nova stepped forward, interrupting me. "Madam Lares. I don't wish to interrupt, but we are running out of time. The portal will open soon and we'll miss our window if we don't get moving."

I bit back an irritated reply. The man was right. But I didn't want to leave the Rev behind. A painful sense of déjà vu was turning my stomach sour. It felt way too much like when I'd had to leave Trish behind in Fairy. "But what if you get stuck here?"

He settled his kind brown gaze on me. "Then I will be pleased at least to have fought in your name and service."

Tears burned in my eyes. I sniffled, rubbing my arms as a shiver threatened. My insides still felt like ice and my outsides weren't a lot warmer. The realm had a perpetual cold dampness to it that was distinctly unfriendly to flesh and blood types. I was sure that was by design. I gave in to the impulse to hug him, surprised to find him as solid as he looked, though his skin was colder than it could have been if he were alive. "Take care of yourself," I told him. "If you're not back in a month, I'm coming after you again."

His smile was sad. "Don't, my dear. If I haven't made my way back to you within a month, find yourself another spirit to round out your council."

I didn't argue. There was no point wasting the time. No matter what he said, I'd be back if he hadn't returned. I looked to Glenn and Matthew, giving them an unspoken command. "We will care for him," Glenn said. "If you could give the Princess something for us?"

He handed me a roll of paper that looked like something from Medieval times. The scroll had been created from thick, yellowed paper that was discolored and ragged, probably from having been carried for a while.

I took it and stared down at the communication, marveling at how heavy it was. "What? There are no post offices in the spectral plane?"

Reverend Dodson chuckled. "I'm afraid the cost of a stamp for a scroll is prohibitive, and the mail keeps falling through the delivery vehicles."

I laughed.

"Aggy?" Trish urged.

I nodded, sniffed, and scraped tears from my cheeks. "I'll see you in a month...or less," I told him.

His smile was sad. "Take care, Aggy. There are more enemies here than you know. Your journey out of here will be fraught with danger."

As if I hadn't already figured that out. We took off running. With a little over two hours to cover a distance that had taken more than twice that before, we'd be lucky if we weren't stuck forever in the spectral plane ourselves.

9

A SUPPLICANT, HER PAIN
MUST BEAR

"Well, I'm not cold anymore. In fact, I'm so sweaty I'm pretty sure my clothes are gonna slide right off me." The words were wheezed out through lungs that had clamped down in defiance of being overused a mile or two back. I stumbled over a rock as I swiped a hand over my face, scraping off a layer of sweat.

Trish threw me a grin, without losing a beat. I suddenly hated her for being so agile and slim and...dry. "Having a hot flash?" she teased.

I narrowed my gaze on her and nearly face-planted as a stick leaped off the ground in an attempt to cripple me. I was so tired my legs had gone numb and my feet were like large, oddly-shaped bunions at the bottom of my body. It was a miracle I was still plowing clumsily forward and I was starting to suspect somebody had magicked my feet so they'd keep moving no matter what. "Let me guess," I wheezed. "The fae don't go through middle-age?"

Her grin widened. "If we did, I'd never tell."

"Ha!" I barked out. It was too much for my weary, sweaty,

swollen body. I stumbled over my own foot and hit the ground at a roll, dust flaring up from the place where I landed and diving into my nostrils.

I was so busy choking and coughing I almost missed the spear slicing the air where I'd been. Suddenly Gren was there, one wing blanketing me as the sounds of battle blossomed around us.

I sneezed and tried to push him away. "What's going on?"

Gren resisted being shoved. "Sit still, Aggy. We're under attack."

"By who...um...whom?" I corrected, channeling His Snottiness, a.k.a. Ferral, who was apparently living rent-free in my head.

"Demons," Gren responded. He shifted to cover me better. His soft grunt of pain reminded me that one of his wings had been badly damaged during his short captivity, but he'd refused to talk about it.

"Let me up," I said, shoving him again. "I can help."

"You have no magic," he argued.

"Neither does anybody else," I pushed on his unyielding chest. "Let me up, that's an order."

He sighed and shoved himself off me, keeping a wing with an arrow sticking out of it between me and the battle. A battle that was severely one-sided given the dearth of weapons on our side.

Armed only with short knives and spunk, Trish and Nova were engaged in hand-to-hand battle with two demonic adversaries who were armed with longer blades. Fortunately, the two fae were much faster and more agile than the demons, which probably explained the growing pile of scaled and horned antagonists around their feet.

As I watched, Nova slashed at an attacker with scaly red

skin, ram's horns decorating the sides of his small head, and tiny sharp teeth that were painted with enough blood to convince me he'd found his target more than once. Nova slashed the demon across the chest and then leaped behind him as an arrow sailed in his direction. The arrow hit the devil instead and Nova took off running toward the distant rock where the archer hid.

"He's a good man to have on our side," Gren said.

I nodded, worried about Trish. She was limping and the arm she'd injured in the cave was bleeding. "Can you get to the other archers?"

Gren nodded. "What about you?"

"I'm going to help Trish." When he hesitated I yelled, "Go!" and took off running. I snapped my arm and the staff I'd yanked from my pocket extended, the orb immediately flaring with golden light.

A smaller demon that walked on four legs and whose squarish form was covered in spikes ambled quickly toward Trish, its spiked tail snapping to the side in anticipation of finding her legs.

I swung my staff, connecting with the meaty little body and sending it flying on a strident squeal. As soon as it hit the ground, the nasty little creature was up and heading my way again.

I spun around and slammed my weapon into the legs of the demon Trish was fighting and it stumbled backward on a pain-filled groan. As it slashed its claws in my direction, Trish took the opportunity to snatch a discarded spear off the ground and impale the beast through the heart.

The thing melted to the ground without a sound. Trish nodded her thanks and turned to the next demon, a formidable creature with oily warts covering its rough black skin and a shock of pure white hair sticking straight up from its bony skull.

I gave the square demon another crack with my staff, following Trish's example and scooping up a spear with my other hand.

Two of the square demons replaced the one I'd sent flying and I put both weapons to good use, my hours of training with the staff coming in handy. I soon fell into the dancelike rhythm of battle, and handily disposed of several more of the small demons.

I was breathing hard but feeling pretty good about myself when I turned around and the world juddered beneath my feet.

I mean literally. It juddered.

The demon was huge. Easily six feet tall at the shoulders and probably twenty feet long. It was covered in thick, black hair and had small round eyes with tiny silver irises that glowed into the growing darkness. Its black nostrils were flat and wet, flaring as it eyed me. If the realm got much darker, those eerie eyes would be all we'd be able to see. The creature would easily meld into the shadows and disappear, never seen until it attacked.

"What is that?" Trish asked, her voice hushed as if a too-loud sound would set the thing off.

"I don't know, but I don't think we're equipped to fight it."

"It's an Iggloc," A deep male voice said. Trish and I looked up to find Nova a few feet away, his head cocked as he examined our new challenge. He was covered in blood, some of it no doubt his own as a wound on his muscular arm and another on his cheek were still bleeding. But aside from a few lines around his eyes, he didn't look even half as exhausted as I felt.

I really hated the fae.

"Is it demonic?" I asked, also eyeing the creature, which stood a mere six feet away but didn't appear to be aggressive.

Nova seemed to be considering my question. Finally, he shook his head. "They're magically created, so technically no. Demonic royalty use them as mounts and pack animals."

I stared into the Iggloc's face and it blinked slowly back at me. As if to verify that it was harmless, the beast opened its wide mouth and yawned, showing me a few flat teeth at the center of its jaw and none on the sides. "It's non-carnivorous."

"So, it won't eat us?" I asked, narrowing my gaze on the oversized teeth.

Nova shrugged. "I guess it could eat us if someone chewed us up first."

Trish laughed. "I'll pass."

I nudged her with my elbow. "Come on, where are your maternal instincts?"

"No thank you."

I laughed. "Okay, well, is that it? Have we dispensed with all the demons?"

Nova nodded.

"Where's Gren?" I asked, looking around as the first ripples of worry bloomed.

"He's over there, talking to that spirit."

I glanced where he pointed and saw my angel, one wing still drooping unnaturally, talking to a tall wispy specter wearing what could only be described as a wrapped skirt. The spirit had a white cloth wound around his head and wore a scruffy silver beard. He was holding what looked like a shepherd's crook in one hand. They seemed to be deep into some kind of bargaining.

"What are they talking about?" I asked.

Nova shrugged again. "Shall we go find out?"

I gave him a smile. "We shall."

I soon realized that just moving closer to the conversation did not help me find out what they were talking about. The specter spoke in a language that sounded as if it might have been from ancient times, a language that Gren, amazingly, seemed to not only understand, but to also speak with admirable fluency.

As we approached, Gren dropped something long and dark into the specter's gnarled hand, bowing as the man took it. Without another word, the specter disappeared.

"What just happened?" I asked.

He turned to me with a grin, pointing behind us. "That, just happened."

A wet snort hit the back of my neck and I yelped, spinning around. I hadn't even realized the Iggloc had followed us over. For its size, the thing was amazingly quiet. "Okay," I said in my most dubious tone.

Gren patted the beast on its hairy shoulder. It grunted softly, its odd eyes rolling back into its head. "*This* is going to help us get to the portal in time."

I eyed it, unconvinced. "*That* looks like it might top out at a couple of miles an hour."

Nova snorted out a laugh. "A little more than that, actually."

Without warning, Gren bent and scooped me up, depositing me onto the creature's wide back. I immediately clutched its fur, fearing it would take off. "Um..." I said, really uncomfortable. "I'll just walk."

Gren shook his head. He nodded at Trish. "Up you go."

She stared at the beast for a bit and then seemed to decide it wouldn't kill her, climbing up behind me.

Gren looked at Nova, arching a brow.

The fae shook his head. "I'll run for a while then we can switch off."

Gren climbed aboard without hesitation. "Ready?" Before I managed to say, "No," he slapped the creature's wide backside. We shot off the mark and proceeded to test the speed of sound as we left my girly shriek behind.

I'd like to say I stopped shrieking by the time we spotted the portal in the distance, but that would mostly be a lie. The hairy demonic pack mule insisted on leaping over trees or clambering over boulders at top speed. Several times during the trip, I saw my life pass before my eyes and realized it wasn't nearly as long as I'd hoped it would be.

The stupid Iggloc seemed determined to shorten it unnecessarily.

Behind me, Trish seemed to thoroughly enjoy the journey, so much so that I figured she must be one of those half-wits who liked plunging from heights on roller coasters, their spleens up around their ears.

Yes, I was getting cranky. It had been a Hellish trip, and I wasn't even coming back with Reverend Dodson. That thought plunged me into contemplations of my worth as a guardian and things devolved wildly from there.

At some point during our journey, Nova had leaped up onto the beast behind Trish, and Gren had taken to the sky. He'd managed to become airborne but his injured wing was only barely functional. I really hoped he didn't do permanent damage by flying, but he'd insisted he needed to scout out our route, looking for a renewed attack as he searched for signs of the portal. Trish watched Gren with an expression that looked like jealousy.

"How come he can fly and I can't?" She finally asked.

I shrugged. "Maybe flight is more integral to his magic than it is to yours."

"Was he flying when he entered the realm?" Nova asked. Trish and I shared a look.

"Yes," she said after a beat.

Nova shrugged as if he'd made his point.

And apparently he had.

"Next time we come, I'm going to fly over the portal line with all my weapons firing," Trish said.

I grinned. "I'm going to blast the ground with my staff and fling magic with my other hand at the same time," I agreed.

We shared a laugh.

Nova said. "I'm going to be eating a large pizza while guzzling a beer."

That set us off and, for the next fifteen minutes, we discussed all the foods we were going to carry across the line if we ever had to return.

An hour later, I was starting to wonder if we'd over-shot our destination when Gren dropped heavily from the sky. To my hypercritical eye, he looked as if he might crash and I tensed for it, my heels touching the Iggloc's sides to spur it into a faster gait. Maybe we could get under Gren and catch him. But my angel managed to stumble to a clumsy landing that took him to one knee, the injured wing sagging over his shoulder. To my vast relief, the Iggloc came to a brisk stop when Gren landed. The thing had good brakes. If it hadn't lifted its head when it skidded to a stop, I'd have flown right over it.

Knowing someone might insist I stay aboard until we reached the portal, I slid quickly off, determined never to plant my buttocks on the beast again. My legs wobbled ominously and I grabbed a handful of the Iggloc's fur, just in case.

I bent at the waist to stretch out my sore leg muscles as Trish and Nova slid gracefully to the ground.

Gren joined us a moment later. His handsome face was lined with weariness and his color wasn't good. He was clearly in pain. "I want you to take my spot on the beast for the rest of the way," I told him, reaching up to place a hand on his too-pale cheek.

Gren took my hand and kissed the palm. "I'm fine, beautiful Aggy."

I narrowed my gaze in disbelief. "I don't believe you."

His smile was just naughty enough to make me blush. "I wouldn't lie to you."

"Did you spot the portal?" Trish asked, her gaze scouring the horizon. She frowned.

I couldn't see the tell-tale wall of light and knew we had to be very close to our deadline, or past it at that point.

The fact that he didn't respond was worrisome.

"Gren?"

He sighed. "I did not see it, no."

My stomach twisted with dread.

Trish reached into her pack and pulled out the magicked timer. She frowned down at it.

"What?" I asked, dread spreading outward from my middle. The last thing I wanted was to get stuck in that goddess-forsaken place.

She looked from the timer to the horizon and back to the timer again. Then she smacked the side of it on the heel of her hand.

"Trish?"

The fairy finally sighed. "The timer stopped. I have no idea how much time there is."

Gren wearily lifted his wings as if testing them. He turned a strange shade of green, his jaw clenching as if the pain were too much. "I'll fly ahead," he said, his voice tight. "It's got to be there."

I grabbed his arm before he could move. "Nope. Not gonna happen. You get to take my seat on the beast."

"Aggy..." he said, clearly planning to argue. I shook my head. "That's an order."

Heat flared against my hip and I looked down to see light oozing from my pocket. "What the...?" I pulled out my staff and blinked in surprise as golden light flared from it, bathing all of us in its glow.

"What does that mean?" Nova asked.

I was embarrassed to tell him I had no idea. "Um..."

Agony pierced my temples, white-hot pain that pulsed against my skull. I rubbed my head and sucked in a breath, determined to wait until it passed and not give in to it. I was so buried in the agony I nearly missed a different type of pain. A pain that seared my chest, robbing me of breath.

It's done, said a familiar feminine voice. *She's gone.*

LeAnn. My heart ached for her. I literally felt her pain. But there was hope behind the pain. The first threads of acceptance that soothed her emotional devastation.

She was ready to go, Madam Lares. She was at peace.

You did the right thing, I told her, tears spilling from my eyes. *You were so strong.* I sensed her pleasure at my words. And, though I found it hard to breathe, I was proud of her.

It was really hard, she said, her words thick with tears. *But I gave her peace. I'm holding tight to that.*

Yes, I agreed. *That is the most important thing, LeeAnn. You released her from a pain she couldn't overcome. Hold onto her in your thoughts and memories. Embrace the beauty that was her soul. Be kind to yourself.*

She cried softly, but I felt each word sinking deep into her thoughts easing emotional balm into the fears and pain and horror of loss. *Through your memories, you'll always have her in your life.*

I know. Thank you, Madam Lares. Thank you for being here for me. For hearing me when I called out to you.

I sobbed, realizing finally, why the final stage of my seating was so important. *Response.* Really hearing those who came to me for help. Embracing their pain. Soothing their fears. Not in a physical sense, but emotionally, cerebrally. Being available all the time. Connecting with them in a wider sense.

Warm hands pulled me off the ground and I looked up at Gren. His eyes were kind as he scraped tears off my face with his warm thumbs. "Aggy?"

I reached up and clasped his wrists, squeezing them. "It's okay. I made a connection. It feels..."

"Wonderful?" he asked, a sweet smile on his face.

Yes. I thought. It did feel wonderful, despite the pain throbbing through my supplicant's voice. I'd helped her with her problem. I'd supported her...encouraged her. And, more importantly, I finally knew what it really meant to reach my final hurdle.

Response.

10

A BARGAIN STRUCK, A PRICE MOST FAIR

"The portal's closing!" Trish screamed from a distance, pulling me from my thoughts. I jolted into awareness of our current problem, glancing toward my warrior fairy.

"You found it?" I asked, slow to switch gears and grasp the urgency of the current situation.

She was running toward us, her expression taut with fear. "It's over there, behind that ridge. The reason we couldn't see it is that it's nearly gone. The walls are barely rising above the ground."

Gren straightened to his feet, stumbling as he moved his damaged wing. His face turned ashen and for a moment, I thought he was going to pass out.

"Gren!" I reached for him, sliding an arm around his waist. "Nova!" I screamed when Gren's knees buckled and he nearly took me down to the ground. The fairy was suddenly there, supporting Gren's other side. "We need to get him on the Iggloc," I said, my voice desperate. I couldn't shake the feeling that, if we didn't get my angel home, he would die.

"No," Gren mumbled, trying to get his legs underneath him. "I can fly."

The fairies and I shared a look. There would be no flying. "Trish, hold the beast."

The Iggloc had grown restless. It was shifting and chuffing, looking as if it might make a run for it. I didn't know if it heard more of the demons coming, or if the distant portal was spooking it. Either way, we needed to hurry. "We're out of time," I said to no one in particular.

Between the three of us, we got Gren onto the beast and I climbed on behind him, wrapping my arms around him to hold him on the Iggloc. Trish and Nova leaped on behind me as the beast danced and snorted, clearly out of sorts.

"What's wrong with it?" Trish asked.

I glanced toward the faint illumination of the portal. "Maybe it's the portal magic."

"No," Nova said, his tone dire. "It's probably the hundreds of demons literally hoofing it toward us with blood in their eyes."

We all turned to find a horrible sight.

Hundreds was not an overstatement. Demons of all shapes and sizes swarmed across the open ground behind us. Twisted, hooved, and winged monsters spread as far the eye could see across the ground and through the air. When they noticed us noticing them, a battle cry rose within the hoard, the sound fierce and wild and vibrating in my chest.

"They're heading for the portal!" Trish yelled.

My pulse spiked. My heart pummeled my ribs. It had been bad enough when I'd thought they were coming for *us*. But Trish was right. The monsters would be happy to kill us along the way, but their goal was the opening between the spectral realm and the human world.

"Goddess!" I breathed.

We could make a stand to stop them. We'd miss our chance to get through the portal, but that would be okay if we could save our loved ones at home and thousands of other humans. Unfortunately, our chance of even making a dent in the force raining down on us was zero.

No. We needed to make a run for the portal and try to get through it before the force arrived.

Decision made, I kicked the beast in the sides and it leaped away as if it had barely been holding itself back.

Then it was all wind, thundering hooves, and wildly rolling eyes as we tried to do the impossible and make it to the portal without bringing a thousand demons through with us.

A cacophony of sounds exploded behind us, throbbing on the air and rolling toward us like a physical force. A strident squawk drew my gaze to the sky, where one of those giant Pterodactyl-type birds cleaved the air in an effort to catch up. I'd first encountered the demonic bird when we'd battled the Trickster and I'd quickly learned it was nothing like the ostrich it resembled.

The sharp-beaked predatory bird looked like something from prehistoric times, its lethal-looking beak mirrored by the horn-like protrusion on its small head. The bird's big body was covered in frilly gray feathers that reminded me of an ostrich's plumage, and its legs were unusually long.

But the threatening red gaze told me it was no ostrich.

Its eyes glowed with the color of old blood, its enormous beak opening to emit a strident scream.

The Iggloc's big head turned and its eyes were almost entirely white, the color in the center having shrunk down to almost nothing. It's sides heaved and its big feet navigated the uneven ground with a lightness that was like flying.

A spear flew toward us from the chasing hoard behind.

Nova gave a short, sharp cry as it sliced through his thigh and embedded itself into the Iggloc's rump. As if it had been waiting for the distraction, the demon-bird dove sharply downward, its claws opening to reach for the lightest of us, and therefore the easiest prey.

Razor sharp claws slid through Trish's flying blonde hair and caught her shoulders, digging into her flesh as she screamed. The bird flapped its huge wings and Trish's body lifted a few inches off the Iggloc. She kicked and screamed, her good arm swinging to punch at the monster.

I swung around and smacked my staff into the creature's leathery leg. It shrieked, lifting higher and carrying a screaming, thrashing Trish with it.

Nova leaped to his feet, balancing on the pack beast's wide back, and wrapped his arms around Trish's slender waist. Her screams turned frantic as Nova fought to keep her with us and the bird fought to take her away.

Flapping its bat-like wings, the monster lowered its head and stabbed at Nova with its beak, barely missing him as he ducked and twisted away. But the maneuver almost cost the bird its prey. Trish slipped back toward Nova and was nearly free.

Flinging up an arm, I screamed, "Illumine!"

Golden light flared from the orb and I focused it into the beast's eyes. The bird reared back from the light, screaming again as its ugly leathery wings flapped to keep it airborne. Then, inhumanly fast, Gren turned and flung one of his blades toward the beast. The knife sank deep into the bird's feathery chest. The monster jerked once, tried to lift higher, fought the pull of Trish's weight dragging it down, and then plunged toward the ground as the fire in its eyes winked out.

Unfortunately, it still had one claw wrapped around Trish, nearly pulling her off the Iggloc's back as it fell. But

Nova still had hold of her. With a final, herculean effort, he yanked her out of the bird's grip and down onto the Iggloc's wide back just before the bird fell the final six feet and hit the ground, sending a wall of dust skyward.

We thundered on, toward the quickly dissipating portal.

Arrows flew past and over us. A spear found the dirt directly in front of the frantic Iggloc and the beast jerked slightly before digging in and leaping the still-quivering spike.

Claws found the beast's heaving side. The Iggloc grunted, its eyes rolling wildly as its tongue waved in the air. It was clearly spent, and the ground just behind us was thick with desperate demons.

But as we neared the portal, the demons stopped trying to attack us. They set their terrifying gazes on the thin ribbon of illumination still showing and dug in, trying to beat us to it.

I knew I needed to do something. We couldn't just allow all those demons into my back yard. There was really only one thing I could do. So, I threw my arm into the air, screamed for more light, and painted the boiling crowd behind us with as much illumination as I could conjure.

The light flared brightly, it power exploding over the heaving crowd, and then bucked in my hand as pure, golden energy replaced the light.

The air around us spun and bit down on my skin as the foul, grayness of the spectral plane gave way to the heat and light of a bright sunny day.

Behind us, blood-curdling screams cut off as several demons got caught in the closing of the portal and were ripped in half.

I grimaced, extinguishing the staff's power with a

thought, and then sagged downward onto the Iggloc's thick neck.

The creature slowed to a stop and stood panting, the smell of sweat and wet fur wafting over us. After the chaos of what we'd just left behind, the silence of home wrapped me in a comforting embrace, soothing the frantic beat of my heart against my chest. I sat quietly for just a beat, cherishing the feeling of being home. Birds trilled and sang around us, fluttering around the feeder Wanda had put up near the back patio so we could enjoy the variety of birds calling the church and its grounds home.

I took a deep breath, savoring the sweetness of the flower-drenched air.

I smiled, my muscles going soft with relief.

A soft groan reminded me that I still had work to do. We had injured. I sat up, flinching in surprise as I saw that we weren't alone.

Mavis stood near the patio holding a kitchen towel as if she'd been wiping her hands with it. Niele, covered in rich black dirt, stood naked as the day he was born. Wanda's pale face stared at me from the porch, where she stood holding a glass of milk in one hand and a cookie in the other.

Every eye was fixed, not on us, but on the beast we were riding. "Honey," I shouted, groaning as I slid down the Iggloc's heaving side. "We're home."

The back door opened and a small, black and tan projectile shot outside. Monty's tiny form bounced toward us with ears flying and tail beating the air. Wraith didn't bother to leave her spot on the fence post to come and welcome us.

I stepped around the pack beast and intercepted Monty before he could spook the animal and get himself kicked or trampled.

My dog gave me a quick swipe of his tongue across my chin before fighting to get free, his brown eyes locked on the Iggloc. "No," I told him. "Be still."

I looked at Mavis, who'd finally given in to curiosity and walked over. "Gren and Trish are hurt." I thought about the arrow in Nova's thigh. "Actually, we're all pretty banged up."

My adopted mother blinked and belatedly seemed to realize I was speaking. "Huh?"

"We have injuries," I said.

She blinked again, her gaze going to the two injured and scraping to a halt on Nova. "Um...That's not Reverend Dodson."

"No. That's Nova," I told her.

Nova bowed his head in her direction.

"The Rev wanted to stay where he was for a while. Long story," I said. "I'll explain it all later."

I glanced at Niele. "Can you get Gren inside? We need to call a healer."

For a beat, I thought Niele was going to ignore me too, but he seemed to rouse himself and moved carefully toward Gren. "Is this..."

"An Iggloc," I told him, getting impatient. "It's gentle. You needn't worry."

He nodded and carefully scooped Gren up, draping him over one shoulder and heading toward the house.

Nova did the same with Trish and we limped toward the house. I looped an arm through Mavis's and towed her along with me. "Are you all right?" I asked my shell-shocked mom.

She was trying to look back over her shoulder at the pack beast. "You're just going to leave it there?"

I set Monty down on the ground with a sternly-worded reminder to mind his manners. He ignored me as only a dachshund can do, and ran toward the big beast. But when he grew close, he dropped to his fuzzy butt and contented himself with barking at it rather than trying to approach. Apparently he had more sense than I credited him with.

I realized they'd be fine when the Iggloc put its head down and started happily cropping grass. "We'll tend its wounds and bring it a bucket of water. Maybe the Crone will take it under her wing."

Mavis nodded and seemed to snap out of her amazed fog. Squeezing her arm over mine, she grinned at me. "I'm so glad you're home, honey. We were worried."

"We?" I squeezed her back and then was nearly barreled over by a skinny teen with a milk mustache. "You're home."

She caught me off guard. Wanda wasn't generally one for displays of affection. When she held on for a minute, I squeezed her back, tears burning my eyes. "It was hit or miss there for a while."

Wanda's skinny arms tightened around me, surprising me with their strength. Finally, she released me and stepped back, scooping up Wraith, who'd finally deigned to join us, and preceding us into the house. "Caleigh's been calling and texting like every hour," Wanda told me. "She said she had a vision. Something about a black lion." The teen shook her head."

"Been there. Done that," I said. Then I realized what Wanda had said and gave her a gobsmacked look. "The crone texted you?"

Wanda nodded, settling the big cat on the floor and going to wash her hands. "I told her she needed to learn how so we could communicate when we needed to."

Mavis and I shared a look. "You told her to do something and she did it?" I asked, still gobsmacked.

Wanda rolled her eyes. "You want something to eat?"

I shook my head but my stomach growled, embarrassing me. "I have to check on Gren and Trish." I started that way, my thoughts on who we could get to help Gren if his injury was as bad as it looked. I knew he'd gone to a healer once when he'd been near death from a demon attack. But he'd never told me who'd helped him. Then it hit me. I turned to Wanda. "Will you call Caleigh and ask her to come? I think Gren's injuries are beyond what any of us can fix."

Wanda pulled her phone out of her pocket and punched it with a finger tipped in shiny black polish. "Hey, girl-friend," she said into the phone as I was leaving the kitchen.

I shook my head. If I addressed the crone that way, she'd turn me into a garden slug and drop me into a pile of slug bait.

Niele had placed Gren on my bed and covered him with a quilt and several blankets. I figured out why when I sat down next to him and felt the icy air surrounding my angel. He'd brought the cold of the spectral plane back with him. Gren groaned softly, shifting restlessly as he slept. Frantic eye movements behind his eyelids told me he was mired in an uneasy sleep. Despite the unnatural cold surrounding Gren, his face was covered in sweat and his dark hair stuck to his neck and face.

He shivered violently and I pulled the covers up to his chin, unable to keep from running a hand over his chest, tears of worry filling my eyes.

"She's coming," Wanda said from the door. When I glanced her way, I saw the fear in her expression before she schooled it. "I'm sure she'll be able to help him."

I nodded, not sure I could talk without crying. "Where's Mavis?"

"She's tending Trish. Bev's coming over too. Between

them, Mother Mavis was pretty sure they could heal the wounds on her shoulders."

"Good." My lips curved upward. "You know you make her sound like a nun when you call her that." The kid had started referring to Mavis that way after she'd moved into the church with me. Mavis had wanted Wanda to call her gramma, but the teen hadn't been comfortable with that. So, she'd come up with her own term of endearment.

"Tilly brought double chocolate muffins over this morning."

My stomach grumbled at the prospect. I could almost smell the delicious confections as my mind conjured them. "Yum," I said.

Wanda came into the room and sat down in the chair by the door. It was my "boots and leathers" chair, the one I sat in to work sticky leather up my legs and over my outsized booty.

"Meow," Wraith drawled as she slunk into the room. The big black cat dodged my touch when I reached for her, always playing hard to get, and jumped up onto the bed. I tried again to grab her when she climbed onto Gren and sprawled over his chest, but my fingers somehow found empty air rather than silky black fur. I would have made a more determined effort to get her off him, except that he seemed to settle with her warm weight on his chest and I decided to let her be.

Niele appeared in the door. "I'm going out to take care of the demon parts in the yard. I'll give the Iggloc water and brush him down."

I nodded. "Thanks, Niele. Can you tend his wounds too?"

"Yes, ma'am."

"I think we should have Caleigh test Wraith," I told my ward when the gnome had left.

Wanda seemed to pull herself out of her thoughts, frowning. "Test her for what?"

"Magic," I said, scratching the big cat's back with my short, battered nails. The touch earned me a hiss and a whip against my wrist of her long tail. "I swear that half the time when I reach for her, she turns into air to avoid me."

Wanda nodded but didn't respond. I knew what she was thinking. The cat hated me. She never tried to avoid Wanda's touch, and the teen didn't really like cats. Although I was pretty sure Wraith was growing on her.

The kitchen door slammed and a familiar arrogant voice called out. "I'm here." A cacophony of barking accompanied the crone's announcement and a trio of tiny elephants pounded down the hallway on big paws, their floppy ears sailing out behind them.

Wraith hissed as Monty and his two girlfriends bounced into the room and the cat jumped off the bed, disappearing into the shadows.

The crone came into the room as I was greeting the two girl doxies whose names were Laverne and Shirley. I didn't know which was which because when I'd asked the crone which one was Laverne, she'd looked disgusted and told me it was the one that responded when I called the name. Since neither dog responded when I called them, I'd decided I might never know which was which. The little dogs were sweet, but they'd clearly been around their independent owner too long.

The old magic woman shooed me away and took my place next to Gren. She pushed the covers back and held a hand over his chest for a moment, a kaleidoscope of colorful magic illuminating her palm as she, presumably, tried to read his injuries. Finally, she looked up at me. "Tell me how he was injured."

I winced. "I don't know. It was during a battle and I didn't see exactly what happened. But it looked to me as if one of his wings was damaged."

"Yes, of course it was," she said, her tone impatient. "But that's not what's affecting him now."

I bit back a smart retort. "We were hoping you could tell us."

Her gaze slid to the teen standing next to me and softened. "Wanda, can you get my bag? I left it with the horse." When Wanda left the room, the crone moved her hand to Gren's shoulder and cinnamon-colored energy burned into the long, bloody tear. The magic must have been caustic, because Gren winced in his sleep and grew more restless. "That's a nice Iggloc you've got out there. How'd you get it across the barrier?"

I started to respond and then stopped, realizing I needed to tread carefully. If I came out and asked the crone to take the Iggloc off my hands, she'd refuse just to be contrary. But I could tell by the shifting of her gaze and her studied nonchalance that she wanted the beast. So, I bit back my excitement and feigned indifference, shrugging. "We were riding full out with a thousand demons on our heels. I guess it just happened."

"Oh?" She moved her magic to Gren's other shoulder. I noticed he seemed to be less restless. "How did you acquire it?"

Really, the woman was a terrible trickster. She kept giving me side-eye and her questions were too eager to be disinterested.

"Gren bartered for it with a passing specter. I have no idea what he bartered with."

The crone ran a finger along Gren's arm, bending closer and eying a narrow red line I hadn't noticed until she examined it. "I think I know." She looked at me. "He gave the creature a feather. Maybe two."

I felt my eyes go wide. "Why would he do that?"

"Angel feathers are worth a lot on the spectral plane. Many spirits believe having one all but ensures a rich life in that horrible place."

I grimaced. "They must have been observing a different place than I was. If I never go back, it will be too soon."

To my surprise, the crone nodded without comment. A beat later, she said, way too nonchalantly. "If you have no use for the pack beast. I could be talked into taking it off your hands."

I looked down so she couldn't see me smile. "Yeah? What will you give me for it?" Who ever said I was a bad negotiator?

11

THE LARES' FRIENDS ARE WORSE THAN FOES

I pushed off the flagstones of my patio with one foot, my other leg folded beneath me, and stared up at a full blue-tinged moon as the glider swayed underneath me in a soothing rhythm. The mudroom door opened and softly closed. I looked up to see Gren, still moving stiffly, making his way toward me with a glass of wine in one hand. "Are you supposed to be drinking that?" I asked, teasing. "There might be an interaction issue with the crone's healing magic."

His smile was weary. "This is for you. If I drank wine I'd probably fall asleep."

He handed me the wine and lowered himself carefully to the glider, sighing as he sat. "I'm not going to lie, beautiful Aggy, that healing took something out of me."

I sipped and made a sound of pure pleasure. "Thanks for this. I wanted some but didn't have the energy to go get it."

He clasped my hand in his and pulled it to his lips for a kiss. "It was my pleasure." The weary smile turned devilish. "Mavis already had it poured. I'm just the delivery boy."

Laughing, I snuggled close, waggling my brows suggestively. "Delivery boy, huh? I've had naughty dreams about delivery boys."

He looked shocked, which only made my teasing more fun. "You jest."

I shook my head, toeing the patio stones to set us into motion again. "I do not jest."

He unexpectedly took the wine from me and took a big drink.

"Hey!"

"I'm sorry, but I'm appalled. I've just learned my woman hungers after males who deliver. I fear I've taken up the wrong career."

I made a grab for my wine but he held it above his head, out of my reach. "Not another drop until you tell me what it is about the delivery man that appeals. Is it the uniform?"

I sighed. "I always did love a man in uniform."

He grew pensive, gliding silently for a minute with my wine glass clutched in one hand. "I'm beyond heart-broken."

I couldn't help it, I laughed. Spurred by the teasing glint in his molten chocolate gaze. "If it's any consolation, I like my delivery men *out* of their uniforms even better."

His brows lifted north. "Now that has possibilities. I can deliver and not wear a uniform. It sounds like we have a workable solution to the problem."

"Yes," I agreed, a laugh dancing on my lips. "Now, can I have my wine back?"

He stood and bowed, offering me the glass of rich red blend with a flourish. "My lady. I deliver this, your wine."

Rather than take it from him, I circled a finger on the air in front of him. "What happened to that whole being out of uniform thing?"

He sat back down. "I'll have to take a...What is it that

you call it? Raincheck? I'm afraid I'm too knackered to pull that off at the moment."

I lay my head on his firm shoulder and sighed. "Me too, so I'll give you that raincheck."

We glided in comfortable silence for several moments. I was so happy to be home, I never wanted to leave again.

A sinuous black shadow leaped from the ground onto a fence post and fixed us with an accusing, yellow gaze. Wraith glared at me for a few beats and then turned her sleek back on me and commenced to cleaning her paws, acting as if I didn't exist. I couldn't help thinking the cat was blaming me for not bringing her buddy, Reverend Dodson back. "She hates me," I told Gren.

He started as if he'd been deep in thought. "Wraith?"

"Mmhm," I said, my eyes growing heavy. Gren had been the smart one. Drinking wine when I was tired was a mistake.

"She doesn't hate you," he said thoughtfully. "Like all the women in this place, she just has opinions."

"That's certainly an understatement."

From my pocket, a random male voice suddenly bellowed, "ANSWER THE PHONE!"

"Ah!" I screamed, sitting bolt upright. "DO YOU HEAR ME?! ANSWER THE BLASTED PHONE!" As Gren chuckled, I shoved my hand into my pocket. My fingers got lost in the folds of cloth and I couldn't get to the stupid phone. I growled my frustration, not able to cut off the obnoxious screaming fast enough. "ANSWER THIS DA%@ PHONE! YOUR MOM IS CALLING! SHE WANTS TO TALK ABOUT THAT TIME YOU TOOTED IN FRONT OF THE ENTIRE FAMILY AT CHRISTMAS!" I managed to get hold of the cell and got it halfway out before it slipped from my frantic grip again. "ANSWER THIS PHONE OR SHE'S

GOING TO PLAY ALL YOUR BABY VIDEOS FOR YOUR BOYFRIEND! DO THE WORDS POOPOOS MY POTTY MEAN ANYTHING TO YOU?!"

Gren threw his head back and laughed.

I finally got hold of the slippery rectangle and fumbled to answer it, my hand shaking. "I'M NOT KIDDING, YOU'D BETTER ANSWER…!"

"Oh, my goddess!" I yelled into the phone.

Mavis was laughing so hard she couldn't speak to me for a minute.

"Very funny," I told her, grinning despite myself. "You need to change that before I have to go out in public again."

She took a breath and was off again.

"You suck," I told her, sounding too much like my favorite teen.

Mavis wound down enough to speak. "I wish I could see your face."

"So do I because that would mean you'd be within thumping distance."

She went off again. When she finally stopped laughing, she said, "I just wanted to tell you I'm glad you're home. I missed you."

My heart turned all gooey. "I missed you too, mom. But I didn't miss the ringtone thing."

She giggled happily.

"Wait. Where are you? Gren said you just poured my wine."

"Walking through your front door, heading out to my car."

"Why'd you call instead of poking your head out the door?"

"Honey…do you have to ask?"

I really didn't. "You're going to pay for that ringtone, you know."

"You've been saying that for months. So far there's been no retribution."

"Revenge is a dish best served cold."

"Well, you go ahead and let it get cold. In the meantime, I've got a folder full of colorful ringtones to torture you with."

I shook my head, grinning. "You're terrible."

"I love you."

"I love you too, mom. See you in the morning."

Disconnecting, I lay my head back on the swing and looked at my angel. His smile was wide and his pretty eyes were sparkling. "She's a digital genius."

I snorted. "Don't ever tell her that. She's got a big enough head as it is."

He slipped his warm hand into mine, giving it a squeeze. We swung in silence for a beat and then said, "Poopoos my potty, huh?"

I smacked his arm and he laughed until tears slid down his cheeks. I fought my own laughter, eventually losing.

Gren pulled me closer and sighed. "It is good to be home."

"Yes," I sighed. "It is."

We sat like that for several minutes, enjoying the normal night sounds of owls hooting and Bathilda fluttering about chirping as she consumed, hopefully, copious amounts of mosquitoes. I blinked. Bathilda? I sat up, my gaze sliding skyward. "Hey, air rodent. What's up?"

There was more chirping as she fluttered past above our heads.

Gren's posture turned expectant. "Is she speaking to you?"

"Of course not. Does she ever?" The truth was, she did occasionally tell me things. Cryptic things. But I knew there was more she could tell me. The goddess-danged bat apparently spoke to my favorite teen every day. They had a relationship I couldn't exactly say I envied. I mean, who'd want a bat for a friend? But it was irritating. The bat knew things. Like how she'd managed to save my kid from a house fire a while back, then turned into a biker-babe lookalike and given me bossy but sage advice about being a role model to the parent-challenged kid. And, yes, she had pulled one over on my snotty advocate, who'd come out of the situation firmly convinced he'd been the one to carry Wanda out of that fire. I'd give her points for that. But, I knew she could be more helpful if only she would.

Like currently, when I somehow knew she had something to tell me, but she just fluttered around chirping like a bat, rather than passing whatever it was on to me. "I'm not a mind-reader, you know," I shouted into the darkness as she fluttered off toward the graveyard.

Chirp!

I sighed, leaning back and snuggling into Gren. "That bat is the flying rodent equivalent of Mavis's ringtones."

He chuckled warmly.

A beat later, when I started to dose off again, Gren shifted on the glider, getting to his feet. "Come on, sleepy-head. To bed with you."

I murmured sleepily, not wanting to get up.

Without warning, he slid his arms beneath me and scooped me off the glider. I gave a surprised little squeal. "I can walk."

He somehow got the door open while still holding me and carried me inside. "Apparently not."

I gave up, snuggling my face into the warm column of his throat. "This is nice."

He laid me gently onto my bed and tugged off my sneakers, placing them beside the bed before tugging the extra quilt I kept folded at the bottom of the bed over me. The soft pillows pulled me toward sleep with downy fingers. I sighed and felt myself sliding into unconsciousness.

Warm lips touched my forehead, lingering. The touch woke me enough to realize I didn't want him to leave. I clasped his hand. "Stay with me?"

His hesitation was brief. "I'd love nothing more."

The Princess needs to speak to you.

Snuggling up against my angel, the comforting lullaby of night sounds wafting softly through my room, I wasn't exactly sure if I'd heard the bat speak, or if the words emerged from my own busy mind. Either way, I figured I'd forget them by morning. Still, I was too tired to care.

And, with that thought, I let myself fall.

"I CAN'T BELIEVE Batty talked to you," Wanda said with a grin.

I rolled my eyes. "Maybe I imagined it." We stopped on the rise of a small hill, and I sighed, enjoying the relative coolness provided by the shade from an ancient tree. We'd walked miles into the Mystical Wood and found ourselves in a sea of grass and flowers, with only the occasional tree to give rise on the horizon.

"She talks to me sometimes," I said. "She just doesn't tell me much."

I fanned my heated cheeks. Despite the cooling fall

weather at home, the woods seemed to keep constant warm temps no matter what time of year we entered it.

"I'm pretty sure Layla does need to talk to you," Wanda said. "And it seems like it might be dire."

I cast a look at my teen, raising a brow in question.

"I checked my super-secret, indisputable source this morning," she said by way of explanation.

"And that would be?"

"Her crystal ball," Bev said with a smile in her voice.

"Hey!" Wanda objected. "Do you not understand the meaning of the term, super-secret?"

We'd used the magical device during my seating when we needed to know the extent of the next challenge so we could prepare for it. I'd totally forgotten about the crystal ball and was a little surprised Wanda still had it.

Bev reached over and patted Wanda on the shoulder. "It's okay kid. Aggie won't tell anybody."

"She won't have to with your big mouth around," Wanda mumbled crankily.

"Hey," I corrected automatically. "Show some respect for your elders."

"She *is* really elder," the teen replied.

Bev smacked herself on the chest in mock horror. "Hurtful."

Wanda snickered.

"Okay, magical historian," I said to my teen, "Did your crystal ball say where this compound is?"

She gave me a disgusted look. "Do I have to do everything?"

"We could call the crone," Bev offered, carefully not looking at Wanda. She knew the kid too well. Wanda had been training under the elder witch for several months and, as all teens did, she thought she knew everything. She'd take it as a personal affront if we contacted Caleigh over something Wanda could help us with.

Aaannnd, right on cue...

"Why would you do that? I don't need her help."

"Maybe not," I said. "But we need somebody's help. Daylight's burning."

"It would have been ever so much more helpful," Bev lamented, "If Layla had just sent somebody to guide us to her compound."

I nodded in agreement. I got that she was trying to keep her location secret...like Wanda's crystal ball...but she *asked* us to come and then left us hanging.

Wanda stopped on a patch of bright green grass and dropped gracefully to the ground, crossing her legs and opening the big book she carried everywhere with her. Spreading it on the grass in front of her, Wanda closed her eyes and held her hands, palms down, over the aged tome.

I recognized it as one of the ones the crone had given her when they'd started their training. It looked to be hundreds of years old, maybe thousands, and had scrawled notes on nearly every yellowed page. I wondered if the notes were the crone's, or if there'd been a magical librarian before the crone who'd handed it down to her.

Bev and I shared a look, both of us fascinated by what Wanda did as a historian. We rarely asked her questions about it because that was the surest way to get her to clam up. The opportunity to watch her do her thing was too precious to miss.

To my surprise, the words on the page lifted beneath Wanda's magic, swirling on the air in a soup of pale-yellow magic that smelled of pears for some strange reason.

The swirling words fought and jockeyed for space, eventually forming themselves into two sentences which I couldn't read. At first I thought it was a different language, maybe an ancient one, given that historians are born with the innate knowledge of all times in magical history.

Given that she was searching through relatively recent history—the period of time encompassing the Lost Princess's leaving the demonic realm and settling in the earthly realm—it didn't seem likely the instruction in the book would be in an ancient language.

But what did I know?

Wanda frowned and finally looked up. "This doesn't make sense."

"What does it say?" I asked, my gaze locked on the still-shifting words.

"It can't be," she said, moving her hands and re-swizzling the words in front of her.

"Talk to me," I said. "Maybe we can help."

She shook her head, her silky dark hair dancing around her slender shoulders. "No. This is right. But it doesn't make any sense."

"Where is it?" Bev asked, looking around.

"Here," Wanda said. "We're on top of it."

12

WITH WEAPONS THROWN THE TENSION GROWS

"It's underground?" I asked, looking stupidly down at my shoes.

Wanda frowned, swirling the letters hanging in the air once again. "No. At least I don't think so. It's more like..."

"Hey, guys?" Bev said.

"If we're on top of it, then it has to be below us, right?"

Wanda stared at the book, clearly flummoxed. "I know that seems logical, but..."

"Aggy," Bev said, her tone impatient.

High above our heads, a raven cawed out a warning, but I wasn't paying attention. I'd stepped away from the teen and was trying to find an entry...a door...a tunnel...anything that would tell us we were in the right spot.

"Aggy!"

"Caw! Caw! Caw!"

A thread of something slipped over me...something that bit at my skin like magic. I absently rubbed at my arms. "Should we call Caleigh?"

Wanda shook her head. "No. I've got this."

"Pee!"

My gaze jerked skyward as I realized the big black bird, which had dropped to a lower branch and was dancing sideways, its wings flapping with apparent alarm, was not just some random bird. "Ray?" I stepped back so I could see him more clearly among the leaves. "What are you peeing about?"

"Caw!"

"Aggy, watch out!"

"Ah!" Wanda screamed, diving away from the historical records she'd been perusing as an ax sailed head over handle in her direction.

The deadly weapon cleaved the ancient tome in half, and Wanda landed behind a thick tree trunk. In a blink, Bev was standing in front of her with magic dancing in her hands.

I spun, finding a line of angry-looking lost ones holding spears, carrying bows nocked with arrows, and brandishing the biggest swords I'd ever seen. "How dare you attack my ward. Are you declaring war on the Lares' council?"

The largest one, his scaled skin a charcoal gray so dark it gleamed in the sunshine that beat down on them, stepped forward and whipped his sword in my direction, its point finding the tender spot beneath my chin. "Why do you disturb the privacy of the Lost City, home and succor of Princess Layla of the earthly dimension?"

I stared at him for a beat, vaguely aware of the fluttering of wings as Ray dropped down and landed on my shoulder like Blackbeard's parrot.

"Rude!" the raven exclaimed, always one for vast understatement.

I held up my hands. "Princess Layla asked us to come. She has something she needs to discuss with us."

The devil's eyes glowed angry red, his big hand tightened visibly on the hilt of his sword. I tensed, pulling my magic forward in case we needed to fight our way out of there.

I threw up a hand and my staff smacked into my palm, the orb on the end already spitting with angry magic. You could have killed my kid," I snarled.

"She was perfectly safe. We are better at throwing than that," a gravelly voice said behind the lead devil. The big guy did a slow turn, a growl rumbling in the back of his throat.

The guard who'd spoken held his gaze, not backing down.

Magic spit behind me. Bev was breathing fast and hard, as if she'd run a mile uphill.

Wanda was as quiet as a mouse.

Ray's feathers rustled softly as he shifted on my shoulder, claws digging painfully into my flesh.

I didn't speak again. I'd said my piece. The guards would either take me to Layla or attack. If they attacked, I fully intended to make them regret it.

Finally, the lead devil guard, fully ten feet tall if he was an inch, nodded to one of the smaller guards in the line behind him and the creature turned on her heel and started running.

I didn't watch her go. My full attention was locked on the leader. His movements would signal the movements of the others. He stared back at me, body on full alert and eyes brimming with devilish fervor.

Ray rose off my shoulder in a chaos of flapping wings and smacked me in the face. I bit back a curse, knowing I needed to project a calm and confident manner in the face of the devils' aggression. That was no easy task when your bird friend was busy smacking you on the face with his wings.

Ray danced across my shoulder and noisily clacked his beak, drawing the attention of the guard. I used the helpful distraction to catch Bev's eye and give her a small nod. She returned the nod, affirming we were both ready to battle if it was necessary.

Finally, when I thought I'd go stark raving mad from the taut silence, the runner returned and gave her boss some kind of complicated hand signal.

"Rude," Ray repeated.

I nodded in agreement. "Are you going to take us to the princess or not? If you're not, then we'll go. We came at her request."

The guard didn't respond. He simply stepped aside, as did the six other guards behind him, and motioned us forward.

With a sense of danger filling the air around us, I reluctantly motioned to Wanda to join me. I wanted her close enough to cover if things went butt-cheeks up. The teen gave her skewered book an unhappy look and then glared up at the devil brigade. "You guys owe me a new book."

"Stay close," I whispered to my kid, and then, with Bev taking up the rear, magic spitting in her fists, we passed through the devil gantlet, and into a magical place.

13

A FRIEND WHOSE FAMILY NEEDS
HER AID

The feeling was like a large rubber band stretching until it couldn't stretch anymore and then breaking, the sting of its rebound a quick bite against my skin. I winced, my arm going protectively in front of Wanda. But she gave a soft little yelp anyway, the magic ignoring my protection.

I blinked in surprise as we walked into a nightscape, the sky above a dove gray, with wispy clouds skidding across a crescent moon. High above us in the trees, an enormous owl hooted its mournful song and broke from the covering branches to spread its wings and flee.

Just for a minute, I enjoyed the irony of the owl fearing us and apparently not batting an oversized eye at the monsters following us.

"This way," the lead guard said, his too-deep voice rasping through the unnatural silence. We fell in behind him, our strides easy on well-worn paths winding through trees not unlike those in the Mystical Wood, except that they were…more. More abundant, extra large, denser.

Behind us, the magic snapped again and the guards jerked to a halt, spinning around with weapons drawn. All eyes slid downward as a low black shadow stalked silently in our direction.

"Meow." Wraith didn't even spare the enormous devil guard a glance as she rubbed against Wanda's legs and did a figure eight around my ankles. Her purr throbbed through the otherwise silent night.

"What is that beast doing here?" the head devil growled.

Wraith hissed in his direction and then twined herself around my legs again.

I shrugged, hiding my own surprise that Wraith had joined us behind a show of disinterest. "Wraith goes where Wraith chooses to go." I hesitated. "But if you're thinking about trying to hurt her, you'll answer to me first and your mistress second. The princess happens to be fond of this cat."

The guard growled again, one scaly gray lip curling with disgust, and then nodded to the female who was leading the way. We walked on, my legs beginning to tire and my lower back screaming at me. I'd been bad about working out lately. I preferred food and beverage athletics, with muffin lifting and coffee slurping in the morning and fork yoga with wine tipping at night to the more strenuous types of training. I was paying for that laziness, and vowed to do better starting the next day. Maybe I'd lift an extra muffin.

After all, there was no need to get crazy about the training.

Wraith suddenly shot forward and the night lit with a crack of silver magic as she disappeared into a shadowed spot tucked into the arching branches of two enormous trees. I jerked to a halt, torn between caution and a strong desire to rescue the cheeky feline from her own curious nature.

"What was that?" Bev asked, her magic spitting around her raised fists.

The guards turned on my sister, weapons at the ready. "Lose the magic," the head devil barked.

After a tense moment comprised of the two factions glaring at each other, another snap of magic had us all turning to find Wraith skulking back toward us. She was licking her lips and I had a terrible feeling some poor mouse wasn't going to make it back to his den.

"Tell us what that was," I ordered the guard. "Or we're not moving forward."

The devilish soldier's blood-red eyes looked, for a beat, as if they might roll. Then he said, "That beast creates her own magic. We cannot be held responsible."

My gaze scanned to Wanda's, then Bev's.

Wanda did an eye roll. "Stupid cat. She's always creating drama."

Wraith twined around the teen's skinny ankles and purred.

Bev narrowed her gaze at the feline. "There's something odd about that cat."

I couldn't argue. "Okay, let's move on. I need to get back home."

The guard frowned. "Move on to where?"

"To see Lay...the princess."

"But..." the guard looked thoroughly confused.

"They can't see past the glamour," a familiar voice said. We jumped and I gave an unmanly yelp that I wasn't proud of. Layla stepped out of the darkness and then pulled it around her, rolling it up like a carpet and flinging it away. I stared at her, dumbfounded as sunlight replaced the darkness and stone cottages replaced the trees. Well, not all of the trees, but a lot of them.

Heat rolled over us and my body reacted by immediately breaking into a sweat.

I looked out over the sunny horizon at the quaint little village. The picturesque place was built on rolling green hills with a narrow dirt road and a wide creek. Clear blue water wound through what looked like hundreds of stone cottages of all shapes and sizes. A pretty stone bridge arched over the creek at the road, and the lane on the other side led up a verdant green hill to a castle that really just looked like a bigger stone cottage.

My eye caught on the abundance of flowers which seemed to grow everywhere, even from the tidy thatch roofs topping the buildings.

"Layla, this is lovely."

The look of pleasure on my friend's face made her even prettier than she normally was in her human form. Extremely tall for a woman, with delicate features and feminine limbs, Princess Layla of the Lost Ones had once worn a devilish form like her soldiers. But something had happened when she was helping me escape a deadly vortex and she'd lost her preferred form, reverting to the part of herself that was human. To my eyes she was beautiful. But to her and her people, she was all but hideous. Still, Layla wasn't one to dwell on the negatives life threw her. And she had, in fact, been working to return to her devilish form. I'd seen flashes of her previous appearance during battle. A fact that gave her hope she'd be able to return to her devilish form for good. Eventually.

"It's home," she said after a moment. "Would you walk with me?"

I nodded and the guards stepped back, following at a distance as Layla led us to a small park with a pond and a fountain. "How's furry butt?" the princess asked with a grin. "I haven't had a chance to kick his posterior lately."

She was referring to my advocate, Ferral. The two of them trained together often, a practice that had begun with a fight that Layla insisted she won handily. The fact that Ferral didn't deny her win told me she wasn't lying. But what had probably started on Ferral's part as an attempt to regain his pride and on her part as a fun diversion, seemed to have turned into a relationship of mutual respect. Maybe even friendship.

"He's as annoying as ever," I said, grinning. "I've been keeping him pretty busy. I'll tell him you're in the mood to kick his butt again."

"Please do." Her eyes sparkled with good humor.

As we drew close to the fountain, I realized it featured a naked devil rather than a naked human. Water spouted from the devil's upraised sword and ran down his muscular body to gloss the heavy goat-like legs.

A pretty, flower-drenched gazebo sat a distance away, the tables beneath the vine-covered roof laden with trays and bowls. A delicious savory scent wafted our way on a warm breeze and my stomach growled embarrassingly.

Layla grinned my way. "You're starving as usual, I hear."

"I worked through my giant chocolate muffin in the long walk to see you."

Layla's eyes went wide. "I don't suppose you brought me one," she asked hopefully.

"No," Bev said. Then, when the devil princess's happy smile turned upside down, Bev laughed. Reaching into the oversized bag she had slung over one shoulder, she pulled out a white cardboard box. "We brought you a dozen, assorted flavors. Tilly wanted you to try the new peanut butter and chocolate flavor and let her know what you think."

Layla gave a little squeal and grabbed for the box, then seemed to realize that squealing wasn't very princess-like and sobered. She gave us a regal bow. "I will accept this as a token of your loyalty and friendship."

I grinned. "Good. Because that's exactly what it is."

Layla sat down on an oversized concrete bench near the pond and opened the box. "Sit. Share a muffin with me."

I sat, but Bev and Wanda strolled down to the pond, twin expressions of delight blooming on their faces as a pair of swans swam toward them across the glistening water. Like everything else in Layla's compound, the swans looked to be twice the size of normal swans. But what was most interesting was the fact that one was blue and one was pink.

"Interesting swans."

The princess grinned, her teeth covered in peanut-butter frosting. "They mate for life, you know. We magicked them pink and blue at the request of a council member's daughter."

"And the bow tie?"

Layla laughed, the sound musical as it carried across the pond. "That was all me. The unfortunate result of too much grog."

I laughed. "Grog, huh?"

"A favorite in my realm."

I knew she meant the demonic realm, but the realization that she'd misspoken stole her smile. Layla really seemed to love being on the earthly plane. At least she seemed determined to love it because, from what she'd said in the past, her life in the demonic realm had been rough. Though, I assumed she had family there she no doubt missed.

The princess sighed, setting the half-eaten muffin into the box and closing the lid. Like magic, a young human woman hurried over and took the box, carrying it back to the gazebo and adding it to the food there. "We have a problem, Aggy."

"I assumed," I said, trying not to throw a wishful gaze toward the white box. "What's up?"

Layla watched Wanda and Bev, who were sitting on the grass throwing hunks of bread they'd been given out to the swans, and chatting. "You spoke to Matthew and Glenn?"

I nodded. "They said you needed to speak with me."

She chewed her bottom lip. Her expression was tense, which was out of character for the cocky princess. "Did they give you something for me?"

I had a face-palm moment. "Ugh! Yeah. Sorry." I glanced toward the pond. "Bev, can you give Layla that scroll?"

Bev reached into her bag and pulled it out, walking it over to us. She stood as Layla carefully unrolled the scroll and read the message. Surreptitiously, I tried to read it over her shoulder but the characters of the text were strange and I couldn't decipher them.

When she finished, she carefully rerolled it and dropped it to her lap, her long fingers wrapped protectively around it.

To my shock, tears slipped down her cheeks.

"What's wrong, Layla. Talk to me. I want to help."

She shook her head and scraped a hand under her eyes, drying her cheeks. "It is bad, Aggy. Really bad." She turned a tear-drenched gaze my way. For a moment, I didn't think she was going to tell me what was wrong. But she pulled air into her lungs and released it slowly. "My people are in great danger and I don't know how to help them."

I couldn't help it, I glanced around the bucolic paradise

she'd made her home. I couldn't see a problem. Everything looked calm and happy.

As if reading my mind, she shook her head. "Not here. My compound is secure. But I'm afraid those who I love in the demonic realm are in great danger. And they will not allow me to help."

14

A DASTARDLY FOE HIS PRESENCE MADE

"Talk to me, Layla."

"You saw what was happening in the spectral realm?"

I nodded. I had no idea what it meant, but I was starting to put the pieces together. "Is your family part of the group trying to get here through the spectral realm?"

"I wish it were that simple. The last thing they want is to come here. They still haven't forgiven *me* for coming."

"Okay." I had a feeling it wasn't the right time to get into that with her. But we'd definitely have to have a girl's night out and probe that tender spot in her heart. "So, they're not on the spectral plane?"

"Not yet. But they are afraid they will be forced out of the demonic realm and won't have a choice."

I frowned. "Who is trying to force them?"

Her gaze lifted to mine, the intensity of her copper gaze willing me to understand. But I didn't understand. "Are they getting pressure because of the mass migration into spookdom?"

I'd hoped to wring a smile out of her, but she simply

shook her head. "The person who is setting them up for expulsion isn't even involved in that. It's not an organized migration. Just a bunch of regular demons who think things will be better here because they think humans are weak and can be overpowered and controlled."

"Okay, so the two aren't related."

"They are though. Sort of."

I shook my head, lifting my hands to show I was lost.

Expelling a harsh breath, Layla said, "The Commander once led Hell's army. He was the one who led them through the Hellmouth that opened outside of town."

My eyes went wide. "The vortex at the old folks residence?"

"Yes."

Memories assailed me of that terrifying time. The drone of a distant army on the march. The terror of Layla's instructions as we prepared to go inside.

"Before we go in there," the princess told me, her tone dire, "you must understand. Under no circumstances should you allow yourself to get separated from me. That's critical." She looked down at me, lines of worry creasing her brow. "If you're not with me when I'm thrown back out, you'll be left behind, and you will not be set free. An ancient warrior guardian is too fine a prize to release. Do you understand?"

I *had* understood. And her words had painted my spine in icy dread.

"He's probably pretty mad that we beat him, huh?"

To my surprise, Layla laughed. "That's a vast understatement, Aggy. "The Commander has been scheming ways to get to us since the moment the Hellmouth collapsed and his mission failed. A demon like the Commander does not take defeat well, and I can only imagine he took the loss as a personal affront. He would have suffered greatly from our beating him."

"His wittle feelings were hurt?" I grinned at Layla, trying to take the shadows from her face.

"His feelings. His body. His fortune. His family."

When I didn't understand what she was telling me, she clarified. By the time she was done, I really wished she hadn't. "He was demoted to the rank of lowly soldier. The skin of his back was peeled away beneath the relentless spiked whips the demon lords prefer. His vast fortunes, including three homes, were taken and his family was flung into the streets." Her cheeks paled and she added, "His wife was shared among the soldiers until she died and his children were given to the poorest family in the realm."

I closed my eyes, realizing how lucky I was to have been born human. "Goddess. How horrible."

Layla didn't respond.

I opened my eyes and reached for her hand, finding it icy. "I'm sorry. I didn't know."

She shrugged. "As you can imagine, the Commander wishes to serve up the same sour stew to us. And my family is the most obvious place to start."

"We need to get them out of there," I said.

"And take them where?" Layla asked, her tone brittle. She stood and paced in front of the bench, wringing her hands as she walked. "That, Aggy, is the heart of the problem. They aren't safe in the demonic realm. Because of the chaos and confusion caused by those idiots who are trying to migrate, they also wouldn't be safe in the spectral realm."

"They'd be safe here," I offered.

She stopped pacing, glaring down at me. "Have you not been listening? They. Will. Not. Come. Here."

I clamped my lips shut and shared a look with Bev. Wanda joined us, her young features tight with concern. "She's right, Aggy," my teen said. "There is one version of history where the Benedict Royals are slaughtered in their beds."

Layla flinched and her pacing grew more agitated.

I gave Wanda a look, but she frowned at me. "There is another where they are killed in a surprise attack on the spectral plane."

I dropped my head back and stared at the sky for patience.

"And there is one potential outcome that has not been determined."

Layla slid her a look. "Did they come here?"

"No," Wanda said. "That much is clear. Although there's a blank spot in that outcome. A slight connection to this plane."

"That's probably just me," Layla said, sounding sad.

"There has to be a way," Bev said, sliding me a look filled with question. My wonderful sister wanted to ask me if there wasn't something I could do. To her credit, she didn't want to put me on the spot.

That was good. Because I had no ideas at the moment.

"Meow!"

We all turned to find Wraith trotting lightly toward us. She jumped onto the bench and commenced to rubbing her head along my thigh. I reached out and gave her a little scratch between her ears.

She head-butted my hand, purring loudly enough to drown out the conversation of the women tending the food in the gazebo. Without warning, the cat struck, her sharp white canines sinking into my hand.

"Ouch!" I tried to yank my hand away but couldn't, and

before I could consider what that meant, a vision slid across my mind.

I guessed he was over eleven feet tall. The sides of his long, narrow head were weighted down by enormous ram's horns that were a deep red, rather than black. His eyes were wide slits on a scabby face, his nostrils black holes at the ends of a rounded hump of a nose. His face tapered down to a narrow snout filled with square teeth that had serrated edges. Fire burned within the eye slits and a growl throbbed around him.

Unlike the lost ones I'd met, the massive devil didn't walk on heavy bent rear legs. His legs, like the rest of his tall body, were straight and long and bulged with muscle. His arms hung at his sides, reaching to his knees with thick, black claws.

As I took his measure, he took mine. It was all too readily apparent that he wasn't impressed by what he saw.

The scabby black lips opened to showcase a terrifying number of teeth and he smiled, cocking his triangular head. "We finally meet, Madam Lares. I have anticipated our final battle for many months."

I frowned. "I'm not sure why you want to fight, but you and I will not battle."

"Oh, but we will." His mean smile slid away. The flames dancing in his slitted eyes jumped with renewed vigor. "We will fight and you will die. But rest assured. Your death will not be swift. And it will not be easy."

Behind him, in the distance, a man and a woman bent underneath heavy chains, their expensive clothing, like something a royal family from human history might have worn, was heavy with mud and hung in tatters from their slender forms. The heavy bent legs appeared to be nearly too weary to carry them forward.

Behind them, already loaded into some kind of prison conveyance led by an Iggloc, were a young girl and boy, whose fluffy blond hair, though matted and spattered by something dark and slimy, reminded me of a certain princess.

"Leave them be," I told the enormous demon. "They did nothing to you. Come find me if you want a battle."

The triangular head cocked again. "But you said you wouldn't be fighting me."

My fingers clenched and I wished for all the world that I held my staff. "Apparently, I lied."

The creature stared at me for a beat and then threw back his head and emitted a howl that made me want to whimper and pee myself. It took me a minute to figure out he was laughing.

I shuddered. "Tell me where you are and I'll come to you. Just let them go. They did nothing to you."

I didn't realize he'd moved until his clawed hand was twisted into my shirt. Wrenching me off the ground, the beast pressed his ugly face close to mine, his breath smelling like spoiled meet and sour beer. "My family did nothing to deserve their fate either," he growled. "Yet they suffered and died." He tilted his head to one side and then, very slowly, to the other. "Do not believe the princess will be the only one whose family will suffer, guardian."

He spoke my title as if it were a pile of writhing worms on his tongue. "I will find each and every one of those you love and tear them slowly to pieces. Then I will roast those pieces over the fire and savor them with a fine grog."

My stomach twisted violently and I suddenly had a terrible need to get out of the vision so I could make sure Wanda and Bev were okay. And Mavis. And Monty. Tears filled my eyes. And Gren. But I couldn't let the demon see my fear. So, I pushed the emotion back and tried for cocky. "That's an oddly specific threat. I can tell you've been thinking about this for a while. Maybe you should get a hobby. I hear wine and painting parties are fun."

The creature lifted me higher into the air, his knuckles digging into my throat and choking off my ability to breathe. I *fought him as he howled again. He wasn't laughing. I realized that as he threw me away from him, my body sailing uncontrollably toward the distant wagons.*

And even before I slammed into them, a familiar pain ripped into my gut and agony took me under.

15

PRISONERS OF THE BEAST AFRAID

Aggy!

A The voice seemed far away, panic filling the sound.

Hands touched my face and I twisted away, my skin burning from the slightest touch. My middle was on fire, an intense pressure making me writhe and cry out.

Pictures slashed through my thoughts. Chains. Crying. Terrified red-gold eyes beneath an unruly cloud of tangled blonde hair.

Flame rose around me, dancing toward my flesh and then arching away as if blown by an insistent wind.

So. Much. Pain.

Aggy?! Come out of it now.

Bev's voice. Cold hands clasping my shoulders and giving me a shake.

"Bev?" Her name broke through like shards of glass, cutting my throat and tongue as the single word passed.

"It's me, honey. You need to pull out of it now. Layla's threatening to heal you if you don't."

I laughed and then moaned, flinging my head from side

to side as the laughter tore from my lips. A trail of fire marked the path the sound had made in my throat.

"It burns," I said, swallowing hard.

"Can someone get her some water?" Wanda. Sounding terrified.

"Here," Bev said, one strong hand cupping the back of my neck and urging me into a halfway seated position. A cool glass pressed against my lips and I opened, greedily swallowing the meagre flow she allowed. "Better?"

The water hurt and soothed at the same time, but I nodded. "Thanks."

"I can call my healer," Layla's familiar voice said. "I promise she's better at healing than me."

I shook my head and my brain slammed from side to side inside the cage of my skull. "Ugh!" I complained. "Maybe just a couple of aspirin?"

Voices, footsteps, then a timid and soft voice. "Here, mistress."

I opened my eyes and found myself staring at a lost one whose kind green eyes seemed to see right through me. Her touch was as gentle as it was sure, and her thick wave of auburn hair tickled my arm as she leaned over me to offer the pills. "Is she still rising into her seating?" The woman asked.

Bev nodded. "She's moving through the last stage. It's been just about killing her."

"For how long?" the healer asked.

Bev looked at Wanda but, before my worried teen could respond, I said, "About a week."

The healer inclined her head, easing me gently back until I lay flat on something soft. It was the first I'd noticed I wasn't lying on the grass outside. They'd carried me into the gazebo and laid me on some kind of pallet. She placed a cool hand over my heart and a pale gray light oozed from her palm. I flinched at first, but soon relaxed under the warm, healing magic. "Your aura is still slightly fractured but you're very close. Have your interactions changed?"

I thought about the woman I'd been able to help through telepathic encouragement and nodded. "I had a vision," I said, the incongruence of my statement making everyone blink in surprise. I reached for Layla and clasped her hand. "Your family is in great danger."

The princess gave me an irritated look. "I realize that. It's what I just told you..."

"No. Immediate danger. I saw them."

Her eyes went wide and she tightened her grip on my hand as if she were afraid I was going to bolt. "Where? What's happening to them?"

"He has them," I said. My response was cryptic but I knew Layla would understand.

She paled, dropping to her butt and looking more lost than I'd ever seen her. "Are they...alive?"

"Yes. But I got a bad vibe. You were right, he has a vendetta."

I'd expected tears, but the information hardened Layla's features. Her aura shimmied and, for the space of a single heartbeat, her devilish form overlaid her human one. "He's not going to get what he wants. I'm going to save them from him and themselves if it's the last thing I do."

I nodded, pushing upright as the pain finally receded.

"I'm sorry," my sister finally said. "But who's this *he* you're talking about?"

Layla and I shared a look, then she grimaced. "He once led Hell's army. He's known as the Commander, though he hasn't officially held that title for a few months now."

I caught my sister's eye and said, "Since we closed the Hellmouth."

"Oh," Bev said. Then, "Oh!"

I nodded. "Apparently, his career as the head evil warrior on the demonic plane was irreparably damaged by our little coup. He's holding a grudge."

"What kind of grudge?" Bev asked. "The kind where he tries to give us an atomic wedgie and rub a noogie on our heads? Or the kind where he attempts to massacre us, our loved ones, and our pets?"

"Your prize is located behind door number two," I told her with a weary smile.

My sister didn't smile. "He's taken your family?" she asked Layla.

Layla looked at me.

"I had a vision and I'm not sure about the timing. He's either taken them or will take them in the near future. Either way, we need to move them to a safer location."

"We should bring them here," Wanda said.

We all glanced at her in surprise. She'd been quiet for so long, I'd forgotten she was there.

Layla frowned. "They won't come. But it would definitely be the safest option."

"Maybe they'd agree to come for a temporary visit. Once things calm down with the Commander, they could go back home."

Layla laughed unhappily. "If only we could promise them that. But we're called the lost ones here for a reason. We're lost to our native lands. Once we come here, we can't go back."

"Can't?" I asked. "What's stopping you from going into the spectral plane and then to the demonic realm from there?"

She crossed her arms over her chest and rubbed them as if she were chilled, which didn't seem possible given that it had to be close to a hundred degrees in her compound. "Once we're lost, we can cross to the spectral realm and back to the earthly plane because we have no spiritual or mental link to either place. Similarly, those in the demonic realm can cross into the spectral realm or any one of several other realms and still travel back home. But the goddess set a barrier between the earthly realm and all others except for the heavenly realm millennia ago."

"Why?" Wanda asked.

"Apparently, she has a soft spot for humans." Her statement sounded only slightly bitter. "You are the most helpless of all the populations. Without magic, you would be overrun and defeated very quickly."

"Then why allow *you* here?" Bev asked. When Layla's gaze snapped to hers, she shrugged. "Nothing personal."

The princess nodded. "It's a good question. The answer isn't simple. As you know, we can generally only pass into this realm through a Hellmouth vortex or a blood sacrifice fed invitation from someone on this realm." She shook her head. "Hellmouths are nearly impossible to open and use successfully. And even the goddess couldn't anticipate that a human would be stupid enough to actively invite creatures into their world that could easily kill them."

"Is that how you got here?" Wanda asked. The kid was like a dog with a bone when she got something into her head. Apparently, she'd decided she wanted the answer to the mystery that was Layla.

The princess fixed my teen with a long, thoughtful look. Finally, she said. "The royal family has an earth witch in their pockets. Working in conjunction with an earth-bound demon and for a large fee, the witch is willing to invite those they are instructed to invite."

An earth-bound demon was one who'd never lived on the demonic plane. They were basically humans with demonic proclivities. Because their interests meshed with the dark realms' interests rather than with humankind, they were valuable to dark royalty. I knew that not because I'd diligently studied demon kind as my advocate had nagged me to do, but because Wanda's father was just such a demon.

"Who's the witch?" Bev asked with a scowl. "We need to stop her."

Layla's gaze slid toward Wanda and quickly slid away. "I do not know who she is."

"If you did, would you tell us?" Bev pushed.

Layla didn't hesitate. "Probably not." When Bev stiffened with anger, Layla lifted her hands. "I understand that you don't like the idea of my people flinging their trash into your realm. I do. But they are exquisitely aware of the danger in doing so. Believe it or not, our people wouldn't send us if they believed we would harm humans."

"Why not?" Wanda asked, her tone implying she was just curious.

"Because it would ultimately come back to bite us. The angelic realm is always looking for reasons to attack the demonic plane."

Thinking of the lost ones I'd come up against during my seating, I wasn't as confident as Layla seemed to be that demon royalty cared a whit about that danger. But it was a discussion for another day, when war between the realms didn't feel as if it was on the near horizon.

So, instead, I said, "Tell me about Matthew and Glenn."

She blinked in confusion. "What about them?"

"Why are they in the spectral plane? And what are they doing with my councilman?"

She frowned. "I have no idea why they were with Dodson. I sent them to keep an eye out for my family and to let me know if or when they arrived." Layla looked thoughtful. "I suppose it's possible they asked him to help. A spirit has more flexibility to move around in that place. And Dodson's been there long enough to have made connections."

"I got the impression they were doing something to stave off the demon hoards from getting through to earth," I said. "But they could do that from this side just as well," I said. "Since the Rev wouldn't come home with me, maybe he did agree to keep an eye out for your family."

"Let's talk about this demon hoard," Bev said. "What exactly happened there, Aggy? You didn't give us any details."

I sighed. "There were hundreds of them. They attacked as we rushed toward the portal. I assumed they were trying to come through with us. But they didn't really try for the gateway until we arrived, so maybe they were coming after us."

"We believed they were pressing the borders because of the blue moon," Layla said, nodding in agreement. "They probably scented the opening of the barrier but were unable to pinpoint it exactly until they came upon you."

"Historically, demons using a portal to breach the earthly plain has never been done," Wanda said. "No demonic being is known to have gotten through the barrier to the earthly plane during a blue moon."

"Historically, that's true," Layla agreed. "But the records are not fully intact. Great wars between the magical races have damaged and obscured records of events." She shrugged. "The best I can say is that it's unlikely...but not impossible. Especially when you basically offered them a doorway into the realm."

I ignored her insinuation. I'd done what I had to do, and we'd taken precautions to ensure that it was as safe as it could be. Still, I'd come back without Dodson in spite of all our efforts.

It was disappointing.

As Bev had asked, I gave them a quick rundown of the events in the spectral realm, soft-balling the attacks and focusing in on our brief conversation with the Rev and Layla's two guards. "The Rev made it very clear he wanted to stay for now. Matthew and Glenn seemed to support his inclinations. Whatever the three of them are up to, they're obviously working together to accomplish it."

Layla bristled. "As I told you, my guards are there to alert me if my family is forced out of the demon realm. They would not do otherwise while under my orders."

I didn't argue. She could be right. But something niggled in my brain. Something about their being with Reverend Dodson at that time and place felt off.

Unfortunately, it probably didn't matter either way. My problem was the Commander and what he'd do in the name of retribution for our coup. Worse, that problem had a secondary level which involved the three men I'd spoken to on the spectral plane. They would make the perfect leverage to be used against Layla and me. And I had no delusions over their ultimate fates if that happened.

16

AN UNPALATABLE PLAN, A FAVOR GIVEN

"So, what exactly do you need from us?" I asked Layla as she walked us toward the entrance to her compound. Bev and Wanda walked ahead, with Wraith winding around their ankles. They chatted easily, walking together so closely their shoulders occasionally bumped.

The sight made me smile.

The princess had looped her arm through mine and grown thoughtful as we walked, her thoughts no doubt lost in concern for her family and friends.

I was distracted too, making our silence companionable.

"If my family is taken to the spectral plane, I'll need to find a way to bring them through." Her copper gaze lifted to mine.

I tensed. "No, Layla. It's too dangerous. What if something dark and deadly came through on their heels?"

She dropped my arm. "I have no choice, Aggy. Of all people, I thought you'd understand."

"I do understand, Layla. But I'm the guardian of the people here. It's my job to protect them against everything and everyone who might harm them. Do you honestly believe I'd stand by and allow you to perform a blood sacrifice at all, and particularly one which might end with demons running loose in Rome again?" I tensed against a shudder at the thought. Between all of us, we'd barely beaten them back the last time, when the Hellmouth had become active and given them an easy doorway into Rome.

Layla stopped, hands on hips, her expression mulish. "I'm not asking for your permission, Madam Lares. My compound is not under your protection. I am just giving you the courtesy of notice."

I reached for her hand but she jerked away. "You're going to offer one of your people as a sacrifice?" I couldn't believe she'd do it.

Her head came up and for just a blink, her devilish form overlaid her human one. "It is not your concern..."

"Layla," I said, my tone gentle. "That will leave a stain on your soul you won't recover from."

She sighed, rubbing her arms. "There is a woman. She has long overseen my comfort and managed my home. She is...my friend." Layla's eyes shimmered with tears. "She has the wasting. It is a common ailment with our people. She is not expected to live much longer. She has begged me to allow her the honor of saving my family. I do not wish it." The tears escaped her iron control, flowing freely down her cheeks.

I fought the urge to pull her into a hug, knowing she wouldn't want her guards to see her in need of comfort. "Are you sure she can't be healed? Maybe the crone could look at her." Caleigh had healed Matthew and Glenn once, when they'd basically sacrificed themselves in an effort to save us from the attack of several Leviathan. Never mind that the great beasts had been Caleigh's to call. She hadn't meant for them to attack...not really...and we'd later discovered she'd pretty much lost control of the enormous fishy creatures. The crone was a phenomenal healer and had brought the two lost ones and Ferral back from near death.

"Nothing will save her, I'm afraid." Layla sniffed and straightened. "Keely will be remembered as a hero to my people. She will have a fountain designed in her likeness and it will decorate my drive. She will be remembered fondly in our literature and all our young will honor her."

I nodded. What she was proposing wasn't something she'd be able to do under my guardianship. Human laws wouldn't allow it. But she was right. Her compound, like the adjacent realm of Fairy, wasn't part of my protectorate. "You'll bring your family here? To your compound?"

Her back straightened, her chin lifting with pride. "Yes. They will hate it." A bitter laugh followed the statement. "But they will be safe, and they'll adjust."

"Okay," I said, expelling a breath. "What do you need from me?"

"I need an earth-bound demon."

I grimaced. "Ugh."

Her lips quivered on a smile she wouldn't release. "He will come if you ask."

"Do I have to?"

She laughed. "You don't, of course. But we will be BFFs if you would do this for me."

I scowled at her, but we both knew I would do as she asked.

She did hug me then. "Thank you, Aggy."

"I'd say it would be my pleasure, but that would be a lie."

Layla nodded. "I understand."

"You'll let me know if something changes in the spectral realm?"

"I will." She frowned, looking toward my sister and my kid. "Aggy, the Commander..."

"I know," I said softly. "We'll worry about him when we need to. But I think it would be best if my council and I were here when you bring your family through. Just in case."

An array of emotions flitted over her expressive face and, for a minute, I thought she was going to deny my request. But she finally nodded. "Yes. That would probably be best."

"WE SHOULD HAVE KEPT THE IGGLOC," Bev complained. "My feet are killing me."

"Are we sure we can't find his house from the street?" Wanda wrinkled her pert nose as we stepped over another magical boundary and the stench of sulfur and worse assailed us.

The Mystical Wood, I'd learned the last time we'd been forced to seek out Wanda's daddy, the earth-bound demon, a.k.a. the local monster judge and jailer. As far as I could tell, Bathos was in charge of finding and locking up escaped demons and serving them a heaping helping of demonic justice. He was bounty-hunter, jailer, and judge all in one. And, gauging by the size and splendor of his home and property, he was paid well for his efforts. Unfortunately, he'd magicked his home to be invisible and inaccessible from the street. We could only find it from the Wood, which presented a plethora of problems, since that meant we basically had to travel there on foot. Unless I was lucky enough to have a magical horse or Iggloc available.

Also, the woods were parceled up between a few dozen different magical groups, some of which were downright nasty. We'd nearly lost our lives the previous times we'd traveled through the different segments, and we'd had access to the White Mare then.

"He likes you a lot," I told my teen. "Maybe you can convince him to join the human world and get a street address," I said, offering a smile. "It would sure be easier on us."

Ahead of us, the earth suddenly exploded upward and Niele burst from the ground, an enormous, slug-like creature attached to his big form, its suckers turning his naked flesh purple where they'd attached.

"Niele!" I jolted forward, golden energy flaring around my hands and my staff snapping into my palm before I even realized I'd called it.

His eyes wide with fear, Niele leaped skyward, twisted his muscular body, and jack-knifed back into the earth with his slimy attacker in tow. Rich, black dirt flew into the air as he hit the ground and the earth opened around him, sucking him back under.

We stood for a moment, waiting, listening.

Silence filled the Wood. There were no pixies buzzing to and fro. No wildlife or flutterflies moved through the trees. There was nothing except a sense of evil magic that made my nerves buzz beneath my skin.

The earth geysered upward again and Niele screamed, his entire form covered in the nasty slugs. The ugly mass hit the ground and disappeared again, a fresh spray of dirt peppering the air.

"Somebody do something!" Wanda yelled. "They're killing him." A small energy glow bathed her fists, but Wanda didn't have a lot of physical energy to call. Her magic was in her innate knowledge of the entire history of magic from the earliest days of its genesis.

Her eyes were wide with horror, and she clutched her

hatchet-cleaved history book as if she might use it to kill a few giant slugs if I didn't do something.

Shaking off my indecision, I stepped over to the hole and looked down. To my chagrin, the dirt had filled it back in and there was no sign of my gnome. I dropped to my knees and started digging, knowing even as I did that I'd be too late. "How can we help him when he's underground?" I asked nobody in particular, panic turning my tone shrill.

The ground beneath my knees rumbled and I threw myself backwards as Niele and his attackers flew skyward again. My councilman was all but invisible beneath the writhing mass of giant mollusks. His big hands flailed over them, trying to pull the sticky things off his body. But they were well and truly stuck on him, and judging by the grayish color of his visible flesh and quickly slowing movements, they were killing him.

"Bev!"

"Don't let them go back under!" she yelled back. "I'm working on a dehydration spell."

I shuddered as the bundle of gross hit the ground and sent a stream of energy into the earth beneath the writhing mass. Niele yelped. I must have hit him. "Sorry!" I yelled, and decided I needed a better approach. Jumping to my feet, I snapped my arm to extend my staff and, my mind set to the goal at hand, I smacked one of the squishy brown and gray suckers with my orb.

Its reaction was more violent than I expected. Its head came up and it squealed, the sound loud and shrill enough to burst my eardrums.

I stumbled backward, my hands covering my ears as pain stabbed into my brain from the invasive sound.

Wanda's scream of pain jerked me into action. I stumbled forward and started whaling on the things with my staff. Injecting more energy than the last time into my strikes, I was happy to see that, in addition to the squealing, at least some of them released Niele. They tumbled backward, feelers violently twitching.

"It's working, Aggy," Wanda yelled. "Don't stop."

I had no intention of giving up, but warm liquid ran from my ears and Wanda's voice was muffled. I was pretty sure the nasty things had burst my ear drums. Growling with determination, I stabbed my weapon toward the still-attached slugs.

Movement on the ground near my feet had me glancing down, but too late. One of the slugs I'd stunned shot off the ground and hit my chest, knocking me to my back. Something slammed into my chest like the blow of a hammer and my lungs seized under the impact.

I was vaguely aware of Wanda screaming my name, but three more blows to my chest made my heart stutter and knocked any air I had inside my body out.

All I could do was stare up at a darkening sky, mouth flapping as air refused to enter my lungs. My stomach roiled with nausea as the nasty sucker pulled my flesh away from my bones.

A small hand came out of nowhere and smacked the slug with a wave of weak but still painful energy into the nasty thing.

It reared back and squealed as Wanda shrieked along with it, and smacked it again. She reached under my arms and tried to pull me away, but I outweighed her by about forty pounds and I wasn't budging.

Somebody was talking but my ears were shot. All I heard was a frantic mumbling sound.

"Help her!" Bev screamed, her strident tone finally cutting through the fog.

I heard that. Realizing what she wanted, I put my feet to the ground and pushed, and finally moved.

I rolled my gaze to Bev. "Kill those things," I wheezed, my lungs finally accepting air.

Bev nodded. She was already crafting a spell, her slender fingers dancing on the air as symbols swirled and dipped and fell into a diamond-shaped pattern that I was beginning to recognize as Bev's signature magic.

A beat later, Bev spread her fingers over the freshly-crafted curse and flung it wide, sending it flying like a net toward the slugs.

"Niele!" I screamed, but my sister was already bent over me, helping me stand.

"He'll be okay," she soothed. "I targeted the slugs. The magic will slide right over him."

I surely hoped she was right, because the net hit the slugs so fast and hard they didn't even have time to squeal before their nasty bodies started to shrink and compress, dehydrating like fat grapes in a drying oven.

17

UNLIKELY ALLIES, BARGAINS DRIVEN

We limped, collectively, over the magic boundary separating the Mystical Wood from the demon Bathos's very fine property. After dealing with the giant slugs, we'd had a brief altercation with a living forest of aggressive trees and, despite winning the battle pretty decisively, none of us had come out of it unscathed.

"I just want to go on record as saying I hate the Mystical Wood," my sister grumbled.

Nodding her agreement, Wanda lifted her hand and they slapped five.

"It's definitely better from the back of a magical mare," I agreed. Though that journey hadn't been without its challenges either. Like nearly losing said magical mare to the poison coating the claws of a pterodactyl-like predator like the one that had attacked us on the spectral plane.

A strident caw sounded overhead and I glanced up to find Ray frolicking in the air above Bathos's mansion. Two giant hawks "frolicked" with him, the three of them apparently playing a fairly aggressive game of avian tag.

"Um," Wanda said. "Is he going to be all right?"

One of the hawks descended on my favorite raven, legs outstretched and talons curved for attack. I frowned. "Bathos promised he'd instruct his demon birds not to attack Ray or us anymore." Ray pitched sideways, one big wing slapping the air just under the hawk's deadly claw. He flapped his wings in an effort to gain some distance from the attacking birds but merely ended up in the crosshairs of the second guardian hawk.

Inches away from a mortal wounding, my favorite raven released the air and performed a perfect barrel roll, dropping beneath his attackers with impressive skill.

"I didn't know he could do that," Wanda said, a smile in her voice.

"I might have given him a couple of magical upgrades," I said, grinning.

Unfortunately, Ray's creative avoidance tactics were only going to get him out of trouble for a moment, because the two hawks were nothing if not determined.

The big black bird found a good air current and used it to hurry our way, no doubt hoping I'd intervene. I fully intended to do just that.

Lifting my staff, I shot a thin stream of golden energy toward the hawk nearest Ray. The air in front of it swirled with electrical energy that stung its chest and head, and the magically enhanced guardian bird reared back with a surprised cry before wheeling sideways and away. That left only one hawk riding the near edges of Ray's backdraft.

I extended my staff and sent another stream of biting energy its way. To my chagrin, the bird anticipated my strike and dodged away from it, the magic catching the end of Ray's tail feathers instead.

He cawed angrily and hightailed it in my direction.

I quickly readjusted my stream and zapped the annoying hawk right on the chest, hurtling it backward on a shrill cry. The hawk rolled on the air currents and plummeted toward the ground as I chewed my bottom lip. "In the heat of the moment, I might have put too much on that one," I murmured.

"Ya think?" Niele asked, chuckling.

The hawk tumbled downward, looking for all the world as if it was going to beak-plant in the garden near the pool, but then somehow managed to pull out of its fall, and fly away on wobbly wings.

"Peeeeeeeeeeeeeee!" a shrill voice screeched, and I looked up just in time to see Ray barreling my way. I dropped the staff and extended my hands just before he slammed into me, catching him in a golden net of magic and easing him to the ground at my feet. The raven emitted several outraged caws and angrily clacked his beak at me. His usual cocky walk was faster than usual and a thin stream of smoke rose from one damaged tail feather.

"Oops," I said, heat filling my cheeks. "Sorry about that." I wiggled a finger over the smoldering feather and it stopped smoking. "I was aiming at the hawk."

Bev barked out a laugh. "You're a menace," she teased, and I flicked her ear hard enough to make her yelp.

"Rude!" the big bird chastised, his head bobbing like a chicken.

"It *was* rude. I apologize," I told him. "Would you like to ride on my shoulder like a parrot the rest of the way?" It was a desperate attempt to appease the flustered raven and it worked. He quickly ascended to my shoulder, his claws biting a little harder into my skin than was strictly necessary. Of course, he smacked me in the face with a wing as I started walking, but I held my tongue, accepting the payback for my magical faux pas.

It was slightly harder to ignore the chuckling of my three companions at my expense.

BATHOS EMERGED from the big house as we stepped off the grass and onto the patio surrounding the pool. As usual, the man's stunning looks came as something of a surprise. Bathos's coal-black hair fell past his chin, slightly longer than the last time I'd seen him, and was parted down the center so the glossy strands framed his handsome face. There was a touch of silver at the temples that made him look very distinguished. He wore a pristine white shirt tucked into dark jeans that melted over his lean muscles. Strangely, his feet were bare.

They were very nice feet.

The demon raised a dark brow when he saw me looking and his perfect lips twitched. Then his black gaze skimmed toward his daughter. His expression warmed and his lips curved in a smile as she wrapped her skinny arms around his waist and hugged him. "Hey, dad."

"Little fiend. How are you?"

Wanda giggled at the name he'd begun calling her and my heart warmed. The demon might be a large pain in my backside...or was that a pain in my large backside?... most of the time, but he seemed to actually make his daughter happy. For that, I could forgive him a lot.

Bathos finally turned his dark gaze on me, the regard in his expression immediately cooling. "Madam Lares. To what do I owe the honor of the *unexpected* visit?"

I didn't miss the emphasis, but chose to ignore it. "I

thought we agreed that you'd inform your avian guards not to attack us."

He shrugged, non-committal. "If I do not know you are coming, I cannot inform them."

I shook my head. "I need to talk to you about something. Do you have a minute?"

He very pointedly glanced at his watch.

I gave him a look, my brows lifted.

He sighed. "Sit. Would you like coffee? Cookies?"

"I'll never say no to a cookie," I told him.

"Chocolate sheet cake cookies. They are outstanding. Tilly has outdone herself."

My mouth watered and I realized I needed to make time to go to the bakery. It had been so much easier, though imminently more fattening, having Tilly with us in the church. When Rome had been under attack from a Trickster, she'd made a temporary bakery in what would someday become my candle shop if I ever had the time and money to complete it. But with banishment of the trickster who'd made all our lives difficult, the brownie had returned to her bakery. I was happy to say that she still delivered fresh muffins to us on Sunday mornings to thank us for giving her a place to go after her bakery was attacked. I tried to explain to her that it had been more our pleasure than hers. But she'd insisted, and who was I to talk her out of bringing me delicious calories?

"I'll get them," Wanda said.

"Thank you, Little Fiend. I'm afraid I have very little in the way of household help these days."

He indicated some nearby chairs and waited until I sat before lowering himself into a chair across from me. Every once in a while, the demon displayed old world manners that caught me by surprise. It was so much easier to just think of him as evil. Although, his genes had produced Wanda, which was a count in his favor for sure.

Ray rose from my shoulder and flew a short distance away, perching on a high branch in a nearby tree. He was no doubt on the lookout for the hawks. Bev and Niele stood a few feet behind me, on constant lookout for trouble.

"You haven't hired new help yet?" I asked, surprised. Bathos had lost everyone who'd worked for him when a dangerous beast escaped from his dungeon and killed them. To my surprise, he'd seemed to take their loss very hard, claiming they'd been with him for decades.

He frowned, crossing his legs and plucking at a string on his jeans. "I'll have to eventually," he said, "But for now, I haven't the heart."

"So, I'm guessin' you eat a lot of Ramen noodles?" Bev asked, humor sparking in her gray eyes.

He studied her for a long moment, then shook his head. "I do actually know how to cook. I just don't enjoy cooking for one." His assessing look lingered on my sister long enough to stir unease beneath my ribs. "*O*-kay."

Their gazes broke and Bathos turned to me. "Okay?"

"Are you aware of the demon migration into the spectral realm?" I asked.

"Of course. Knowing that type of thing is part of my job."

His job. Yeah. I frowned. "Are you also aware that the Commander has set his sights on revenge?"

Wariness filled his gaze. "I had heard something of that."

"And you didn't think it made sense to warn us?"

He shrugged. "I am keeping an eye on the situation. You are in no current danger."

I narrowed my gaze. "At what point do you decide we're in danger?"

"You'll know when we get to that point."

"*How* will I know?"

He leaned forward, resting muscular forearms on his knees. His black gaze swirled with intensity. "Because I will claim my daughter and bring her into the safety of my home."

I shook my head. "We've talked about this, Bathos. You agreed. This...place...is not safe for her."

"Yes. We agreed. For now." We stared at each other for a long moment. I fought not to show him how much the idea of his taking Wanda away terrified me. Not only because I didn't believe she'd be safe with him. But also, because I'd grown to love her. I could no longer imagine my life without her plucky, determined spirit in it. And my dog would fall into a severe depression if we lost her.

When I spoke, my voice throbbed with the emotions I was trying not to show. "I'll fight you to the death for her."

His gaze held mine. He didn't speak for a moment, and then all he said was, "Noted." He sat back "Now tell me why you've come so I can get on with my day."

"Layla has had word that her family is in danger. Apparently, the Commander has people inside the royal palace who are loyal to him. She is certain he'll make a move against them."

Bathos turned thoughtful. He sat back in his chair, the intensity of his black gaze focused on a spot beyond me. He placed one large hand on each knee and sat in silence for a few beats. Finally, he said, "The people of the realm believe their royals were at fault for the Hellmouth failing."

"Why would they blame the royals?" Niele asked.

Bathos spared the gnome a quick look, grimacing in distaste as he took in Niele's earth-painted nakedness. I gave my gnome a quick look and thought he was being more chaste than usual. At least his big hands were folded in front of his stick and berries. Maybe our sensibilities were rubbing off on him.

"The demons and devils are all too aware that Princess Layla lives in this realm. They are aware that she's made a home here. That she has human friends and even humans living in her compound, working for her. They believe the royals' loyalties are split and that they are protecting the human realm."

My eyebrows flew north. "But, that's ridiculous."

He shrugged again. "You know the strength of rumor and half-truths. The Commander may have been cast aside professionally, but the people remember him for the many times he fought on their behalf. Not for his many cruelties. They mostly do not blame him for the Hellmouth failing. They believe he was undermined and misled by those he should have been able to trust."

"The royals," I said, nodding.

"Yes. Layla is correct. Her family is in great danger." He cocked his head. "What does she want from me? If she's looking for information, I believe she has eyes and ears in all the right places already."

"That isn't necessarily what she needs. Though, she and I would consider it a favor if you'd keep us apprised of any danger to her people in the realm."

He didn't commit to that. He was much too political to make such a promise before he saw what was coming. "What else?"

I stared at him for a moment, trying to read his body language and expression for signs that he'd be willing to help. Unable to read anything from his expression, I finally just put it out there. "Layla wants to open a gateway into the demon realm. She wants to bring her family into her compound."

He blinked, clearly surprised. "The princess is willing to perform a blood sacrifice and you're going to let her?"

I nodded. "It's a special situation. She has someone who's willing to do it." I frowned, letting my displeasure show. "I don't like it, of course. But I have no control over her."

"I'll admit I'm shocked." He shook his head. Then his gaze sharpened. "She needs an earthbound demon."

"Yes. Will you help her?"

"The real question is, why are you helping her?"

The answer to that was very complicated. I took a moment to organize my thoughts and then said, "Because her parents are in real danger. And because she will do it with or without my help. If I help her, I'll be in a position to make sure there is no breach beyond her family. If I don't help, something much worse than a dying friend helping her bring her family to safety may well happen."

The door from the house slammed open and shut, and Wanda's fast footsteps scraped across the concrete patio. Bathos held my gaze for a long moment. I bit back the desire to plead my case, knowing that Wanda would quickly pick up on the subject of our conversation. I didn't want the kid to think about ugly things like blood sacrifice. I didn't want to think about them myself.

"You had two kinds of cookies in there so I brought both. Did Tilly make these cinnamon ones too? They look amazing." Wanda didn't seem to notice when we didn't respond. She'd already broken a cookie in half and stuffed it into her mouth.

Bathos's black eyes held a pinprick of fire in their depths. I reached for magic in case I needed to defend myself. I had no idea why he was reacting so strongly to my request, but demons lived by a different set of rules than we did.

"I brought a piece of bread for Ray," Wanda said, and then proceeded to break the thick slice of what looked like homemade bread into pieces, flinging them to the concrete. Ray gave a happy caw and descended eagerly to peck at the offering.

Finally, the fire left Bathos's gaze and he inclined his head, just the tiniest bit.

I followed suit, sealing our agreement.

With that, the tension broke, and we ate cookies.

18

REGRETS AND REVELATIONS SOUR

We arrived back home just in time for dinner, which I could smell all the way out to the edge of the woods. Judging by the number of lights glowing in windows, it appeared my council had arrived in force.

Though I was tired from a long day that had been fraught with magical mishap and mystical mayhem, I perked up at the thought of spending the next couple of hours with all my favorite peeps.

"What are you smiling about?" Niele asked.

"She's looking forward to seeing her sexy angel," Wanda said, making kissy noises at me.

I flailed a hand at her and she ducked away with a laugh. "I'm happy to see everybody," I objected.

"Uh huh," my sister said dryly. She inhaled deeply and her expression turned blissful. "I, for one, am really looking forward to getting intimate with that lasagna I'm smelling."

"Lasagna!" Wanda squealed, and with the energy of youth, she was off and running.

I sighed. "I really wish I had that kind of energy."

Bev threw an arm around my shoulders. "Don't. She'll get there before us, which means mom will put her to work setting the table and pouring drinks. By the time we get there all the work will be done."

Laughing, I raised a hand and we bumped knuckles.

The back door opened and Gren came out, his lean form distinctive in the dim light. He spoke to Wanda as she ran past and then turned his full attention on me.

"Madam Lares," Niele said. "I'll be in later. I need to do a check of the grounds."

I opened my mouth to respond but he'd already dived beneath the grass, a spray of soft dirt the only sign of his departure.

Gren leaned against the wall and crossed his arms, patiently awaiting my arrival.

"I...um..." Bev didn't finish that thought. She hurried past Gren and into the house, where an uproar greeted her as everyone spotted a new victim.

I smiled at my angel as he straightened away from the wall. "Hey," I said, my voice warm and inviting.

"Hey, yourself," he responded.

"Are you trying to escape the chaos?"

He pulled me against his wide, warm chest and wrapped his arms around me. Gren lowered his lips, stopping a breath away from mine. I waited eagerly for the kiss I knew would rock my world. "There's something you needed to know before you came inside."

"Oh? What? Did something go wrong? Is everybody okay?"

I tried to step around him but he held me tight.

"Everybody's fine and there's nothing wrong. What you needed to know is that I've been waiting all day to do this." His lips lowered to mine and heat flared from the gentle touch. My body warmed and molded to his as my arms lifted to twine around his neck. The kiss deepened, turned molten, and infused me with naughty thoughts that definitely couldn't be acted on with a house full of people.

When he broke the kiss several minutes later, I sighed with regret, resting my forehead against his. My heartbeat was fast and my pulse elevated. And every inch of my body was screaming for more. "How about we take Air Lungren to a spot without so many people and you can give me a clearer picture of just exactly what you've been thinking about doing to me all day?"

His chuckle was sin personified. The deep, throaty sound wound its way beneath my flesh and played havoc with all my important parts. "You're kind of the main feature at tonight's dinner. They're here to celebrate you coming back safe and sound."

His words made me frown. "There's nothing to celebrate. I didn't accomplish what I went in for. And I might have made things worse."

He rubbed a heated thumb over my lips before following it up with a brief touch of his talented mouth. "You saved Trish's friend, perhaps saving Fairy in the process and bringing Trish home where she belongs."

When I simply shrugged, he added. "And you brought an Iggloc home."

I laughed at the teasing note in his voice. "Which Caleigh promptly stole." I ran my tongue over his bottom lip, tasting evidence of something sweet on his skin. "Mmm. Besides, the Iggloc was your idea."

"I'll agree that I bartered for the beast. However, my intention was to ride it to the portal and then leave it in Spirit." His grin widened. "But you brought it here." His delight was infectious.

"I know you're just trying to distract me from my failures, but I'll admit that everybody's reaction to the beast was fun."

He nodded. "They're all in there talking about it. Your favorite teen is beside herself. She insists she's going to go stay with Caleigh for a few weeks so she can ride it."

My eyes flared with surprise and dread. "We'll see about that."

"So," he said, settling me closer and holding me tight. I laid my head on his chest and sighed. Gren's heart beat steadily against my ear and his heat and strength soothed me like home. "What's really bothering you?"

I couldn't tell him that. If I admitted that Layla was going to do a blood sacrifice to bring her family here...a family that would not be happy for her efforts and might be dangerous if they decided to rebel...he'd probably want to stop her. I couldn't explain why I thought we should let the princess do it. Not when it was simply a gut feeling based on nothing concrete.

Maybe it was my newly forming *Response* magics that were telling me to let it play out. Or maybe I was just being a coward. The last thing I wanted was to alienate a good friend and ally. "I'm just tired. Layla sent me on an errand that turned out to be exhausting as well as irritating."

"What errand?"

I sighed. "She wanted me to intervene with Bathos, asking him to help her with a project."

"Ah." His warm lips touched my hair, trailing down to place a heated brand on the skin below my ear. I shivered with delight. "Your favorite demon. No wonder you're feeling off."

I nodded, remembering Bathos's threat to take Wanda. I pulled away, looking into Gren's sexy brown gaze. "He's threatening to take Wanda away from me if the demons find a way into this realm."

Gren stiffened. "That's not going to happen. The child would be in constant danger with him and he knows it."

"That's what I told him. But he threatened to go to war with me about it."

Gren's square chin tightened. "Then war it will be. But I assure you, lovely Aggy. It is a war he will lose."

I nodded, but the frown wouldn't release my facial muscles. "I can't lose her, Gren. I just can't." Tears slipped from my eyes, glossing a warm trail to my chin.

"You have my word, Aggy. The demon will not take that child. First, because we will not allow it. And second, because the demons will not get a foothold in this world. You have my word on that too."

The door opened and Mavis stuck her head out. "Hey, you two, dinner's ready and wine is poured. Get your backsides in here."

TO MY VAST ANNOYANCE, I ended up in a chair next to Ferral. I wasn't sure if my friends and family had done it to tweak me, or if it was just that nobody else wanted to sit next to the crabby advocate. I bit back a sigh and dropped into the seat, grabbing my wine and taking a healthy sip before turning to the sour face next to me. "Ferral."

He glowered in my direction, his body language even tenser than usual. "Madam Lares. Why didn't you return with Reverend Dodson?"

I took another sip of wine.

A plate full of lasagna, salad, and garlic bread appeared

in front of me. Mavis patted my shoulder. "Ferral, what did we discuss?"

His dark silver gaze widened slightly, just enough to tell me he didn't want Mavis to yell at him.

I hid my smile.

"I am simply asking what we all want to know," the advocate said.

Mavis looked down the long table I'd recently bought to accommodate my council. We'd had to put it in the sanctuary because it was so big, but it looked pretty in the huge, beautiful room. "Anybody here want to quiz Aggy on the Rev?"

Reactions ran from mumbled negative responses to definitive denials and even one chirp from the bat that was currently hanging from a light near the window.

Mavis turned a quelling look toward my advocate, complete with one arched blonde brow. "'Nuff said?" she asked the angry moon hound shifter.

Ferral simply picked up his wine glass and held it aloft. "To Madam Lares and her triumphant and safe return." The table erupted in cheers and I groaned softly. I went for another sip of wine only to discover that it was gone.

I'd sucked it down like it was water on a one-hundred-degree day.

Mavis set the bottle in front of me, patting me on the arm. With a final glare at Ferral, she went to take her seat at the other end of the table. Niele hurried into the room, calling out his apologies for being late. I was happy to see he'd cleaned up, combed his frizzy gray locks into a semi-controlled state, and was wearing a pair of the moss shorts Bev had made him.

"Hey, Niele," Trish called out. "How was your adventure to Bathos's mansion?"

The gnome slid a quick look toward Wanda and headed for the chair my werewolf shifter, Luke, added to the table for him. "The demon was on his best behavior," Niele said. He smiled at Mavis and thanked her for the plate of veggie lasagna, bread, and salad she handed him. "But we had a little trouble with the Mystical Wood." He proceeded to tell them about the giant slugs.

Everybody leaned forward, listening intently to the story. My council was always interested in stories about the Wood and its challenges and creatures. I didn't know if it was because of the sense of adventure inherent in dealing with the fairytale forest and its often-unpredictable magical inhabitants, or just as a training exercise. Learning how to deal with such a wide variety of monsters was an ongoing challenge. Especially for me, since I hadn't even known that magic existed until I became Lares.

"Were they Bathos's monsters?" Luke asked.

Her mouth full of lasagna, Wanda shook her head and swallowed. "No. But his stupid hawks attacked Ray again."

I observed the girl, wondering at her recent tendency to chime in when someone talked about her dad. She used to defend him. But I suspected that she was uncomfortable being the only one to defend the demon. Still, I hated to see the tightness in her muscles when she spoke ill of him. I added a conversation with her about that to my mental To Do list. Wanda shouldn't feel pressured to bad-mouth her father just to fit in. Even if he was an arrogant jerk at times.

Okay. Almost always.

"If those birds hurt Ray, they'll be dealing with me," Mavis said. "I thought he agreed to call them off when we visit?"

"There was apparently a loophole," I said, stabbing a

bite of lasagna. "We discussed it and I don't think he'll do it again."

Bev snorted.

The table settled into comfortable conversation and I relaxed as the wine warmed my belly and my advocate stopped attacking me. By the time Wanda brought one of Tilly's molten chocolate cakes into the room and started handing out slices, I was so relaxed I was nearly asleep.

"Why didn't he return with you?" Ferral asked.

I'd been trying to listen to several conversations and his words didn't sink in at first. When they did, I turned to him with no anger and nodded. "You're right. We need to discuss this."

I tapped my wine glass with my knife and waited as the room quieted. All faces turned my way with expectant expressions. "In his usual direct and determined way..."

Chuckling filled the room and Ferral's scowl deepened.

"My advocate is correct in claiming I owe you all an explanation regarding Reverend Dodson."

Trish looked relieved that I was finally telling them what I'd asked her not to share until I knew more. Gren's expression gave nothing of his feelings on the subject away. Wanda and Bev nodded, no doubt happy not to have to avoid the subject anymore.

The rest of my council exchanged glances, which told me they'd been talking about the Rev's notable absence among themselves, probably wondering why I hadn't explained it yet. The realization brought guilt, like acid churning through my stomach. "I should have addressed it sooner, and for that I apologize. But I wished to speak with Princess Layla first."

Mavis looked confused. "Why? What does she have to do with this?"

"Maybe nothing," I admitted. "Although the coincidence of finding the Rev with Matthew and Glenn is too much for me to ignore."

Surprised murmurs peppered the air.

I nodded. "Layla, as it turns out, had another reason for sending her most trusted guards to the spectral realm. Her family is in danger." I gave them a quick overview of what she'd shared with me, excluding her plans to open a portal into the demonic realm and bring her family out. "Matthew and Glenn are helping the Rev find out why so many demons have fled their homes and are coalescing in a realm adjacent to ours."

"But I thought the demonic couldn't come here without a blood sacrifice ceremony?" Luke said, his golden-brown eyes dark with worry.

"Normally they can't," I agreed. "But the thinning veil around the blue moon makes them think they have a shot at breaking through."

"What about what the Rev said," Trish asked. All faces turned her way. "You know, about the demons thinking they had something that might help them bust through."

"Some*thing*?" Ferral asked. "Not some*one*?"

Trish looked at me and I shook my head. "He said something."

"What thing?" Bev asked.

"Unfortunately, we didn't have time for a lot of details," I told them. Or any actually. "Our portal was going to open soon and we were still pretty far away from it."

Trish nodded in agreement. "I think we should all hit up our sources to see if anybody heard that rumor and knows what they're looking for."

"Is this object tied to the moon?" Luke asked.

"Unclear," I responded. "And I have no idea how many days we have left of thinning."

"A little less than twenty-seven days," Luke said. "But thinning is strongest in the three days after the first full moon, three days around the fifteenth, and three days before the next one." Like all shapeshifters, Luke was intimately aware of the cycles of the moon and their phases.

"The power of three," Wanda said, nodding.

"As you all probably know, a blue moon isn't called that because of its color," Luke clarified. "It's the relatively rare occurrence of two full moons in one month. Or, approximately twenty-nine days. Doubling the moon's inherent magic."

"So, they're at the end of the first thinning," Wanda said, some of the tension leaving her face. "We should have a few days to prepare, right?"

"Yes," Gren said, his voice soft. Everyone turned to him, eager to hear his opinion. Lungren Maker was generally a man of few, softly-spoken words. But when he shared an opinion it was worth paying attention to. He looked at me, his dark brown eyes appearing even darker than usual under the soft white light in the sanctuary. "But if they've found what I fear they've found, that won't matter."

19

OUR FRIENDS APPROACH THEIR DARKEST HOUR

Tension pulsed through the room for a beat before I asked, "What do you think they've found?"

Ferral sat up straight, his silver gaze darkening with emotion. "You don't think they've gotten their hands on the Gateway Gem?"

Gren caught the advocate's gaze, his own filled with clear concern. "It's the only thing that makes any sense. Why else would demons be flooding the spectral realm?"

Ferral cursed softly.

"Judging by its name, I'm guessing this is some kind of portal device?" I said.

"Not a device," Mavis said, surprising me. She and Gren shared a quick glance and her peaches and cream complexion turned slightly green. She clasped her hands in front of her on the table and stared at them. "It's an icon of sorts. Forged from the sands of the great arena in the realm of the spirits. It was rumored to have been empowered by the blood of the guardian lion and enhanced with the lifeblood of a million magical beings."

The room was quiet following her dire proclamation.

Finally, I said, "That sounds like a fairytale told to children who are misbehaving."

My sister shook her head, the movement making her long, blonde ponytail dance. "It's no fairytale," she told me. Bev fixed a worried gray gaze on me, her lips forming a tight line. "It's a giant red gemstone. A living cult of High Priests who roamed the spectral plane millennia ago created it as a means of moving between the physical and spectral realms. Initially, it only worked for spirits. But it is reputed to be a ravenous creature that constantly needs to be fed. Over the millennia, it has been infused with the blood of creatures from other worlds, allowing demons, devils, and creatures from other dark realms to cross onto the spectral plane and, conceivably, into the human realm."

As she spoke, the dread that had begun to twist my lungs with Gren's and Ferral's words tightened until I found it hard to breathe. "And we think the demons have control of this stone?" I asked.

"It would explain the exodus into the spectral realm," Niele said, frowning.

"And the Commander suddenly making scary noises," I murmured.

Ferral twitched in surprise. "The Commander?" His face paled. "What of him? Please don't tell me you've spoken to him?"

I stared at the advocate, letting my freaked-out expression serve as my response.

"When?" he demanded. "How?"

"In a vision. He's not happy."

Luke snorted out a laugh and shrugged when all eyes slid to him. "You have to admit, she has a way with understatement."

"Describe 'not happy'" Mavis said, her tone dry.

"He pretty much wants to kill me and everyone I love, and bathe in our blood."

"Well." Gren said. "We'll have to kill him."

I couldn't help it, I laughed. "Talk about understatement."

My angel smiled, the sight warming me from my toes to the tips of my ears. "But first, we need to find him," Gren continued. "And I'm guessing when we find the Commander, we'll find the Gateway Gem."

"Where has it been up 'till now?" Niele asked. "Surely it's been hidden somewhere."

All gazes focused on the gnome.

"Does that really matter?" I asked.

He nodded. "If something like that exists, why hasn't this realm been overrun long ago? Has it been hidden? And if so, who found it, and how?"

Ferral made an impatient sound, but I held up a hand. "He's right. That information would probably help us find both the Commander and the gem."

Trish said, "It has always been believed that the Benedict Royals kept the gem hidden in an underground vault. Many have tried to find and liberate it, but no one has ever succeeded."

"The royal family is under assault now, according to Layla. They're on the verge of being taken." I didn't tell my council about my vision. It didn't seem important at the moment. "If the gem was taken, that would explain the Commander's sudden power over the royals."

"It *has* been taken," Trish said. All gazes slid to her. She flushed. "That was why Nova was there."

"But you told me..."

She gave me an apologetic smile. "I know. I'm sorry. I lied." As I tried to come to grips with her admission, she went on. "The seelie queen sent him into the spiritual realm to find the gem and liberate it." Trish flushed when she saw my expression. "It was a test, meant to buy him back his place at his mother's side. Nova didn't intend to return to seelie, but he knew how dangerous it would be if the Commander got hold of the gem." Trish's vibrant green gaze found mine. "As you witnessed, he failed. He was captured and thrown into one of the cells at the arena. But he did hear news of the gem. One of the demons who was thrown into the cells with Nova said the Commander didn't have it yet, but he was on the verge of getting it."

Rage slid through me. "You should have told me."

Trish looked down at her untouched plate. "I'm sorry. I hoped we...the fae...could deal with the issue before it became a problem."

"The fae?" The words came out louder and shriller than I'd intended. "Is that where your loyalties lie now? You share potentially deadly information with them first, then maybe throw it out to us as scraps after the fact?"

"No!" she looked appalled. "But the queen came to me after Nova was taken. She asked me to find and help him. I didn't want to endanger you unnecessarily..."

"Endanger me?" I stood up so quickly, my chair fell backward with a bang. "You've endangered everyone in this room and all of the people I protect. It might already be too late for us to stop the Commander. We might be overrun with demons before we have time to form a plan. If we'd known as soon as you did..." I turned away from the table, too angry to speak and madder still when tears burned my eyes. I blinked rapidly, unwilling to shed them.

"Madam Lares," Ferral said, his voice at my back uncustomarily soft. "Perhaps our time is better spent gaining as much information as possible right now. If the fae know something that will help..." He let the sentence trail off, lifting his palms. The humility and gentleness in his tone stopped my anger in its tracks. And, though I could barely look at Trish because I was so irritated with her, I returned to my seat, which Gren had helpfully returned to an upright position. "Okay, this dinner has just become a battle planning session. Ideas?"

~

THE NIGHT WAS DECEPTIVELY QUIET. Only the soft, intermittent chirping of a bat flapping past overhead disturbed the silence. Behind me, the house was dark and quiet, only the small light over the kitchen sink giving relief from the darkness.

The house wasn't empty. The teen was in her room, pouring over the books Caleigh had given her, with the crone on speaker so they could work together despite the distance separating them. The rest of my council had gone off to perform the tasks we'd outlined for them in the planning session.

Sitting at the table on my pretty little patio, I spun my nearly untouched glass of wine by the stem, my gaze locked on the shadow-filled back yard. Down by my feet, Monty snored softly. Despite the noisy evidence of his sleeping, his head jerked off the patio stones and his gaze slid skyward with every chirp from the busy bat.

She comes, the bat's disembodied voice said inside my head.

I jerked to my feet, rousing Monty into motion, and stepped into the thick grass to await the woman striding quickly across my yard with two guards flanking her.

Monty took off in their direction, barking a warning that they were entering his territory.

I tensed, relaxing as Layla lifted a hand to stop her guards from responding to the noisy threat. If it had been Matthew and Glenn with her I wouldn't have worried. Actually, if it had been those two, who'd worked beside me and my council nearly enough to be one of us, Monty never would have challenged them. But we didn't know the new guards, a male and a female, both so large that they towered above even Layla's six feet plus height.

Monty slowed long enough to lick Layla's toes and then bounced toward her guards, giving the male a growl and a gentle nip on his shin and the female a kiss on the knee.

My lips curved into a smile despite the dire situation we found ourselves in. My charming little man always did have a soft spot for the ladies.

Layla fixed me with a glower as she strode the last few feet and stopped. It was clear she was irritated that I'd summoned her. I'd expected nothing less. But she had information I needed and time was of the essence.

"Thank you for coming, Princess Layla. Would you like something to eat or drink?"

Royal devil civility required an exchange of pleasantries and sustenance before business was started. Normally, I'd eschew the practice in the name of expediency. But the offer told Layla that her visit to me was a formal one. A meeting between two leaders of state, carrying the weight and importance that implied.

She inclined her head in a formal response and said, "Thank you for your kind offer, Madam Lares, Guardian of Rome and all its Subsidiaries. Sustenance will not be required."

I nodded, swinging a hand toward the table where I'd

been waiting for her arrival. "Please sit? We have something of grave importance to discuss."

When she hesitated, I added, "It concerns the royal family as well as my protectorates."

Layla turned to her guards and spoke in the language of the demonic realm. The two turned smartly on their heels and strode into the darkness, stopping about ten yards away and staring off toward the woods.

She sat heavily, her pretty face lined and weary. "Have you word of my family?"

"Nothing new."

She frowned, looked for a moment as if she would stand and leave.

I held up a hand. "First item of business. I spoke to the demon Bathos and he agreed to help with your...project."

Layla's expression softened a bit and she inclined her head. "Thank you, Aggy."

I nodded. "Also, we have reason to believe the Commander has gotten hold of the Gateway Gem." I watched carefully for her reaction.

She jerked violently and her eyes went wide. "What have you heard?"

"The Rev believes the demons have found something to help them cross over. Gren suggested it might be the gem." I hesitated with the last part, my anger threatening to color my words. Finally, I sighed. "I learned tonight that a seelie fairy prince has apparently gotten information the gem is all but in the Commander's grasp."

Layla jerked to her feet and I started to rise, fearing she was going to bolt. But she simply began to pace, her strides rapid and tight. "They should have told me. It affects us all." Anger made her words harsh and she quickly devolved into the guttural language I couldn't understand.

"Who should have told you?" I asked.

She stopped, turning to me as if she'd forgotten I was there. "The timing makes sense. It would explain why my family is suddenly in hiding. But it should not have been possible."

I leaned across the table. "The Commander was a valued subject in his role as head of the demon army, right? Maybe your parents trusted him with its location."

Her dark blonde brows pinched together. She shook her head vehemently. "My parents are violently aware how important it is to keep the gem's location secret. The stone is much too volatile an object to allow it to fall into the wrong hands."

I bit the inside of my bottom lip, unhappy about my next question but knowing it had to be asked. "Could he have... forced...them to tell him?"

Layla didn't curl into the fetal position at the possibility. She simply shook her head again. "The children have no knowledge of the gem. My mother would die to protect it. My father would kill or die rather than tell anyone. No. They didn't tell him. Maybe it's a bluff?"

"It's possible," I said, my tone measured. "But we have a pending breach coming. By all accounts an enormous one. The only way we can hope to survive it is to know exactly what we're up against so we can plan for it."

Layla nodded. "What can I do to help?"

Relief softened muscles I hadn't even realized I was clenching. "Can you contact your parents? Ask them if the gem is secure?"

Layla deflated. "I've been trying to get a message to them. They aren't responding." She lowered herself back into her chair, dropping her head into her hands. "The only knowledge I have of their whereabouts and condition is from your vision." Her eyes went wide. "Can you force another vision?"

"Unfortunately, I have no control over them." Though, Ferral had told me once the final stage of my seating completed, that would be one of the things I should be able to do. I didn't have the ability yet.

"Can you try?"

I didn't want to get her hopes up. "I don't think I'm at that point yet, Layla. I'm sorry."

Her shoulders sagged.

She nodded, standing. "I'll continue to attempt to contact my parents. You should look for other means to discover the fate of the gem."

"What other means?"

"A millennia ago, the gem had to be moved because a historian was able to discern its location through a careful reading of historical records."

"The crone?" I asked, my displeasure dripping from the question. The last person I wanted to depend on to locate the dangerous icon was the crone. The woman was bad-tempered and secretive, and I had no confidence she'd help us even if she could. Unfortunately, she was also the most powerful magical historian in existence.

"Possibly. But don't you have a talented magical historian on your council?"

Of course she knew I had. She also knew Wanda was training under Caleigh to improve her skills. "You want me to ask the kid to find the gem? She's a novice. She'd have about as much chance as I would to find that icon." I realized as the words came out of my mouth that they weren't fair. Wanda was actually very talented. Extremely adept if I considered that she'd done most of what she'd accomplished without much if any training. Her mother, the person the Rev had gone into the spectral plane to find, had been a talented historian. Talented enough that we believed she'd been taken and eventually killed because of her skill. But Wanda was...

"She's just a kid," I said, my heart breaking at the idea of putting that kind of pressure on my teen.

"Have you ever wondered why the crone was willing to take Wanda under her wing?"

I shrugged. "Wanda needed training and the crone needed someone to boss around."

Layla smiled, but it didn't reach her eyes. "Does that statement really describe their relationship?"

No. It didn't, I realized with a start. They worked together like near equals. Which, I realized, was unusual and unexpected. "What are you telling me?" I asked Layla, my weariness and frustration suddenly dragging me down.

Layla reached out and touched my hand. "If you have another vision, will you let me know?"

I stood, nodding thoughtfully. "Don't forget, I want to be at the ceremony when you bring your family in," I told her. She hesitated, looking suspicious. "So you've told me. But why?"

"You might run into trouble. If you do, I want to be there to help."

She seemed to consider my words for a beat, and then she nodded. "I'll keep you informed."

As Layla and her guards melted into the darkness at the back of my property, a familiar thrum pulsed through the night sky above me. I sat back down at the table and sipped my wine as Gren stepped from the sky and strode toward me with nary a hiccup in his stride.

My own personal guardian angel had arrived.

20

A WARNING COMES, ITS VISIONS DIRE

Iflashed Gren a smile because I couldn't help it. He walked directly to the table, grabbed my hand, and drew me to my feet. "Hello, lovely Aggie," he said, his voice husky. His lips found mine and our bodies melded together as if they'd been designed for each other. The kiss was a heated promise, a sensual assault that made my senses whirl from the combination of soft, questing lips and his long body wrapped around mine.

By the time he broke the kiss a few minutes later, my breathing was erratic, my body was on fire and my mind was muzzy with need. I'd have given anything to be able to take his hand and pull him inside. An hour or two of time spent rolling around on my bed was a burning wish I had no right to pursue.

There was no time. Besides, the teen was inside the house and I had no intention of being *that* kind of mother. I took a determined step back and squeezed his hand in silent promise. "Layla was just here. She didn't tell me much about the gem. Only that its location can apparently be found by a historian."

Gren nodded without surprise. "Wanda?"

"Hopefully. Though I can't imagine she has the power or knowledge needed to do something that other, much more experienced magical historians have no doubt been trying to do for centuries."

"Don't sell her short, Aggy," Gren said. He took a seat next to me at the little table. "The crone wouldn't waste her time on a historian with a shortage of magical ability."

I sighed. "That's what Layla said."

He took my offered glass and sipped. "Truth is truth." Handing the wine back to me, he settled back into his chair, wearily rubbing his face.

"Did you find the goblin soothsayer?"

The council members had all been sent to speak with anyone they believed might "see" the gem or the demons' intentions in the hopes we could get more insight into what was happening than we currently had. Which wasn't much.

He shook his head. "I left a message with his intern. Hopefully, we'll hear from him in the morning."

I snorted. "Goblin soothsayers have interns?"

Gren's weary expression brightened. "He also has a housekeeper, a groundskeeper, and a butler."

"I'm apparently in the wrong business."

A soft chirp lifted our gazes toward the leaden sky.

Batty fluttered overhead, yellow eyes like tiny lanterns in the darkness. *A spirit awaits you in the graveyard.*

I pushed to my feet, the wine making my movements sluggish. "Who is it?"

The irritating flying rodent ignored my question and fluttered off in the direction of the graveyard. Gren joined me as I stepped beneath the flower-drenched archway that formed the entrance to my patio—Niele's fine handiwork—and we strode toward the small graveyard at the side of my large property. The white picket fence surrounding the worn and chipped stones was a north star in the darkness. Inside the fence, a translucent, silvery figure waited with an expectant stance.

The young woman had straight dark hair that fell well past rounded shoulders and piercing dark eyes that looked black under the cloud-studded moon. She wore a shimmering white gown that was cinched at her slender waist, and soft, flat slippers on her feet. Her pale fingers clutched the thorny length of a blood-red rose she'd no-doubt picked from the flower beds along the fence.

As I watched, she lifted the flower to delicate nostrils and inhaled deeply, her black eyes closing with pleasure.

"Hello?" I said, offering the ghostly figure a smile.

The woman's eyes snapped open. She stiffened, her gaze rising to Gren's and her features tightening with fear. "I only wish to speak to the Lares. I wish no trouble, angel."

I frowned at her reaction to Gren's presence. "He won't harm you. What business do you have with me?" I stared at the puzzling blue-gray aura surrounding her ghostly form as a memory niggled.

The woman's gaze slid to the church and softened. "I used to bring my daughter to this church. It was a peaceful time. I miss it. I miss her."

Pity tightened my chest. "I'm sorry for your loss." The sentiment had come easily to my lips, but the strangeness of it hit me a beat later. It was, of course, customary to say such a thing to the living who'd lost a loved one. But spirits who were aware and sentient also grieved those they'd left behind. Those they'd lost.

She nodded, seemed to shake off her sad thoughts, and skimmed another fearful look Gren's way before addressing her full attention to me. "I have come with a warning. The demons are amassing. They only await the leader to begin their migration into this realm."

Gren and I shared a look. Though we'd known it was coming, hearing her say the words made it feel more imminent and made my stomach clench with fear.

"Who's the leader?" I asked.

The woman grimaced as if the knowledge physically hurt. "He failed because of you. His position, his reputation, everything was lost when he suffered that defeat. He is very angry. You and your people are in grave danger."

"Who sent you?" Gren asked. Though the question was asked in a gentle tone, the intensity behind it was fierce.

The woman ignored him, her gaze locked on mine. "I've come to right a wrong. You must not let the princess bring her family here. It will create a killing field."

"Why?" I asked, stepping closer. "What do you know?"

The spirit shook her head, her slender form wavering as if she would disappear. "I can't tell you more than that. Even that is too much. But I couldn't let you..." A silvery tear slipped down her pale cheek. A quiver touched her colorless lips. "I wouldn't want this place to be destroyed. There has already been enough pain. Enough suffering." Her gaze once more strayed to the church, then rose to the night sky and the pair of bright, yellow eyes glowing through the dark. "I need to go." Despite her words, she didn't leave.

A beat later, her gaze found mine again and she swayed forward, one spectral hand finding my arm, bathing it in ice. I watched in horror as her eyes rolled back in her head, her lids staying open to expose the eerie whites of her eyes. Her lips began to move.

"When every soul is drawn to see, a place where only death decrees, then life becomes a distant thought, and each torn heart once pleasure wrought, the devil rises on its heels, and every soul its future yields. And only she who guards the day, can stop the demons' deadly play, but when her thunder growls on high, an evil plot must shrink and die."

With that cryptic message, the specter seemed to shake off the vision. But before I could question her further about it, the wispy form sifted quickly away, into the rising mists of the night.

"Well," I said. "That was weird. Do you suppose she was talking about the Commander?"

"I'd say that's a good bet," Gren agreed. "Whoever she was referring to, if Layla's ceremony to bring her family over is the catalyst, we need to stop that ceremony."

I started to nod, my head jerking to a stop as a vision slammed into me, jolting me to a stop as my surroundings dropped away.

Shrieking. Terrified cries and shrill begging. Blood running in thick rivulets down a window with spiderweb fractures. There was growling in the distance, followed by a broken scream of terror and pain. The vision jerked, shifted, showing me busted furniture covered in splashes of crimson and draped with limp, bloodied forms. So much blood. The vision playing across my inner screen didn't feel as if it were something that would happen in the future. Rather, it was as if it were occuring at that very moment.

A shadow fell over the fraction of the scene I could see. It shifted sideways and then jerked again, shooting directly at me. I gasped, wrenching backward from the faceless demon whose claws ripped through flesh without mercy. The shadow fell over an elderly man whose chest was torn into bloody tracks. The man's grizzled gray face filled my vision as he sagged downward. To my shock, he opened his mouth and said, "Goddess...save us." And as he fell, the vision shattered, fracturing into black shapes that spun away from me, and left me sobbing and panting on the wet grass.

I hadn't even felt Gren's warm hands rubbing my back. Or the words of comfort and reassurance he'd been giving me. His voice had been lost behind the violence of the scene I'd been forced to view. But as the vision receded, I finally felt the comforting circles he was rubbing across my back. I heard the terrified concern in his deep voice, made husky from fear. "Aggy, talk to me. What's wrong?"

I swallowed hard and dropped backward, uncaring for the wetness seeping through my jeans. Seated with my legs bent and my elbows resting on them, I panted with emotion, dizziness trying to take me down.

"Put your head between your knees," Gren said, his hand gently pressing my head down. "Try to take slow, deep breaths."

I did as he said, feeling the panic start to ease. My mind slowly cleared and I gave a cry of alarm, trying to shove to my feet.

Gren held me down. "Talk to me," he said. "What's going on?"

"Vision…" I gasped out. I looked at him, my eyes wide with terror. Grabbing his hand, I wrapped both of my hands around it and squeezed hard enough to dent his skin with my nails. "I don't think it was the future," I told him. "I think someone called out for help. I think they need me to save them right now."

"From what?" he asked, helping me stand.

"Demons." I clamped down on debilitating fear as my mind relived the horror of what I saw. "I think the people were being attacked by demons."

I took off for the house, my steps gathering speed until I was running full out.

Gren easily kept up with me, grabbing the door and yanking it open as I threw myself into the house. "Wanda!" I screamed.

The door to my kid's bedroom opened and she came out wearing an oversized t-shirt and boxers with dachshunds all over them. Monty trotted out behind her. "What's wrong?" She asked, one hand shoving a thick wave of black hair off her face. She blinked sleepily and yawned, a pillow crease denting one flushed cheek. "Call everybody. Tell them to meet us at the bar at the edge of Rome. And they need to hurry."

As I rushed out of the house, my heart thudding against my ribs, I was dimly aware of Gren's deep voice rumbling further instructions to the teen as I threw up a hand and snatched my staff out of the air.

Gren ran out of the house. "Should we fly?" he asked.

I hesitated. As much as I enjoyed flying Air Lungren, I decided the car would be a better option in case someone needed to be evacuated from the scene. "No. We'll take my car."

He didn't argue. He simply ran toward the ancient Range Rover that was parked under a security light in my gravel lot and climbed in on the passenger side.

Six seconds and two grinding turns of the key later, I hit the road and took off in a spray of gravel, the screams of my people still ringing in my head, along with the knowledge that for some of them at least, I would be too late.

21

REGRETS RENEW THE LARES IRE

I slammed my foot on the brake in the gravel parking lot of a bar called, Clay's Place Bar, flinging gravel and sending the Range Rover skidding sideways before coming to a stop mere inches from a security light pole. Gren was out of the car and running for the bar as I fought my seatbelt, but I was seconds behind him as he flung open the door and dove inside.

I had the space of a single heartbeat to notice the telltale signs of trouble before pulling open the door.

A dense, black shadow skimmed across the windows, the form unnatural and brimming with evil intent. One window was broken, the splintered remains of a heavy wooden chair half inside and half in the parking lot. Blood painted the inside of the window in the entry door.

But it wasn't until I opened the door and stepped inside, that I felt the full impact of the oily evil overtaking the space. The bar had apparently been cloaked with a sound-dampening spell because, despite the broken front window, I hadn't heard anything until I'd entered.

Screams and terror-filled pleading saturated the bar.

Mixed with inhuman growls and the nightmarish sounds of savagery, the horrific resonance pulled a quiet sob from my throat.

I forced my shoulders back and straightened my knees. Snapping my staff to its full length, I took a step forward, my gaze scanning the bar for a target.

Evil, black as tar, punched me in the chest as I stepped deeper into the place. Bodies lay everywhere, strewn over the soiled carpet, draped over the bar, sagging from several bar stools, and, in one horrific case, pinned to the wall near the hall leading to the restrooms by a thick spike which had no doubt come from a broken chair leg.

My worst nightmare had come true. I'd failed my people. I'd been totally unaware as the demons...somehow... breached the dimensional boundaries and began their orgy of death and destruction.

Tears burned my eyes.

A shadow flashed past and my head came up. No more crying. I needed to stop the killing before it spread beyond the bar's walls. A guttural scream came from the back of the bar, in a second room where I could see pool tables and an empty stage where a band probably played on Saturday nights.

First, I needed to contain the problem. Lifting the staff, I screamed, "Enclose!"

Golden magic streamed from the orb at the top of my staff and filtered away from me in a wide, thin wash that hit the walls, the door, and the windows and painted them in sparkling energy.

My spell had barely had time to lock down before a wave of putrid brimstone stench swept over me. I reacted without thinking, whipping around and sending a thick column of golden energy into the shadow demon preparing to attack me.

The thing was enormous, its vaguely man-like form rising on bent legs nearly to the ceiling and spreading across the majority of one wall.

My magic made it fade slightly, but the thing quickly recovered. The demon sent me flying with a punch in the chest by an enormous clawed hand. Expecting to slam into a wall or table, I instead hit a firm but malleable chest and was immediately engulfed in charcoal gray wings.

Gren bent his head to look at me. "Are you okay?"

A wet growl kept me from responding and Gren slapped a wing out to send a nasty-looking demon with pale pink, warty skin flying. Thick strings of slobber slapped at us as the monster's body left the ground.

I pushed off Gren as the shadow demon rose again from the floor and stabbed my staff toward its body, aiming for the approximate location of its black, black heart. "Infuse!" I screamed, and sent as much energy as I could muster into the thing. I had no illusions that I'd be able to defeat the creature alone. The last time I'd battled a shadow demon, it had taken the combined energy from me, Layla, and several of her guards to kill it.

The shadow's thick arms swung away from its body and I ducked as one of the shadowy limbs swung in my direction. Before I could retaliate, it slid upward on the wall and along the ceiling, descending again on the other side of the bar.

Sneaky demon.

Gren had moved away to deal with what sounded like several more of the monsters. I doubled down on my attack, yanking magical energy from my surroundings in an attempt to weaken the demon enough that, with help from my council when they arrived, we could hopefully put it out of our misery.

I thought I was making progress in weakening the beast when it suddenly disappeared, its shadowy form sinking below the floorboards beneath my feet. "Curse!" I yelled, panting and sweaty from my efforts.

Pounding shook the front door and it took me a beat to realize it was my team. I shoved wearily to my feet and stumbled over, touching the door with a fingertip and murmuring, "Release," before stepping back.

The door flew open, nearly knocking me to the floor. I caught it with my hands, and pain thrummed up my arms from the impact. "Ease up," I said crankily.

Bev blinked in surprise and immediately looked guilty. "Sorry. I thought the door was spelled so we tried to blast it open with magic."

A wolf shot past me and, within seconds, Luke had leaped onto one of four demons Gren was fighting.

Mavis and Bev pushed past too. "Where do you need us?"

"There's a shadow demon. I think it's going to take all of us to defeat it."

Mavis opened her mouth to say something, but never got the chance. A shadow rose out of the floor behind me and roared. I started to turn as dense, sulfurous arms wrapped around my middle, yanking me off the ground. The demon's grip tightened until I could no longer breathe, and my instinctual kicking had little effect on his dense, spongy form.

A large, silver dog leaped through the door with a snarl on its sleek muzzle. Ferral caught the demon in his formidable jaws and wrenched his muscular body sideways. To my shock, a piece of the monster's arm ripped away with a wet, meaty sound and the demon released me to focus on the hound.

I hit the ground and rolled, coming up with my staff and more than my share of irritation.

Mavis and Bev flanked me, their fingers vigorously building spells on the air. Bev tied off her first spell and sent it flying. The spell was a dark mist that ate holes in the creature, turning it to black lace wherever it touched.

The demon threw back its head and screamed, the sound shattering bottles and glasses all along the bar, and breaking out what was left of the windows. Mavis flicked her spell toward the beast's legs and I watched as pale green strings of magic shot toward the thick, shadowy appendages, hitting them like string, and immediately thickening to something more the width of one of my arms. The dense threads twined around the shadow demon's legs and tightened.

The creature teetered in place, wavering and fighting to stay upright as Ferral proceeded to tear more chunks off its arms and torso.

Black clouds of sulfurous magic rolled off the monster, a choking mist that made it impossible to see the demon we were fighting. Bev flicked another lattice spell at the demon and then succumbed to the mist, doubling over in a violent coughing attack.

Mavis swirled her fingers in the air and made a chopping motion across the magic she'd formed there. A beat later, she flicked a magical face mask toward me and another at Bev. She slid three fingers over her own face, and a mask covered her from eyebrow to chin. Then she got back to the business of defeating our demon.

I could barely feel the mask she'd given me. Like hers, it covered me from brows to chin, keeping the choking mist out as well as blocking the demon's cloaking powers so I could see where it was.

Without hesitation, I sent another stream of energy into the beast, focusing on its torso and leaving the legs, arms, and head to my team.

With our combined attack, it took another twenty minutes of constant magical strikes to send the thing crashing to its blank face on the floor. When it didn't get up again, we all collapsed into the few unbroken chairs. All of us, that is, except the two canine members of my team, who dropped to the floor and panted.

Gren lowered himself into a chair close to me. "Well, that was exciting."

We looked around at the mess and I said. "We need to check the victims. Maybe some of them are alive."

Mavis and Bev nodded but didn't move. I knew how they felt. Every muscle in my body felt like spaghetti. A soft groan from behind the bar spurred me to my feet. We found the bartender covered by part of a ceiling beam and dug him out. He was bruised and battered but would live. "Is there anybody else hiding here?" Gren asked the man.

The bartender nodded, pointing to a man sitting on the floor, leaning against the wall. The victim's short, gray-blond hair was matted with blood and he had claw marks across his chest. "The other bartender is down and I saw a bunch of people running to the kitchen," he gasped out through the pain of what I was pretty sure was several broken ribs.

"We'll go see," Mavis said. She and Bev headed that way.

While Gren gave the first bartender water and did what he could to make him comfortable, I saw to the second bartender and then looked around, taking stock of the victims.

Several were breathing, but everybody was pretty beat

up. A deep sadness tightened my chest. It was my fault. I should have heard their cries. I should have known they were in trouble. Why hadn't I? What good was *Response* if it didn't stop things like what happened in the bar from happening?

A heavy, warm arm dropped to my shoulders. Gren's lips touched my temple, lingering there. "You came as soon as they called," he told me in a soft voice. "It's all you can do."

"Is it, though?" I asked, feeling as if I could have done more. Much more.

A burst of silvery light announced the transition of my canine council.

Right on cue, Niele burst from the floor, spraying dirt and small gravel as he surged out of the hole he'd made. He looked around, frowning. "Looks like I'm late to the party."

"You are," I said. "Can you call Chief Marshal please? Tell him there's major cleanup of the magical kind."

"Will do."

Chief Davis Marshal had been like many people in my protectorate when I'd started my seating. He was fully human and, at the time, had zero suspicion that anything magical existed. His learning curve on that had been even shorter than mine as Lares. And nearly as painful. He'd found out when I'd arrived at the Rome Police Station with several demons and a royal devil contingent in tow.

Eye-opening didn't begin to describe his introduction to magic. In the space of only moments, he'd gone from the Magic 101 level to one of expert practitioner with severely sweaty palms.

To the Chief's credit, he'd gotten himself up to speed quickly. And, though we could probably credit his private "tutoring" sessions with the mom of my heart for much of that, Mavis wasn't responsible for the Chief's innate savviness, or his determination to protect the people of Rome from all things evil, whether human, magical, or beast.

I trusted the Chief to bring the right people and equipment to deal with the cleaning and coverup of a magically-caused crime scene.

As for the half-dozen people Mavis and Bev were leading out of the backroom looking slightly the worse for wear, it would be up to us to make sure, if they weren't magical, they had a plausible scenario in their minds for what had happened at the bar while they were there.

Judging by the slightly dazed expressions on the faces of the five men and one woman wearing biker leathers, that work had already been done.

I verified it with a quick look at Mavis and received a slight nod. After a quick discussion with Bev, I learned the group were not locals and had just been passing through. We pointed them to their motorcycles and sent them happily on their way, oblivious to the nightmare that had torched their lives.

It turned out the bartender was a gnome. Niele's fourth cousin on his father's side...or something like that. I didn't even try to keep track of Niele's extensive family. I only knew there were a lot of them, and that the gnome community was vast, well-hidden, and close-knit. They'd stepped in to help in a couple of situations since I'd become Lares, and I had a deep respect for them as a race and an even deeper gratitude for their selfless aid.

Niele offered to take his cousin home for gnome-style healing, which I gathered involved being buried beneath a flower bed and left for a day or seven, depending on the extent of the injury. My groundskeeper and the bartender dropped into the hole Niele had created beneath the wood floor and I sagged, suddenly feeling the weariness of the last few hours.

I stood in the middle of the bar, noting the distant throb of the sirens as Davis and his officers approached. Despite the distance, the siren's call throbbed beneath my skin.

My weariness turned to an ache, and I absently rubbed a spot over my heart. The ache increased and a jolt of fear swept through me as dizziness assailed. Was I having a heart attack? I opened my mouth to call Gren over and hesitated. It wasn't the sirens throbbing beneath my skin. I sat straighter, my gaze sliding around the bar.

It was a heartbeat.

Not my heartbeat, but a second one, which had tuned itself to mine and was speeding even as my heartbeat sped. I placed my hand flat over the beating sensation and stood up, looking around. Bev and Mavis were each bent over a victim, their palms glowing with pale green light as they sent healing energy into their respective "patients", who were draped over the debris-strewn floor. Trish...whose arrival I'd missed during the melee...was giving healing magic to a pretty young woman near the door. Luke was outside, pacing in front of the tattered remains of the door, his taut musculature and intense yellow eyes evidence that he was on the watch for more demons. Gren knelt next to a man with gray hair, one hand on the man's head and another clutching a bloody hand. Gren's eyes were closed and I was fairly sure he was praying.

I walked over and knelt down across from Gren, recognizing the man who'd called out to me when the demons had attacked. I took the man's free hand and smiled down at him. "Hello..." I hesitated, realizing I didn't know the man's name. I was going to leave it at the awkward greeting when the name popped into my head, delivered in the man's own voice. *Rob*.

I smiled. "Hello, Rob. Thank you for calling me. You saved a lot of lives today with your quick thinking."

He smiled, his lips bloody but the light in his eyes happy. He squeezed my hand in his cold grip. "Bless you, goddess. I knew you'd come."

I didn't bother to correct his assumption that I was a goddess. It didn't matter a whit and there was no sense wasting whatever time he had left.

Rob's body tightened in a violent shudder. I glanced at Gren and he frowned, giving his head a tiny shake.

Tears burned my eyes, but I wouldn't shed them in front of Rob. His expression was blissful. "You brought my guardian angel," he rasped. "Bless you for that, too."

I blinked hard to expel tears. I nodded. "This is my favorite angel," I told him, giving Gren a watery smile.

Rob's chest rumbled wetly and he shook. Alarmed, it took me a minute to realize he was laughing.

He must have seen my look of alarm because he nodded. "It's okay, goddess. I know I'm dying. I'm fine with that. I get to go to my beautiful wife, Desiree now. That is the answer to my prayers."

I must have looked confused because he added, "I called you to save the others." He fought to lift his head and Gren slid a large palm underneath it to help. "That pretty little girl over there..." He pointed to the woman by the door, who seemed to be stirring. I was happy to see she had color in her cheeks. "That's my granddaughter. Desi would have wanted me to save her. She would have scolded me if I didn't." The wet laughter erupted again and turned almost immediately into a coughing fit. I tightened my grip on his hand and waited while he worked his way through it. Then he lay back, sighed contentedly, and closed his eyes. "I'm going now, goddess. Thank you for saving my lovely little girl."

And with that, he was gone.

I let the tears slide down my cheeks and squeezed Rob's hand one last time before standing. Gren stood too. "Only the man who was pinned to the wall died," he said. "Despite everything, we managed to save nearly all. You should be proud of that."

I rubbed absently at my chest, wondering why the beating sensation was still there. "Proud? No. I should have saved them all."

"Aggy. We've talked about this. You're not supposed to save them all. Only the ones who aren't supposed to die at this time in their lives."

I barely heard his scolding. I'd begun to walk toward the back room. I was only vaguely aware of my movements but I couldn't have stopped myself if I'd wanted to. I didn't want to stop. I was in the grips of my very own siren song.

Stopping at the first table, I scanned a look over the broken cues and the scatter of balls, some of which had claw marks marring their surface. A broken glass lay on its side on the table, golden liquid spilling out onto the torn felt. The window in the back wall was shattered, the glass sparkling on the floor, the sill, and likely outside in the parking lot.

The heartbeat I could still feel in my chest had sped, the thump, thump, thump of its cadence vibrating through my core like rock music.

A tiny sound...a mere whisper of fabric rustling...drew my gaze to a cabinet at the side of the room. I moved in that direction, my gaze locked unblinkingly on one door, which was just the tiniest bit ajar.

The sour stench of old food assailed my nostrils as I bent close to a bin filled with dirty dishes. I pulled magic into my left hand as I reached toward the handle with my right.

Thumpthumpthumpthumpthump...

My heart sped alongside the intruding beat.

Slowly, my senses on full alert, I pulled the door open and jerked to a stop, the magic in my fist sizzling hungrily.

I stared at the creature looking back at me, my breath locked behind my shock.

Large red-gold eyes blinked up at me. A cloud of blonde hair puffed up around straight black horns that stuck straight out at the sides of a triangular head. Dove-gray scales covered a small body and, as the creature tried to shove itself further into the shadows inside the cabinet, cloven hooves dug into the tender wood of the pine furniture.

It was a child.

I crouched down and let my magic die, giving the small creature what I hoped was a disarming smile. "Hello."

The child blinked rapidly, pressing against the back of the cabinet in an effort to get further away from me.

"Who do we have there?" Gren asked, his tone gentle.

I didn't look up because I feared if I looked away the child would run. "If I'm not mistaken, I think it's Layla's sister." I softened my gaze and held my smile. "Is that right?"

Without warning, the creature bunched her limbs and shot out of the cabinet, knocking me to my back and running right over me.

The kid's weight knocked the wind out of me. She wasn't big, but she was heavy and she'd landed on me with some force. As I fought to pull air into my chest, a high-pitched keening sound erupted behind me. Wheezing like an asthmatic, I turned to find that Gren had managed to get his hands on the child and was currently fighting to keep from being bitten while not hurting her.

"Mavis," I wheezed out. Gren somehow heard me over the keening and turned, calling out to the mother of my heart.

A beat later, Mavis had hold of the child's hand and was speaking in her trademark, upbeat mother voice. The child blinked back at her, relaxing enough to take the sucker Mavis had somehow produced.

Gren helped me to my feet and I stood, slightly stooped, one arm across my belly. "Do you think she understands what we're saying?"

Mavis kept her smile in place as she responded. "I think it's just tone of voice," she said, her gray eyes twinkling. "And suckers."

I snorted, drawing the girl's gaze. The kid's eyes narrowed. It looked like she was thinking about bolting again. "Mom."

"I've got this, honey." Mavis gave the girl a gentle tug and they sat down at a fairly clean table together. "Call Layla," she said still speaking through the smile.

But that was the moment Chief Davis's car roared up to the building and screeched to a halt. Fortunately, he'd killed the sirens before turning into the lot, but the cruiser's lights still flared through the night. However, it was the man himself who was the last straw. He climbed out of the car and strode in his no-nonsense way into the bar.

The kid took one look at him and leaped onto the table with another one of those keening squeals, and she was gone in a blur of movement that ended on a wash of air and the soft tinkling of glass from the broken window.

As we looked at each other in stunned silence, my phone rang. I knew who it was from the Monster Mash ringtone—Mavis and Layla's handiwork. I sighed, wanting more than anything to reject the call. But the princess was the person I most needed and least wanted to talk to at that moment. I motioned for Luke and Ferral to go after the girl and, with a sigh, I answered. "Hey, Layla. We have a problem."

22

A TINY FIEND, A MYSTERY BRINGS

"I s this the last one?" Mavis asked, her shoulders sagging as the large creature in front of her shimmered and disappeared, followed by the sound of hooves clacking across the tile toward the door. The back door opened and closed and the room felt empty after the noise and bustle of the previous hours.

She and Bev had created close to thirty obscuring spells for Layla's people and her fatigue was showing in the too-pale color of her face and her wobbly legs.

"It is for you," Chief Davis said, his tone no-nonsense. He scooped her up and looked at me. "I'm going to put her in your room. You're going to get her something to eat and then she's going to sleep for as long as she needs."

"Davis," Mavis complained, shoving at his shoulder. "Put me down. I'm doing a job here."

I held the Chief's determined gaze for a moment, caught between the need to tell him to back off, and my feeling that he was right. Mavis had done too much.

I looked at the mother of my heart. "He's right, mom," I

told her. "I'm going to need your help with the Commander. You need to sleep."

Her lips pinched with irritation but she didn't argue. Which meant she was more tired than usual.

Davis carried Mavis out of the kitchen and I turned to Wanda. "Do we have any of that cold chicken left?"

She nodded. "I'll make her up a tray."

"Thanks, sweetie." I glanced at Bev. She was sitting at the table, head bowed and shoulders rounded, and I sighed. "Let's make two of those sandwiches," I told the teen. "I'll help."

We worked silently, the kitchen peaceful after the seemingly endless line of lost ones needing obfuscation magic so they could search Rome in the daylight for the child. In addition, Bev had made a necklace with obfuscation magic they could put on the little one if...when...they found her.

I put a sandwich in front of my sister and she jerked, her head coming up and her gaze focusing wearily on the plate. She'd apparently fallen asleep sitting up. "What...?"

"Eat," I told her. "Then you're going to sleep for a while."

She started to argue but I shook my head. "That's an order."

Bev's lips curved gently in the corners. "You're not the boss of me."

I grinned at the often-used phrase from our childhood. "Actually, I am."

She shrugged, staring at the sandwich as if she were too tired to pick it up. I sat down next to her. "Do I need to feed you?"

She sighed and grabbed half. "Where's mom?"

"Davis embraced his inner caveman and carried her off to bed."

Her gaze went wide and she grimaced. "Ew."

I chuckled. "Not like that, toilet brain. She needs sleep."

Bev nodded, chewing thoughtfully.

A plate appeared in front of me. I looked up into Wanda's bright gaze. "For you. I'll take Mavis her food and then drop anchor in the sanctuary to study. Caleigh sent me some new books." The teen glanced at Bev. "You can have my bed."

Bev nodded, swallowing. "Thanks, girlfriend."

Wanda took off with a tray containing a sandwich, a cup of tea, and a cookie.

Bev and I frowned. We hadn't gotten cookies.

I got up and went to the pantry, foraging until I found the bakery box from Tilly's hidden behind several cans of green beans. The kid wasn't stupid. She knew that would be the last place I'd look. I hated green beans. The only reason I had them was to supplement Monty's diet kibble in an effort to help fill the giant vacancy that was otherwise known as a dachshund stomach without his gaining thirty additional pounds he didn't need.

"She hid the cookies?" Bev asked, looking a little perkier with food in her belly.

I handed her two of the chocolate chip delights and I took two for myself. Shoving the sandwich away, I started on the cookies.

The first bite melted sweetly on my tongue and I moaned with pleasure.

Davis came into the room and eyed my cookies. I gave him one and stood. "Coffee?"

"Yes, please."

Bev nodded, her mouth full of cookie.

I shook my head. "Unless you want decaf that's a negatory," I told her. "You need to sleep."

She sighed unhappily. "Milk then?"

"That, you can definitely have." I made coffee for Davis and me and poured Bev's milk. Retrieving the cookie box from the pantry, I set it in front of the Chief before sitting back down at the table.

"How's Mavis?" I asked the cop.

He sipped his steaming coffee, made a delighted face, and then shook his head. "She ate half her cookie and then fell asleep."

I grinned. "Sounds right to me."

"Except for the only eating half part," Bev said before popping the last bite of her second cookie into her mouth. She rinsed it down with the last of the milk and stood. "I'm going to try to sleep. Wake me up if anything happens."

"I will." As she left I whispered, "I won't," to Davis.

He grinned and took another cookie. "So, any idea where the kid came from?"

"Layla thinks the demons brought her over."

"Does that mean they already have the gem?"

I'd told the Chief what we were dealing with because there was a good chance we'd need his help. At the very least, he might end up with a few demons in his jail cells.

"Unlikely." I thought about my vision. If it had been real...and I had no reason to believe it wasn't...it told me that the Commander had probably already taken Layla's family. "We'd be facing a full-scale migration and assault right now if they had that rock already."

"Then how did those demons get here?"

It was a good question, and one I was determined to find out the answer to. "I'm not sure. It's possible they came in through a blood sacrifice. Obviously, we need to find out."

He sat quietly for a minute, drinking his coffee and staring out at the rising sun beyond my kitchen window. I suddenly realized how tired I was. It had been a long night, filled with stress and trauma that I feared would keep me awake and my thoughts spinning. Despite that, I'd probably need to catch a couple of hours of sleep soon, or I wouldn't be good for anyone.

As if reading my mind, Chief Davis stood and walked over to the sink, rinsing out his cup and putting it into the dishwasher. He turned back to me and said. "You need to sleep too, Miss Aggy. I'll put a car on the church until your people return, so you can get some rest."

I nodded, fighting back a yawn. "Thanks. If something happens let me know, okay? Even if I'm asleep."

"I'll call the girl and she can wake you."

"That would be great." I stood and headed out of the kitchen before realizing there was no place for me to sleep. I stood in the door to the sanctuary and looked at Wanda. She nodded toward the couch. "I already put a blanket and pillow on the couch. I'll be quiet."

"You're my favorite kid," I told her, stumbling wearily toward my makeshift bed. "Even if you did steal my dog."

She snickered.

But as I draped myself over the long couch, pulling the blanket up around my chin, I heard the pitter patter of little doxie feet and a soft, warm body launched himself up to stretch out beside me. Wrapping an arm around my little man, I closed my eyes on a sigh, and fell directly into the arms of Morpheus.

I'd love to say it was a dreamless sleep, absent violence and terror-filled screams, but that would be a lie. I fought my way through the tortuous nightmares until I couldn't take it anymore, and then woke to find myself alone in the sanctuary, minus one teen and her faithful furry companion.

I shoved the covers down, suddenly too hot. My shirt

was damp with sweat and heat seemed to boil out of my head, cooking the pillow beneath it. I had a moment of stark fear that I was falling into another *Response*-driven attack, but then realized it was probably just a normal pre-menopausal hot flash.

Ugh.

Voices in the kitchen indicated that Mavis and Bev were awake. The spicy scent of taco meat was evidence that Mavis was back at the stove.

The woman really needed to learn to take a break.

But, with a couple of her best-in-class tacos coming my way, I wasn't complaining.

A bright afternoon sun beat through the kitchen window when I entered, the fierceness of it making me blink. "What time is it?" I asked blearily as I covered my eyes.

"Good afternoon," my sister said. She was setting the table while Wanda tossed a salad near the sink. I noticed the teen kept dropping chunks of carrot and red pepper for the bottomless belly with legs standing near her feet.

"It's nearly four. You slept almost ten hours." Wanda tossed Monty another hunk of pepper and settled the bowl into the center of the table. "I think I found something in the books. Or, I should say, Caleigh found it. I just extrapolated out from what she found and hopefully learned something helpful."

"Extrapolated, huh?" I asked, grimacing. "That's way too big a word for my sleepy brain,"

She rolled her eyes. "There are four instances where demons have breached the boundaries between the spectral plane and forbidden dimensions over the last eight hundred years."

Mavis handed me a wine glass filled with a burgundy-colored liquid and I blew her a kiss. "This is why I forgive you for the ringtones," I told her.

Mavis laughed, winking at Wanda. The sight turned my spine to ice. The last thing I needed was the two of them ganging up on me with the stupid ringtone thing.

I sipped my wine as Wanda continued.

"All four instances happened during a blue moon phase."

"Wait," I said, "I thought you said it had never happened during a blue moon."

She flushed pink. "Turns out I was missing some information."

Weasel words that meant she'd been wr...wr...wrong.

"So, they didn't need the gem?" I asked, dread tugging at my gut.

"No. But they needed something magical that had been in the spectral plane to cross the boundary through special circumstances. It isn't clear what those special circumstances were, but I got the sense it was something different each time."

The tiny frisson of dread grew claws and raked the inside of my belly. I looked at Mavis and Bev, my eyes going wide. "The kid."

Bev frowned and Mavis covered her mouth with a hand. "That child can't be working with the demons."

Wanda shook her head. "I doubt she is. There's nothing that said the thing from the spectral plane was a person, or that she was in on it. For all we know, they had a witch summon the kid over the boundary against her will. From what you told me about her, she was too young to be in cahoots on a plan to conquer this world. This thing the books mentioned seemed to be just a precursor for the exodus."

"But Layla's baby sister was in the demonic realm. Did she cross from there?" Bev asked.

I shook my head. "I'm pretty sure, according to my vision, that the family was taken into the spectral realm."

Mavis dropped into a chair at the table, looking gobsmacked. "Did the book tell you how this precursor sets the exodus into motion?"

Wanda shook her head. "I'm still working on that. If you don't mind, I'll take my tacos into my room and keep working."

Mavis stood up and wrapped her arms around Wanda. "Of course, honey. But you're working too hard. When this is over, I demand you go to a movie or something with your friends. Okay?"

Wanda's grin was wide and smug. "Well, if you insist."

I laughed. "You've been played," I told my mom.

Mavis blew air through her lips and flapped a hand. "You don't seriously think she's fooling me, do you? After all, I've already raised three teenagers. I know a thing or two."

Wanda turned her grin on me. "I'm so weary and put upon, I might need extra cookies too for the next couple of weeks."

Mavis flicked the teen's ear, earning herself a pain-filled yelp and more laughter. "Get out of here you little hoodlum. Or I'll put raisins in your cookies."

Wanda made a gagging noise and slouched out of the room.

Our smiles left with her. "I can't believe Layla's baby sister is in the middle of this mess," I said. Then my eyes went wide. "Layla's going to have kittens when she finds out."

"You should call her," Bev told me.

I sighed, pulling out my phone. Before I could dial,

however, the door in the mudroom opened and Layla herself strolled inside. And, from the expression on her face, I feared I wouldn't like what she was about to tell me.

"Did you find her?" Bev asked.

"No." Layla didn't look away from me as she answered. "But I think we're close."

"That's good, right?" I asked, confused by her dire expression.

Layla finally glanced away, her demeanor fraught with guilt. "I'll be pleased to find my little sister. She's probably terrified." The princess moved over to the sink, leaning against the counter and crossing her arms over her chest.

She stared hard at me until I finally asked. "Did I do something to irritate you?"

Layla flinched, looked away, and frowned. "You did nothing wrong. It's me. I've done something...inadvisable. And I'm afraid I'm going to pay a huge price for it."

The stiff formality of the princess's speech told me she was uncomfortable with what she was about to say.

"What is it?" I asked, even though I had a horrible feeling I already knew what it was.

She filled her lungs and slowly emptied them before saying, "I performed the blood ceremony last night."

Silence pulsed through the room, all of us staring at Layla in shock. Finally, Mavis said, "Well, I guess that explains how the kid got here."

I glared at the princess. "Then you lied to my face when you were here?"

She returned my glare. "No. I simply chose not to tell you." To my surprise, a tear slid down Layla's cheek. "And, as far as Desmean arriving because of the blood-ceremony, I only wish that were how she got here. But the ceremony failed. None of them came through."

I knew virtually nothing about blood ceremonies. But it was clear Layla had expected a hole to open up in front of her and her family to walk out. "Are you sure?"

She all but stamped a foot in frustration. "Well, obviously not, since my baby sister just turned up in a human bar. What if the rest of them are here somewhere? What if they ended up all spread out or in the wrong dimensions?"

Her fear and tension were so strong I could smell them, like burnt toast, in the air.

"When we find her we can ask about the rest of your family, right?"

Layla scowled at me for a beat and then finally shrugged. "Desmean is very young. She may not understand what happened to them. Or to her."

"If they're here, we'll find them," Bev said. "But we have a bigger problem, I'm afraid."

Layla gave her a disbelieving look. "A bigger problem?" she fairly shrieked. "Bigger than me misplacing my entire family?"

I winced. "Actually, yes." I filled her in on what Wanda and the crone had found. "There's a good chance your family...or at least your sister...will be the catalyst for releasing a hoard of demons into the world."

"Curse!" Layla swore, finally stomping her foot. "What else could possibly go wrong?"

And, right on cue, my gut threatened to rip in half, and I fell over the table as agony flared through me.

23

OUR HEROES PLAN, A LOVED ONE SINGS

The Commander looked so real, I thought he'd appeared inside my home. If he wasn't standing seven or eight feet away from me, then my visions were getting much stronger.

I'd basically gone from rabbit ear antenna picture quality to Ultra HD.

Monty was sounding the alarm in the distance, his barks sharp and angry in frantic warning. My mom and sister were shouting and I had the distinct impression they were gathering magic to attack the Commander.

But the demon only had eyes for me. Red, slitted eyes to be exact, and his smile was more teeth than lips. As I remembered from before, he was enormous and terrifyingly demonic. But it was the confident way he moved that really got the razors slicing through my middle. He acted every bit as if he'd already defeated us. As if he knew something we didn't.

And I was horrified that he did.

"Madam Lares. We meet again. Have you prepared for my arrival?" He looked around my kitchen, nodding, *"It is small, but*

it will do. And there is plenty of land for me to build a finer home. I think perhaps a castle."

"You're not going to be here long enough to move in," I said, sounding more confident than I was.

"Ah. It appears you haven't been paying attention. I'm standing on your very doorstep. It is only a matter of hours before you and I meet face to face." He cocked his head like an ugly, oversized bird. "Is it possible you don't know?"

"I know you think you can use the kid to invade the human realm. I also know that I'm not going to let that happen." If only I was as confident of that outcome as I sounded.

"Ah. The girl. Yes. Pity she was sucked away from her family like that, isn't it. I can assure you they miss her horribly." His laugh was darkly smug. "Their grief may prove quite fatal."

I ground my teeth, wanting to strike out at him and end everybody's suffering at his hands. But it was only a vision and my sole weapon was my words.

"You are a pathetic creature," I said. "We beat your butt before and we'll beat you again. I don't think your followers will be so eager to give you their loyalty when we humiliate you a second time, do you?"

His eyes flashed with the colors of fire and his teeth vibrated on a feral growl. "I will rip you from stem to stern and feed on your entrails, puny guardian. Then I will flay the skin from your tattered body. As you scream in pain, I'll roast your council over a fire pit and invite all my friends to feed."

His words made the razors in my belly double down on their attack. I wondered that I was still upright as warm wetness flowed from my nostrils and my legs turned to lead beneath me. I briefly wondered if the demon could kill me from within a vision. And then realized he wouldn't even need to. My own body was going to be the end of me.

"Good luck with that," I managed to wrench out. "I don't think it's going to be as easy as you think."

"Ah, but you are wrong, Madam Lares. I will follow your very footsteps into the human realm and defeat you before you even know I am there". He reached toward me, swiping a claw beneath my nose and eyeing it with interest. "I shall enjoy feasting on you. Until we meet again," he growled. And then he was gone.

I blinked, coming back to the present and the twisting agony in my belly. Mavis was standing over me, her hands outstretched and pale green energy spitting from her palms. I groaned and she looked down at me, the magic disappearing and her expression going from rage to worry in the blink of an eye. "Honey! Are you all right?"

I shoved off the floor, using Mavis's arm and the table to get to my feet. The world twisted and went sideways and nausea bloomed as vertigo swirled in my brain. I dropped into the nearest chair, taking deep breaths and releasing them slowly. "Well," I said. "That was fun."

"Here," Bev said, a stack of tissues appearing in front of me. When I looked up she pointed to her nose. "You're bleeding."

I pressed the wad of tissues to my face and rested my head back on the chair.

"How long have you been communing with the Commander?" Layla barked out.

I twitched in surprise. I'd forgotten she was there. I still felt woozy and nauseous, and didn't feel like defending myself to the irritable princess. "I don't 'commune' with him. It's more like he gets all up in *my* grill. Besides, this isn't the first time he's forced himself on me. You do remember me hitting the ground at your compound, right?"

"Yeah," Bev said, nodding. "But this *is* the first time you produced him in nearly solid physical form, whole and audible, for the rest of us to experience."

I blinked. "I... Really?"

Mavis nodded. "He was standing right there in the doorway to the hall, looking all hostile and demony."

I wrapped an arm around my middle as a wave of pain slashed through it again. "It must be a side-effect of *Response*."

"What can I get you?" Bev asked, her warm hand finding my shoulder and gently squeezing.

"A glass of water?"

She patted my arm. "Coming right up."

"What are you going to do about the Commander?" Layla demanded.

I closed my eyes and tried to wish her away. Unfortunately, when I opened them again she was still there. I sighed. "*We* are going to find your sister," I responded with only a smidgeon of the irritation I was feeling. "She's the key to them getting through the barrier. She needs to be found and isolated so they can't use her."

Layla's anger didn't soften one bit as I reminded her the next step was really up to her. My people were helping with the search, the kid was her sister—her responsibility—and she presumably knew Desmean better than any of my people. "Where could she be?"

Layla stood and began to pace. "I have no idea. If my parents had time to instruct her before she was taken, she would be looking for me."

"How good are her tracking skills?" Mavis asked.

Bev set a glass of water in front of me and I took a tentative sip, waiting to see how well it sat on my stomach before drinking more.

Layla frowned. "I haven't seen her since she was a baby.

I'm ashamed to say I don't know her at all." Tears glistened in Layla's eyes and she blinked rapidly to clear them. "But members of devil royalty are generally very good at tracking. We have elevated senses of smell and hearing. She might have scented me on you. If she did, she'd be scoping out this place. Hiding nearby."

"That's good, right?" I asked. "I can call Luke back to track her..."

Layla shook her head. "She'll run if you set the wolf on her."

"Right," I said, mentally having a face-palm moment.

"If she saw you come in, she might show up here?" Bev suggested.

But Layla shook her head, anger suffusing her cheeks with color. She spread her arms. "Do you think she'll recognize me like this?"

She was right. Layla's devilish form was gone. She looked just like any human. "Then we'll need to post your guards around this property. Will she approach them?"

"I don't know but it's the only thing we can do. I'll choose those of my guards who are best at scenting. Maybe we'll get lucky."

"Good." On an impulse, I stood and wrapped Layla in a quick hug. "We're going to find her, Layla. We have time." I had no idea if I was right about that, but it felt like the right thing to say.

She nodded, not looking at all convinced. "I'll arrange for the guards. Please inform your council not to attack them."

As soon as Layla was outside and beyond the patio where I knew she wouldn't hear me, I said, "We can't wait for Layla to find her sister. We need to lock down the graveyard now."

Both Mavis and Bev frowned. "The graveyard? Why?" Bev asked.

"Because of what the Commander said. He's going to follow my footsteps into the human realm."

They thought about that for a beat and then two sets of eyes widened. "He's going to use the portal," Mavis said. "But how? It's not like a doorway that can be opened and closed multiple times. The magic that opened it is gone. We made sure of that as soon as you were back."

I shook my head. "I don't know how. But we can't afford to ignore that tidbit. Either he's very smug about his chances, or he misspoke. Either way, I believe that's where he's going to attempt the breach. And we need to be ready for him in case he manages to do it."

A high-pitched, off-key voice entered the hallway. We all turned to see Wanda, ear buds in place. Her face was screwed up and she was dancing toward us, oblivious. She was looking down at an ancient tome as she approached, singing along with the song she was playing way too loudly. I had to give her credit. The kid could really multi-task.

Wanda jolted to a stop when she saw me, bloody tissues still clutched in my hand. She removed an ear bud sending the distant strains of rock music into the otherwise quiet kitchen. "What happened? Why are you bleeding?"

Bev, Mavis and I shared a look and burst out laughing. We weren't really laughing about the vision. Conjuring up the Commander in my kitchen definitely wasn't funny. But what can I say? We'd had a heck of a twenty-four hours. "Nothing." I pointed to my nose. "It's just a nose bleed. Nothing serious. Did you find anything new?"

"Huh? Oh. Yeah. I found another mention of the gemstone. Most of it was the same info as the other books had. But there was a small section...just a couple of paragraphs, that mentioned breaches without the icon." Her expression grew intense. "Aggy, it says the object I mentioned before...the one that breaches through a special circumstance and allows entrance?"

I nodded.

"The breach is going to happen in the same spot where that object passed from one dimension to another."

"But how are we going to find out where that is?" Bev asked, looking as frustrated as I felt. "We can't find the kid and we'd need to ask her where she came through."

I sighed. "I guess it could still be the graveyard. But it seems like we would have noticed if she'd popped out there."

"Yeah, and if she had, how did she end up at the bar? I don't know how or why she would have gone there when this place probably reeks of lost ones," Mavis said.

We sat in silent thought for a few minutes. Finally, I said. "I'll see if anybody has a lead on the kid's whereabouts. If I come up blank, I guess we're going back to that bar."

Bev grimaced. "Yeeha."

24

A DEMON'S THREATS STRIKE THE CHILD MOST DEAR

I n the end, we decided the hospital made better sense. If a crossing happened in the bar, somebody had to have seen something. After a quick call to Chief Marshal, we'd learned that the owner, who'd been one of the injured, was the obvious person to ask.

I brought Mavis with me into the man's hospital room in case he proved recalcitrant. Mavis was both easy on the eyes and soothing to the soul. She was also around his same age, so he related to her more easily than he would to me. I'm not above using what I've got to get information in an emergency.

Or, in this case, what Mavis has.

Our man's name was Clay Oxford. It turned out he was the owner of Clay's Place Bar, as well as the second bartender we'd tended.

In addition to running the bar, Clay rebuilt antique cars, liked small dogs, favored wine over beer, and enjoyed long walks on the beach and lazy Sundays in bed.

We'd learned many things about Clay. Too many things. In the end, I decided it might have been a mistake to bring my mom. The two of them hit it off like they were lifelong buds. I was pretty sure Chief Davis would *not* appreciate how well they got along.

Finally, I gave Mavis a discrete signal to cut the small talk so we could ask about the important stuff. For some reason, she rolled her eyes at my finger across the throat and tongue out of the side of my mouth signal. I'd thought I was being subtle.

"So, Clay," I said by way of smoothly segueing from the topic of favorite bodywash scents to rampaging demons (In case you're wondering, Clay stated a preference for vanilla lavender but he'd be willing to consider switching to Mavis's rose-scented brand. Clay was a man who was very secure in his masculinity. And, apparently, he smelled good too.) "Did you see anything unusual in the bar before the fight broke out?"

Clay, it turned out, wasn't human, so he knew about demons. He had some kind of shifter genes, but I wasn't rude enough to ask what kind. However, after the body wash conversation, I was dying to know.

"Unusual how?" he asked unhelpfully.

"Oh, I don't know. Like, a flash of light or a giant split in the air that vomited demons?"

Clay stared at me for a long beat and then laughed heartily. Apparently he thought I was high-larious.

When I didn't laugh too, he looked at Mavis. She patted his hand. "We're worried about a breach. Anything you can tell us about those demons would be a great help."

"Oh. Well, I can't tell you much. They just walked through the door like the rest of my customers. They were glamoured to look human. I'm not sure when they dropped the glamour. It probably happened when that guy with the long, shaggy gray beard went after the skinny, dark-haired guy with a pool cue. Things went pear-shaped shortly after that." He frowned as he spoke about it. "I sure hope my insurance will cover the damage."

Mavis patted his hand. "They certainly should. If they don't, you just let me know and I'll wiggle my fingers at the person in charge." She winked and Clay laughed.

"When did the kid get there?" I asked Clay, wanting to give my mom a stern glance for promising to use her witchy ways on the insurance company.

"Kid?" Clay asked. "What kid?"

"The one with hooves," I said. I started to tell him who she was and decided against it. There was no good that could come from anyone in the human realm knowing a royal devil child was around and unprotected. "Did she come in with the demons?"

Clay's frown seemed to show genuine confusion. "I never saw no kid. Kids aren't allowed in the bar. Chief Davis would have my license if he knew there was a kid there."

"Are you sure?" I asked. My questions were cut off as my phone rang. I looked at the ID and saw it was the teen. Giving Mavis a lift of my brows to indicate I wanted her to keep trying with Clay, I walked out to the hallway, out of Clay's earshot. "Hey," I said when I answered. "What's up?"

"Aggy!" The tone of her voice was a warning.

"What's wrong? Please tell me the Commander's not already here."

There was a beat of silence that had me motioning to Mavis. I started toward the elevator, my heart pounding like a bass drum. "Wanda? Honey, talk to me."

"It's not the Commander," she finally said. I relaxed fractionally. The kid still sounded upset. "It's my dad. He says I have to go with him."

I TOOK the final turn onto my road on two wheels. The church rose above us on a verdant, heavily-treed hill, the sun a golden paintbrush gilding the stark white walls and softening their harsh lines.

In the distance, a thick wall of clouds looked even more onerous as a backdrop to the brightness of the sun. As I threw on the brakes, sending a spray of gravel into the air behind us, I couldn't help seeing the threatening wall of clouds as a portent of things to come.

Mavis was already unbuckling her seatbelt as I ground to a gravel-strewn stop in my small lot, my ancient Range Rover crooked and panting as we leaped from its seats.

The grounds were empty as we ran toward the front door. The air around the church smelled sweetly of flowers from the lush beds Niele had created around the heavy front door. I barely noticed the flowers, but the distant call of a raven made all the hair rise on my body and gooseflesh pebble my arms.

I slammed the door open and dove through it, already screaming Wanda's name. Mavis followed on my heels, her hands weaving a spell in case Bathos was there. I had no idea what the spell would do, but if it would keep my kid there, I was willing to invite every witch I knew to the church to join her.

"Wanda?" I peeked into her room and mine on my way to the kitchen and jolted to a stop in the sunny room that was the heart of my home. No. That wasn't quite right. My family and friends were the heart. Wanda was the heart. The kitchen was only a room we all loved to gather in.

I threw out a hand to stop from falling into a puddle on the floor. My palm fell on the cookie crumb-laden tabletop and I thought of the kid hiding the sweets so I wouldn't eat them all. In that moment, I realized I was nothing more than a woman-shaped Monty. All stomach, hair, and attitude.

I sobbed as I realized she was gone. "I'll kill him," I growled out as I held onto the table to keep from punching something. "I'll tear him into tiny little demon pieces and laugh while I'm doing it."

A soft whine sifted toward me from the mudroom and my pulse shot into the danger zone. I pushed off the table and ran, taking the two short steps down into the long, narrow space where I hung my coat, left my wet and muddy boots, and stored extra food and supplies for the house.

I stumbled on the last step and fell, landing hard on my knees as I saw him.

Monty. His long nose pressed to the door. His body motionless as he cried softly for his favorite teen.

Tears slid copiously from my eyes and I crawled to him, pulling him into my lap and burying my face in his soft, fragrant fur. "We'll get her back, buddy," I promised my little dog. "We'll bring her home."

"Aggy, honey. I think you need to see this."

I kissed Monty between his sad, brown eyes and shoved to my feet, my legs feeling like lead as I climbed the two steps.

I jerked to a stop, blinking rapidly at the sight before me. In the center of the room, their transparent bodies intersected by a chair and part of the table, Wanda and Bathos squared off in obvious disagreement.

The guardian isn't your mother, the demon said, his lips curved in an angry smile. *She isn't your family. I am.*

Wanda's pretty face folded into sadness. *Aggy loves me. And I love her.*

A sob clung to the back of my tongue and I pressed my lips tightly closed, trying to hold it back.

Bathos slammed a hand down, the sound of flesh hitting wood was weirdly incongruent since they were standing a foot or two away from the table. *You're an obligation to her. Nothing more. You don't think she'd be thrilled to have you out of here? She and her boyfriend could have the house to themselves. If you truly care about her, why wouldn't you want her to be happy?*

I growled low in my throat, magic surging from my core at his words. He was shamelessly manipulating her. And my heart broke when I saw her face. It was working. She was starting to believe she was a burden to me.

"I'll kill him!" I screamed, frightening even myself with the vehemence of my vow. Down by my feet, Monty growled, his lips curling in a snarl as he eyed the magical memory Mavis had created in the room.

Wanda wrapped her arms around herself and nodded and my heart shattered into a million pieces. Okay. I'll go with you. But I need to call her. I can't just leave without telling Aggy where I'm going.

The demon clearly didn't like that idea, but he nodded. "Quickly." His gaze slid in my direction. My heart skipped a beat. For a minute, I thought he was looking at me. That should be impossible given that he was simply a memory Mavis had conjured from the magic residue he and Wanda had left behind. But then I realized he wasn't looking at me. He was looking into the back yard. Into the trees lining the side yard. Why would he be looking there? Had he brought someone with him? Someone who'd ensure Wanda had to come with him?

Another raven call filtered through the background and I ignored it, too engrossed in watching Wanda's plight playing out in front of me to investigate. I watched the kid pull out her cell and hit a button. I couldn't hear my own voice answering, but I heard it in my memories.

"Aggy?" Silence followed as she listened to me, her worried gaze sliding to Bathos.

"It's not the Commander," she said after a few beats. I remembered relaxing at the assurance, happy in my temporary ignorance.

It didn't last long.

"It's my dad. He says I have to go with him."

Bathos dove for the phone, snatching it from her fingers as she turned and started to run. Mavis and I followed them down the hallway and watched the teen dive into her room and slam the door closed on her father, the deadlock I'd insisted on sliding into place.

Wanda had called me paranoid at the time. I'd been embarrassed because she'd been right. But our lives were filled with dangerous people, monsters, and things that go bump in the night.

Watching the demon kick and pound the door to no avail, I said a prayer of thanks that I'd been paranoid.

As Bathos pounded on the door, screaming her name, I ducked through his vaporous image, the magic biting at my skin as I stepped inside her room. The picture I saw there would stick with me for the rest of my life. Tears fell in sheets down my face.

In the memory, Monty was sitting on the bed, his gaze sliding nervously toward the door and the angry demon who was trying to break down the door to get to his daughter. He was screaming something about not having any time.

Wanda was ignoring him. She bent down and kissed Monty on the nose. "I love you, buddy." She told my dog.

Behind me, Mavis sobbed softly.

I chewed my lips to keep from screaming.

"I'll see you again someday, I promise. In the meantime, you need to hide." She covered the little dog with a blanket and patted a book sitting on the bed beside him with her hand. *"Tell Aggy to read this and she'll understand."* Then she lifted her gaze toward the door, the telltale glow of magic showing beneath it. Bathos was going to break in soon. Wanda's gaze swung to look directly into mine. *"One of the most useful things Caleigh has taught me is that history always repeats itself,"* she said. *"Nothing we see, or feel, or do is new. Millions of people have done the same, felt the same, seen the same before us. That's very important, Aggy. Don't follow me. I'll be back as soon as I can."* She yanked the window open, kicked the screen out, and scrambled through, stopping only long enough to stare back at us, though we hadn't even been there when she'd lived that moment. *"I love you guys."*

And then she was gone.

"No!" I screamed. Even knowing it was useless, I ran to the window and placed my hands on the windowsill. The window was still open and the painted wood was dappling with raindrops as the rain began to fall. I stared out into the darkening day, my vision clouded behind the rain and my tears.

An arm slid around my waist and Mavis rested her head against my shoulder. I gasped under a barrage of deep sadness. "She's gone."

Mavis cried softly, tightening her arm around me. "I know, honey. I'm so sorry."

"We have to find her," I said.

Mavis just nodded, continuing to cry.

There were a hundred things I needed to do. Thousands of people depending on my next move. I had responsibilities to be handled and information I needed to get. A literal world I had to save.

But all I could do in that moment was stand there, staring out at the rain and crying.

My heart was broken. And I didn't think I could move.

I don't know how long I would have stood there if my grief hadn't been interrupted by the sound of a clearing throat behind us. I turned tear-filled eyes toward the intruder and nearly swallowed my tongue.

The demon Bathos stood there, his evil spawn of Hell self stiffly held and his coldly handsome face tight with emotion. He didn't say a word. He only stood there, his hands folded in front of him and his expression unreadable. As if he knew I needed to tear him into bits and was making it easy for me.

I was happy to comply. With a roar of rage, I flew across the room and launched myself at him.

25

THE LOSS OF HEART, THE LARES' FEAR

We went down in a tangle of limbs, me shrieking like a banshee and him simply covering his tender bits as I clawed, punched, kicked and screamed into his hated face.

Even when Monty joined the fray, nipping and growling and lunging at Bathos, the demon didn't fight back.

A few minutes later, my rage spent, I sat back, panting. "Defend yourself," I yelled.

He stared at me through angry black eyes, one of them swelling and purpling from my fists. "There is no defense for what I've done."

I blinked my surprise. "This is some kind of trick, isn't it?"

He shook his head, his silky black hair fanning out on the hardwood floor. "I have done a lot of terrible things in my long life, Madam Lares. But I count this as among the worst. I have run my daughter off just when she needed my protection the most. I am shamed and have come to you to plead your help."

I pushed to my feet, scooping Monty up before he could

bite the demon someplace where his instincts would force him to retaliate. "Get out of my house. Don't ever contact me again. You have put yourself outside the circle of my protection and you are forever dead to me."

He casually stood—annoyingly much more gracefully than I had. Brushing imaginary dirt off his behind, the demon fixed me with a look that was tailor-made to throw me off my game. Cold, calculating, or evil Bathos I understood. Kind, regretful, pleading Bathos made my skin itch. "I understand your anger. In your position I would feel the same. I only wish to say one thing. Will you listen?"

Narrowing my eyes at him, I reluctantly nodded. "Say your piece and go."

He sighed. "I don't expect you to believe me, but I was trying to protect the girl from what is coming."

"And what, exactly is that?" Mavis asked.

He slid his black gaze her way. "Surely you understand that you are standing on the precipice of another battle in the war with the demons?"

"We do," Mavis said. "Surely you haven't forgotten that we've battled them before, with Wanda's help, and you didn't run to protect your daughter then. Why now?"

He clasped his hands, the knuckles white as if he were trying not to punch something. "I was protecting her in my own way. Behind the scenes. Keeping watch from afar. But that is not the point." He stepped closer, his black eyes narrowed with intensity. "There is more happening here than you understand, Lares. Much more. And I fear some of it directly affects my daughter."

Fresh anger stung my cheeks and made my stomach roil. "Stop talking in riddles and tell me what I need to protect her from."

"Her mother."

Silence throbbed between us, severed only by Monty's restless whining. I set him down and he trotted back to Wanda's bed, climbing the stairs and curling up on her pillow with a mournful sigh. My heart broke a little bit at the sound, but I kept my focus on Bathos. "Explain."

"It isn't just the Commander who comes to battle. He has long kept a slave at his side. A woman who has the knowledge he needs to gain access to certain magical artifacts and form the means to cross forbidden barriers. She is a powerful witch. She is also a historian whose soothsaying prowess is overshadowed only by the crone's. In fact, the two women have long been stark adversaries. Rumor has it that the crone was the one who sold this historian to the Commander in the first place."

"Why would the crone do that?" I asked. "Simply from jealousy?"

Bathos shrugged. "Jealousy was definitely part of it. But there was something the crone wanted even more than getting rid of a rival. Something far more personal."

"What?" I asked, losing patience with his riddles. "Net this out, Bathos. As you know, we have a battle to prepare for."

"Have you not already figured it out?" he asked, his voice taut with irritation. "The crone has lived a long, lonely life. Millennia with only her dogs and her work…"

Mavis held up a hand. "Wait. Are you saying that Laverne and Shirley are a thousand years old?"

He frowned. "More than that, I should say. Several thousand."

Mavis and I shared a look. "They had dachshunds several thousand years ago?"

"How would I know. Will you pay attention?" Bathos barked.

I held up my hands, secretly wondering if Caleigh could make Monty live as long as I did. That was definitely something worth considering.

"...intern."

I blinked, realizing I'd missed what he'd said. "Sorry. What about an intern?"

His lips formed a tight line. "I said...the crone had been seeking an intern for centuries. She was very picky about the candidate. In fact, as much as I admire my daughter's skills, I was shocked when the crone took her on."

"What does this have to do with Wanda being in danger? If anything, I'd think the crone's interest would be another layer of protection for the kid."

"It would be," he agreed. "If it weren't for the fact that Caleigh doesn't like competition and will do almost anything to remove it."

My head was spinning. "So, what you're saying is that the crone will harm Wanda because she fears competition? That's ridiculous. Why train her in the first place if she doesn't want the girl to be a good historian. They're like peas in a pod. I can't believe..."

"It is not Wanda she will harm," he interrupted.

He let that hang there for a beat and then went on. "I am concerned the girl with throw herself in the middle of the coming battle and be killed by accident."

"Curse, curse, swear!" I muttered on a growl. "You're breaking my brain, demon. Just tell me what the danger is."

"Willow will be coming with the Commander."

I blinked at him for a few beats, my weary mind trying to attach a person to the name. When it hit me, I gulped. "Wanda's mother is coming back?"

He nodded. "And she will attempt to take Wanda from the crone. If she succeeds, the crone will level the world. If she doesn't succeed, Willow will lay waste to the realms. And, either way, I am nearly certain that Wanda will try to fling herself between the two women to protect them both."

"Which will guarantee she'll get herself killed," I finished for him.

Goddess in a gondola. I hadn't thought things could get any worse.

THUNDER BOOMED overhead and I jumped. With everything I had on my mind, my nerves were shot. The back door slammed open, the wind catching it and yanking it out of the hand of the water-logged princess who entered, herding a smaller form covered in a raincoat that puddled around her small feet.

I jolted to my feet. "You found her?"

Mavis whipped around hopefully, probably thinking I'd meant Wanda. Her face fell, but she forced a smile at Layla. "Princess. It's a terrible time to be out and about."

Layla pulled off her yellow rainslicker and reached to take the slicker off the small royal next to her. Desmean blinked up at us with terrified red-gold eyes, her arms wrapping protectively around herself.

"She found *me*, actually. The guards discovered her waiting by the magical border, unable to cross without their assistance."

Relief slid through me at the sight of the royal child. "I'm so glad. But you should have left her at your compound where..." I cut myself off before I said the Commander's name. Desmean might not understand our language, but names are names in any tongue. "...someone bad can't find her."

Layla shook her head. "I know. But I needed you to have this." She pulled an object wrapped in cloth out of her pocket and handed it to me. "Our parents sent my sister here when I summoned them." She frowned. "They are refusing to come, but they worried for Desmean because she is young and can't protect herself."

"You mean someone did come when you did your blood ceremony?"

Layla nodded, her cheeks flushing. "I not only didn't manage to get them all, poor Desmean ended up in the wrong place." She frowned. "And I may have been responsible for those other demons at the bar." She looked so miserable at the admission that I didn't have the heart to yell at her. Besides, after raging at Bathos, I was beyond my quota for beating people up for mistakes at the moment. I fixed her with a stern look. "You and I will discuss that later. When little ears aren't around."

Her lips pressed into a firm line but she nodded.

I unwrapped the cloth and gasped. A gem the size of my fist glittered under the overhead light of my kitchen. I showed it to Mavis.

"How did the child get that?" Mavis asked. She was making hot chocolate and filling a tray with cookies for the littlest princess.

"Mother gave it to her. She knew the Commander was searching for it and wished to get it out of the demonic realm. Her request was that it be given to you. Desmean insisted on coming with me to be sure you received it."

I smiled at the small princess and she looked away with embarrassment.

Mavis walked to her and bent close. "Desmean, would you like hot chocolate and cookies?"

Layla repeated the question in their strange, guttural language and Desmean nodded.

When the child was happily munching her snack, Layla, Mavis, and I moved further away so she wouldn't hear what we were talking about.

"Bathos was here earlier," I told Layla. "He said the Commander is coming very soon. And he'll have a magical historian with him. A witch nearly as powerful as the crone."

Layla's shock mirrored ours from earlier when I told her about my teen and who was coming. "Do you wish my people to search for Wanda?"

I was oh so tempted to take her up on the suggestion. But I trusted Wanda to take care of herself for the time being and we needed to focus on keeping the Commander out of the human realm. "Thank you. That will have to wait, I'm afraid. Since you no longer need my people to search for Desmean, I'll send them to the bar to wait for the crossing. In the meantime, you should take your sister to the compound and keep her there so they can't use her to open the barrier."

Layla nodded. "I'll send you my best fighters. Thank you for helping me find her. It is wonderful having her here with me and I intend to keep her safe no matter what happens."

I silently wished her well. I couldn't count the number of times I'd had the exact same thought about Wanda. And in the end, I'd been unable to keep her safe at all.

"I'd appreciate the fighters. If Wanda turns up at your compound, can I ask that you keep her safe for me?"

"Of course. It would be my honor."

Layla gave me a hug that was long enough to let me know how much she appreciated our help with her sister and then bustled her reluctant sibling back into her slicker.

Mavis filled a bag with cookies and the small royal left the church with a wide smile on her face.

Gren arrived only moments after they left, looking wet to the skin and as tired as I'd ever seen him.

Mavis took one look at my angel and said, "I'm making coffee."

"Thanks, Mavis," Gren said, then wrapped me in a very moist hug.

I ignored the water soaking through my clothes and held on tight, fresh tears sliding from my eyes. His response was to hold me tighter. "We'll find her. In the meantime, Wanda is very smart and well capable of taking care of herself."

"I know. I was just thinking the same thing. But it won't stop me from worrying about her."

As he drank his coffee and ate a sandwich Mavis forced on him, I showed Gren the gem and told him what Bathos had told us about Wanda's mom. He looked appropriately grim. "That's not ideal. But we'll figure out how to deal with the problem once we get the demons buttoned up. In the meantime, we need to hide that," he nodded toward the gem sitting on the table between us," somewhere safe.

"Do you have any suggestions?"

He thought about it for a beat and then smiled. "I do, actually." He held out his hand. "Do you trust me?"

With my life. I nodded, dropping the gem into his hand.

"Caw!" My gaze whipped to the window where Ray perched, pecking insistently on the glass. "Caw!"

I started to stand but mom waved me off. "I'll get him." Mumbling something about pushy birds, Mavis hurried over to open the door for him. The big black bird flew inside, landed on the rug in the mud room, and proceeded to expel as much water from his feathers as he could.

Mavis squealed as she got caught in the crossfire and

grabbed a towel to dry off her legs. "Birds are supposed to deal with that kind of thing outside," she groused. "You're turning into quite the weeny."

Ray lifted his wings and flew over the steps into the kitchen. "Rude!"

I suddenly remembered the cawing from before. Had it been him? "What's up Ray?"

Without warning, my vision went wonky and I was looking into the cloud-drenched distance in a gray, pouring rain. A small, stooped figure huddled low over the neck of her mount, a galloping white mare. Speeding along behind them was the familiar bulky form of the Iggloc.

As quickly as it had changed, my vision returned to normal and I staggered from the usual bout of vertigo. "I hate it when you do that," I told the raven, who'd flown up onto the table and was pecking at the crumbs Desmean had left behind. At my scolding, he danced sideways, ruffled his feathers from top to bottom, and then stubbornly returned to his crumb feast. The little girl had left so many crumbs on my table I wondered if any of the cookies had gone into her mouth.

"Did he show you something?" Gren asked.

"Yeah. The crone riding the White Mare, and they brought the Iggloc."

"Has he been able to do that before?" Mavis asked, frowning at the bird. She motioned to Gren's mug and held out her hand.

"Not a memory, no. He's only hijacked my sight to show me what he was seeing. I'm guessing this new trick is a side effect of engaging *Response*."

"Handy," Gren said, giving Mavis his empty cup so she could refill it.

I nodded, my mind haring off in ten directions at once.

Thunder boomed again, followed by a bolt of lightning that lit up the yard.

It was a really bad night to be riding through the night. But I was sure the crone had good reason to do it.

And I wasn't looking forward to the showdown that was about to come.

26

A BATTLE COMES, A KILLING GROUND

T he door to the belfry opened and Gren stepped down into the kitchen, brushing rain out of his dark hair as he closed the door.

I looked at him, widening my gaze in question.

He just smiled.

She comes.

My head jerked up at the sound of Batty's voice in my head.

"What is it?" Gren asked, disconnecting his call with Ferral.

"The crone's here."

Gren nodded. "What do you want me to do?"

"Stay by my side in case she attacks?"

Gren reached out and clasped my hand. "She cares for the girl. If she's angry, it is because she is frightened."

"I know. But that won't keep us safe until she cools down."

"Agreed."

"Do you really think she'll attack?" Mavis asked, her expression shocked.

That she could be surprised at the idea that the crone was unstable and dangerous told me we'd spent entirely too much time in the viper pit. We'd gotten acclimated to the poison surrounding us and had forgotten how deadly it was.

That was about to come back to bite us. No pun intended.

The mudroom door flew open and the crone stormed through. There was no sign of the frailness she sometimes exhibited. The rounded back, the stiff gait. The woman who flew into my kitchen fairly bristled with magical energy, and she flung it at us without even giving me a chance to explain.

Hot, silvery magic shot from her gnarled hands like a tornado, spinning its way through my kitchen and ripping up everything in its path. Three potted herb plants were sucked from the windowsill and pulled into the tornado, the violent energy flinging dirt and tiny pieces of ceramic pot around the room.

The curtains were yanked from their rod and ripped into pieces.

The rod shot toward Gren, looking as if it would impale him, but the deadly projectile was wrenched to a stop by a lasso of pale green magic. My gaze flew to Mavis in time to see her yank her hand back and catch the errant rod, flinging it away.

Dishes flew off the table and spun away, smashing against the walls.

I took a plate in the temple and nearly went down under the resulting wave of wooziness. Gren caught me before I fell and wrapped a protective wing around me.

A sconce was ripped off the wall and shattered against the floor. The wires that had been anchoring it danced and sizzled with live electricity, spitting like angry snakes beneath her power.

Mavis's fingers worked fast and furious in the air, creating a spell that the crone's magical tornado nipped and chewed on even as she created it.

Monty ran into the room barking and the crone fixed her enraged gaze on him, lifting her hands as if to attack.

That was the end of my patience. Yanking my own power forward, I shoved Gren's protective wing aside and straightened to my full five feet six inches. "Stop!"

The single word roared from my lips, smacked into the walls and reverberated inward, sending power vibrations over the entire room.

The energy tornado died. Everything that had been trapped in its rotation crashed to the floor in a chaos of sound, and the energy started to disperse.

The crone still stood in the doorway, her expression murderous and her gnarly fingers still curved like claws in front of her. "Where is the child?"

I had to bite down on the desire to send her after Bathos. He was the one to blame for Wanda's running away. And he certainly deserved to be pummeled about his rock-like skull and shoulders with the crone's rage-magic. But siccing her on the demon didn't fit my long-range goals. I needed the crone's respect and help to find my teen. And, as much as I hated to admit it, I might need Bathos's help too. "She ran away."

I swallowed hard at the look on the crone's face. Not her rage. I could handle that. But the fear and helplessness that played across her features...just for a beat...was almost my undoing. Because I knew how she felt. I was feeling it too. "I believe it has something to do with her mother," I risked telling her. "She didn't tell me what she was planning. I just found out a little while ago."

"How did you find out?" the crone growled.

"I crafted a replay spell," Mavis said, drawing the ancient witch's full attention. "We saw her leave."

Neither of us told her about the book Wanda had left for us. I hadn't had the heart to look at it yet. Whatever was in those pages, it wouldn't bring Wanda back. And, until I dealt with the demon incursion, I couldn't plan a rescue for my kid anyway. Gren was right. Wanda was smart and capable. Before coming to me, she'd survived on her own for years because she'd been caught in a Groundhog Day spell, reliving the same day over and over again. But she'd been lonely. I had to assume she'd also been scared. I didn't want that for her again. I refused to let her live that way. But I'd need the crone's help to avoid it. "As soon as we stop the demons from coming through. I'm going to need your help to get her back," I told the crone. "We need each other, Caleigh. Let's not fight."

The old woman's face turned sour when I used her name. Her body stiffened. For a beat, I thought she'd retaliate. But she didn't. With a visible force of will, she forced herself to soften and nodded. "Let's get this done, then. So we can go after the girl."

I nodded. "Shall we get the horse and the Iggloc settled in the shed out back? I have hay and feed in there for them." I'd had an oversized shed built at the back of the property when the White Mare became a regular fixture in our lives. I kept it clean, stocked, and ready at all times because I didn't always know when the horse was going to show up.

The crone nodded. "We'll get them out of the weather. But no food. They'll need to be ready to fight if necessary."

"Let's go then."

"I'll come with you," Gren said, giving me a meaningful glance.

I nodded. "Thanks." Looking at Mavis, I said. "Can you check on the team at the bar? As soon as we're done settling the animals, we'll be joining them there."

"Of course." She grabbed my arm as the crone ducked out into the rain again. "Are you sure you don't need me out there too?"

"Mostly sure." We shared a smile. "I don't think she'll blow up again. She just needed to blow off some steam."

Mavis nodded. "Be careful anyway. You know how volatile she is."

"I certainly do." I grabbed a rain slicker off a hook in the mud room and headed outside. Caleigh had the mare's reins in hand and was leading her toward the shed. I looked around for the Iggloc. "Where is it?" I called to the crone.

She stopped, turned back, and shrugged. "It's around."

"Uh, Aggy," Gren said.

I turned and saw him staring toward the side yard. "What?"

He didn't speak, so I followed his line of sight. What I saw made all the blood in my body turn to ice. "Curse!" I screamed. In the next moment, all three of us jumped into action. Gren launched into the air, wings a bass throb beneath the thunderous rain. The crone yelled, "Haya!" and performed a running leap onto the White Mare's back. I started to run, calling my staff to me as I screamed. "Mom!" I put power into my call. Lots of it, so she could hear me over the pounding rain.

Mavis opened the door. "What's wrong?" I could barely hear her with the heavy drone of rain slamming down on us. "Call the team. It wasn't the kid. It was the Iggloc. The demons are here!"

Mavis's gaze slid toward the side yard, where the Iglocc stood facing a giant split in the air, its coat glowing with a silver illumination that painted the graveyard behind it in a surreal light.

As we watched, the slit spread wide, showing the charcoal perspective of the spectral realm behind a veritable army of demonic creatures pressing through the breach.

Thousands of them.

And most of my team was fifteen minutes away at best.

We were toast.

Gren landed at a run, his blades already slicing the air as his feet touched down. He danced lightly over the ground with the two, sword-like knives he favored, their blades so sharp the demons who lost their heads in the first five seconds probably died before they felt the sting.

The crone rode the horse with her hands in the air, the clawed fingers spraying copious amounts of magic that painted the battlefield in exploding demon parts and black blood.

I pulled energy from my core, channeling it into the glowing orb at the end of my staff, and then used it like a flamethrower to spray the lines of invading demons before they even got through the slit.

Still, we couldn't keep them back. They came on, using the bodies of their fallen as shields to avoid our attack. As the demons breached the realm, they spread out and took refuge in the trees that formed a thick, living boundary along the side of my property.

At some point, I became aware of Mavis joining us. She crafted a huge, magical net and dumped it over the rampaging demons. Then we sprayed the netted monsters with killing power before they could get free.

As soon as she dropped a net, Mavis would start

another one and we'd do it all again. But then the monsters got smart. They shoved the biggest demons to the front, including helpless creatures like the Iggloc to force the net to stretch higher, and many escaped from the sides and back as the bigger creatures struggled with the net.

We fought our humanity as much as we battled the demons. It wasn't in us to kill the helpless beasts they shoved to the front. And that reluctance cost us time as well as safe space.

Suddenly, the battle was inches away instead of yards. Three demons launched themselves at me, fighting with brawn and speed instead of skill.

Using claws and teeth, they needed to get in close to their prey, and I needed space for the maximum effectiveness of my weapons.

But I lost that space. So, I adjusted. As a scaly black creature with orange eyes and six horns placed around the top of his skull like a crown threw itself at me, I jabbed it hard in the gut with my orb and sent a slicing dose of magic through his body. Fire erupted in the demon as my magic hit, and he fell screaming to his knees as it consumed him from the inside out.

I had no time to prepare for the next monster. A pale-skinned demon, standing only hip high but outfitted with bladed claws for hands came up behind me when I was busy setting the ones in front of me on fire. The monster made a weird ticking noise as it slashed at the back of my legs with its claws. I spun to attack it, only to be hit with the force of a runaway train by a larger demon barreling into me.

I hit the ground on my back and tried to rise, but the monster stomped a massive foot on my middle and the world went charcoal around the edges as my breath was stomped out of me and bones cracked beneath the assault.

I barely managed to get my staff up between us as the monster threw itself over me, teeth snapping inches from my throat. All I could do was get the staff and my arms between his teeth and my flesh and pray.

"Aggy!" Gren screamed my name and started toward me, but was overwhelmed from behind by what looked like a dozen monsters. He went down under a wave of snapping, slashing demons.

"Gren..." Tears slipped down my cheeks and I fought my body's need to pass out, the lack of air and stabbing pain in my ribs quickly taking their toll.

A shrill scream ripped my attention to Mavis. She was standing on a gravestone, her fingers painting the air with a complex spell, and one of the monsters had hold of her ankle. As I watched in horror, the beast ripped her foot off the rock and she fell backward, smacking her head and shoulders hard on the stone. She went limp, the spell falling away like spilled sugar as she was pulled like a sack of flour to a circle of slavering beasts.

"Mom!!!!" I tried to push the beast off me but couldn't move it. In rage and fear, I poured energy into my staff, infusing it with as much magic as I could yank forward, and slammed it into the demon's thick, scaly body. The creature reared back, roaring in pain and stumbled backward. I drew on my remaining power and used it to leap off the ground and stab the orb downward, into the creature's chest.

The orb split the thing's flesh like butter and imploded it from the inside.

Clawed hands grabbed my legs and arms. Snapping teeth ripped at my clothing, tearing my flesh along with it.

I threw back my head and screamed, my last nerve

twanged. Power rolled away from me like a thick, golden fog, knocking demons and devils and ghouls and blood-drinkers and an assortment of monsters over like pins in a bowling alley.

Beside me, the earth burst upward and Niele, wearing his flower-covered vest of battle, flew skyward. He landed on a cluster of monsters and began tearing them apart with claws that could make confetti out of rock.

A long, mournful howl burst through the storm. A breath later, an enormous wolf shot past me, joining Niele in his demonic rip-fest.

I tried to see past the sea of demons to find Mavis.

I couldn't find her.

Ferral loped up in his moon-hound form and stopped next to me. He lifted his gaze and fixed me with a questioning silver regard.

"Mavis is down. I need to get to her." I took off running in the direction I'd last seen her. Ferral leaped in front of me and cleared a path as I jumped over beastly bodies and rammed my shoulder into anything that got in my way. Seeing her small, crumpled form in the blood-covered grass tore something apart inside me. "No, no, no, no!" I screamed. I dropped to my knees next to her, panic making it hard to breathe. "Mom," I pushed bloody strands of blonde hair off her too-pale face and felt her throat for a pulse. She was too still. Unmoving and barely breathing. "Wake up!" I pleaded, the world blurring behind my tears.

The shadows at the tree line split in a dozen spots and Layla ran out, her sword extended above her. The princess's voice rose in a warbling, high-pitched cry that sent her warriors into battle.

"Aggy!" I turned to find Bev running toward me. Behind her were two other witches from their coven. Bev dropped beside me. "Mom?" She took in the blood pooling beneath Mavis's head and her hands came up, hanging in the air above Mavis without touching her. "Aggy, she's bleeding badly."

"I know," I said, snuffling loudly. "I can't heal her. We need to get her a healer."

Bev turned to the other witches. "Healer!" she screamed.

"Watch out, coming through," said a familiar voice that allowed me to breathe. Bev and I looked up at Trish in her tiny warrior form. The fairy burst into full size and dropped down on Mavis's other side. She did a quick assessment and then slid her hands on either side of Mavis's head and sent magic into the wound, a soft green glow lighting the chaotic night.

Three demons tried to get past Ferral and get to us. They were quickly wrapped up in a thick wave of magic and lifted into the air, screaming as the magic cut them in half.

I turned to the witches and nodded my thanks.

Wilhelmina Marks, a.k.a. Willy waved at me and went back to her spell work. Her fellow witch, Pietra, gave me a worried smile.

"Is she going to make it?" I asked Trish.

The fairy spared me a quick look but didn't respond. She bent closer, the soft glow around Mavis's head deepening to dark green, spitting wildly as the intensity increased. Minutes passed like hours. Our hands tightly clasped, Bev and I were oblivious to the battle around us, our tense gazes locked on the woman struggling for life before us. Trish never faltered. Though, by the paleness of her skin I knew she was exhausting herself. Finally, Mavis's cheeks started to gain color, only a faint blush at first, and then turning a pale pink. But she was so quiet. So still.

"Trish?" I asked, worry making it hard to breathe.

"Give her a minute," the fairy said, her tone not unkind.

Mavis's eyelids fluttered, and then she moaned, her fingers twitching as Trish sat back on her heels. The fairy looked totally worn out from the healing. "She needs fluids and rest."

"She's going to be okay?" Bev asked, her voice filled with hope.

Trish gave her a pitying look. "I hope so. She needs time."

I fought despair and forced myself to thank the fairy. "I'll never be able to repay you..."

She held up a hand. "You owe me nothing. Except, maybe a chance to apologize? When this is over.

I nodded and squeezed her small hand in mine.

As I tried to decide what to do next, a pair of thick goat legs with cloven hooves appeared behind Trish. We all looked up, and up, into Matthew's welcome face. I smiled. He gave me a strange grin that looked bizarre in his triangular devil face. "Matthew. You're back."

He jerked a head toward the slit, which might have looked smaller than it had before. "Is that shrinking?" I asked.

"The crone is closing it. She sent the Iggloc back so the breach has lost its focus magic."

I nodded, feeling so tired.

"Madam Lares. May I have the honor of taking the witch Mavis to your home where she will be safe?" the lost one asked with a bow.

I nodded, feeling such a wave of gratitude that tears slid from my eyes. "Yes. Thank you. Will you stay and watch over her?"

He inclined his head. "It would be my honor."

I watched as he carefully scooped Mavis up and started running, so fast he was little more than a blur on the air.

Bev stood and helped me up. I looked around and saw that, while we'd worried about Mavis. My friends and allies had gotten things well in hand. Only a few dozen demons remained, and many of those were making a break toward the quickly closing breach. But there was one person missing. And it was a very special person. I grabbed Bev's arm. "Have you seen Gren?" She spun where she stood, looking all around and frowning. "When was the last time you saw him?"

I remembered watching him go down. Overwhelmed and unable to fight back. It had been too many demons for even Gren to handle. My stomach twisted with fear. "I have to find him."

I took off toward the spot where I'd last seen him. He'd been near the breach, mere feet away from the sizzling slash in the air.

I found one of his blades sticking out of a nasty-looking demon with tentacles instead of arms. I yanked it out, wiped it off on the dead beast's clothes, and moved on. There was a pile of demons where Gren had been standing, but no Gren. I took that as a good sign and kept looking.

I was five feet away from the breach when I heard his voice.

"Aggy!" I spun around and grinned when I saw him. He looked a little beat up, a little bloody, but he was coming for me with strong, ground-eating strides.

I started toward him, a relieved smile on my face.

"Hello, Madam Lares."

I turned to the woman standing in front of the breach. I wasn't sure if she'd come through it, or walked across the battle ground. "Hello." I frowned. "Do I know you?"

With long, straight black hair and eyes of such dark brown they looked black too, she seemed familiar.

Then it finally hit me. It was the woman in the grave-yard. The one who used to bring her daughter to the church where I lived. But something was wrong. She was flesh and bone, where before she'd appeared to be a spirit. "How are you here?"

She smiled. "It's a long story. I'll tell you later. But right now, there's someone who needs to see you." Before I realized what she was going to do, she wrapped the long fingers of her right hand around my arm and yanked.

Gren's blade fell from my hand as the world shifted, grayed out, and turned backwards. Suddenly I was looking through the breach *to* my yard instead of through the breach *from* my yard. My tired brain took a frustrating moment to accept the change and understand it. When I finally did, I looked around, horror filling me as I found myself inside the spectral realm again.

"Aggy!" Gren called, his voice filled with fear.

I could see him through the quickly shrinking breach, but he seemed to be searching for me.

"He can't see you," the woman holding my arm said. "The breach looks closed to them. It will be closed soon enough anyway." She shrugged.

"No." I tried to yank my arm from her grip.

She held on, her hold reinforced...I realized...with magic. "Uh, uh. You need to stay here. He wants to talk to you."

"He who?" But I knew. Terror turned my spine to ice. I knew who *he* was. And all I wanted to do was run.

I jammed a hand into my pocket and found my staff missing. I must have lost it during the battle somewhere.

"Hello, Madam Lares. We finally meet face-to-face."

I reluctantly turned my gaze toward the enormous devil I'd spoken to only in visions. The sight of him alive and real turned my gut to ice. He was standing there, flesh and blood. And I was going to die. But I forced a calm expression onto my face and simply said, "Commander."

27

AND IN THE FIGHT A CLARITY FOUND

The demon smiled and I shuddered at the sight. "I'm so glad to have you with me at last," he said. "We have much to...*discuss.*"

"Please tell me you didn't do all this just to get hold of me?"

"I won't tell you that. It's not completely true after all. This was simply a dry run for a much larger event. I think you'll enjoy watching it unfold." His smile oozed oily evil. "If you're still alive."

Fighting to keep my expression neutral, I skimmed my jailer a look, taking a chance. "What do you think Wanda would say if she knew what you were doing?"

Willow blinked rapidly, seemingly shocked by my question. Or that I knew who she was. "Stop talking. I'll ask the questions. Where is the gem?"

"The gem?" I feigned confusion. "Why do you need that?"

She snorted. "Surely even you can figure that out."

Unfortunately, I could. If they had the gem they could come and go to the earthly realm anytime they wanted. "I don't know what you're talking about." I leaned close, speaking into Willow's face. "She's in danger, you know. Because of you."

Willow's grip on my arm tightened. "I said, shut up!"

"Willow, get yourself under control." The Commander's voice was a growl.

She made a visible effort to regain her calm.

I wasn't going to let that happen. "She'll hate you for this. She's been sad about you going missing, you know. But this will kill any feelings of love she has for you."

"Shut! Up!" She slapped my face hard enough to make me stumble. I used my falling weight as leverage to wrench my arm free. As soon as I hit the ground, I yanked energy into my hands and launched myself at her, slamming my palms against her chest. Willow jerked and twitched, her eyes rolling back as my power flowed into her.

"Enough!" The Commander wrapped his claws around my arm and yanked me away from his minion. Willow crumpled to the ground, still twitching. I tried to slap him with energy and earned myself a clawed slap that ripped the flesh of my cheek and jaw. I hit the ground, rolled, and tried to climb back to my feet.

He laughed, easily plucking me off the ground. "Time to go to your new home. I think you'll love it. There are lots of rooms where we can play." The demon made a thoughtful face. "Although, to be honest, I'm not sure you're going to enjoy it as much as I will."

My thoughts spun, searching for ways to delay the inevitable. "I thought you wanted the gem," I said. "I can get it for you. But I need to go back to my house." With any luck, we'd never make it that far. Gren and the rest of my council were out there, on the other side of the quickly-closing breach. They were looking for me and would be ready for trouble.

"You don't really believe I'm that stupid do you? I don't need the gem. When I'm ready to come back here, I'll have lots of leverage." He slid a smug, speculative look over me, from stem to stern. The look left me feeling soiled and more than a little terrified.

The breach spit and sizzled, drawing the Commander's attention to the woman who walked through it. Layla stood inside the breach, her devilish form in place. She held herself straight and proud, her manner screaming of royal birth. "Hello, Father."

I wasn't sure which of us was more surprised, the Commander or me.

A quick look from Layla reminded me the element of surprise worked in both of our favors. We needed to make full use of it.

I settled my feet, putting my weight in my toes, and waited.

"Daughter. What a nice surprise. Have you finally come to take your place by my side?"

The thought must have been horrifying to my friend. Her devilish image wavered for a beat before sharpening again. "I've come to trade myself for the Lares. I was the one who stopped the Hellmouth from opening completely. I'm the one you want."

I was pretty sure Layla shrank into herself a little more with each word. My heart broke for her, and I couldn't let her give herself over to the demonic creature who'd let thousands of his people die just to get something he wanted.

"No, Layla. I'm not going to let you do this."

She gave me an angry look. "You don't control me, Lares." Her tone was so bitter, I almost believed she hated me. She lifted her gaze to the Commander. "Let her go and I'll stay."

He seemed to be considering her offer. I glared at Layla, letting my eyes tell her what I couldn't say out loud.

Her gaze flicked slightly. Not much. I only noticed because I was staring closely at her. Suddenly, her devilish form blinked away and human Layla was left standing there.

The Commander sucked in a quick, surprised breath.

"Did I forget to tell you? This is the real me now. This is what your Hellmouth did to me." Without warning, her hand came up and she screamed, "Down!"

I dove as best I could, the devil's clawed grip digging deep into the tender flesh of my forearm. Layla's blade hit true, burying itself to the hilt in his chest. But he barely seemed to notice. He was too powerful to be downed by a single blade.

I grabbed hold of my power and slammed it against the arm holding me there, infusing him with deadly levels of pure energy. His eyes widened and his body twitched under the magic's impact, but even that wasn't enough to kill the demon.

There was a quick flash of movement behind him and instinct had me ducking.

Light flared off a silver blade as it swung toward the Commander's neck...and then nothing. My heart thumping wildly in the silence, despair overcame me as I realized the blade wielder had missed. Or had he?

A slender line of black oozed across the Commander's throat and his head skewed sideways, before sliding slowly off and hitting the ground with a gruesome crunch.

As the demon's body crumpled to the ground, it revealed Glenn and Reverend Dodson, both grinning widely.

"Come on, Aggy," Layla said. "The crone can't hold this open for much longer."

I hurried forward, pausing only briefly to consider Willow, draped across the gray, rocky ground. I gave brief consideration to bringing her out with me, and then decided my favorite teen already had one too many bad parents. She didn't need a another one.

I stepped through the breach and turned, happy to see the Rev and Glenn stepping through with me. Then, with a high-pitched twanging sound, the breach snapped closed and the assorted warriors gave a hearty, if weary, cheer.

AN UNSEASONABLY WARM breeze carried the sweet smell of flowers across the graveyard. My team and I had spent several days repairing the grounds and the grave markers from the demons' deadly breach. Happily, the Rev had been part of the effort, helping us match bodies with markers where stones had been obliterated or blown away.

Niele had directed repairs and added a few very nice improvements, such as the stone bench I was currently sitting on with Monty and Wraith. The big, black cat was sprawled belly up across my lap, purring, and Monty was lying next to me, his entire demeanor droopy.

I stared at the starry night sky and sighed. The world was quiet and peaceful. Too quiet. Too peaceful. It made me sad, like Monty

I'd come out there to collect my thoughts about Layla. Her revelation that the Commander was her real father explained the tension and heartache that had made her come to the human realm, leaving behind a family situation that likely was very painful. I didn't know if her pain had been physical as well as emotional, but I suspected from some of her statements that it might have been. One day I would ask her about it so I could understand. Maybe talking about it with me would help her heal. Maybe not. But I'd offer a shoulder to lean on. It would be up to her if she accepted it.

"I see Wraith approves of the new furniture."

I glanced up and smiled as Trish settled next to me. The bench was located beneath an oak tree near the graveyard. I'd requested it be large enough for at least three people because even if I had no human-shaped friends with me, I never traveled far without my little dog and, lately, the big black cat.

Lifting his head just long enough to swipe a tongue over Trish's nose as she bent down to kiss him, Monty immediately dropped his head back to his paws with a sad sigh.

Trish scratched his ears. "How's he doing?"

I shrugged. "He's miserable. If I didn't miss her so much myself, I'd be jealous that he loves her more than me."

Trish nodded and tickled Wraith's belly. The cat gave a playful growl and clamped Trish's hand between her teeth. The feline's tail snapped a few times and then she batted the fairy on her jeans-clad knee.

"She'll come back," Trish said. "If she doesn't, we'll go after her."

"I'm afraid she won't come back because of Bathos. He's made a move to force her to live with him until she's an adult. He's not the sort to give up on something once he's set his mind to it."

Trish nodded. "Have you spoken to Caleigh?"

I knew why she was asking. If Wanda wanted to go somewhere her father couldn't get to her, any of the crone's well-hidden homes would be good choices. "Caleigh claims she hasn't seen the kid, but I suspect she has. She was just too calm and disinterested the last time I spoke to her."

I didn't tell my friend about the passage in the old history book Wanda had left for me to read. Marked with a receipt for Monty's dog food so I'd be sure to know it was for me, the passage read simply, "*There shall come a time when the magic requires the keepers of history to coalesce and embrace its arts together. For if the one who professes the ultimate power in wielding her talents does not teach others of her skill, what earthly good is it to the world? One expert is a very nice thing to have at cocktail parties. But two or even three experts can the world save if they are so inclined.*"

My lips curved upward.

Trish cocked her head. "You seem calm too."

"I am, strangely. If she's with the crone she's happy." I smiled a secret smile. "And, if I just happen to drop by and visit the old witch in the next day or so..." I shrugged.

Trish laughed. "Great idea. What's going to be your excuse?"

"I don't know. Monty's sad. He needs a play date with Lavern and Shirley for his emotional health." That was the reason I would give the crone and my teen when I saw them. But there was another, more important reason. I needed to talk to Wanda about Willow. While I was relieved beyond measure that the kid hadn't intervened at the battle as Bathos had predicted. I had no doubt she'd been nearby. She would know that I had attacked Willow. For all I knew, I'd killed her. And Wanda needed to know exactly what had transpired to bring about that outcome. My chest hurt at the thought. It was possible the kid of my heart would never forgive me for what I'd done. It was equally possible she'd hate me. But I knew I had to take that risk. Because she had a right to know.

Trish and I fell into silence, staring out over the beautiful property my groundskeeper had made for me. It had been a week since the battle and my final seating phase drama hadn't recurred. There'd been no more crushing pain. No menopause-type symptoms. I'd had a few low-level visions and even more mental requests which felt a little too much like prayers for my comfort. I'd also learned that I needed a shut-off valve in my brain for those times when more than a couple of my people reached out to me at once. It had only taken one episode with a dozen people talking in my mind at once to convince me of that.

My advocate was currently helping me with a block, making the process as painful as possible in his usual way.

On a happier front, Trish was back with us. Mostly. She still had duties in Fairy as they prepared for Nova's coronation as king, but she managed to escape for an hour or so every day and had used the time to move my bathroom project forward. And eat copious amounts of Tilly's baking.

Life was beautiful. Mostly.

Layla had stopped by to tell me her little sister was staying with her for the foreseeable future, which seemed to make her very happy. The two of them had visited a few times because Desmean had taken a liking to both Monty and Wraith. It turns out royal devils were not big on having pets. Layla had grown to appreciate the charm of having small, furry creatures underfoot and she was happy to introduce her sister to those delights.

The interactions between my fur-babies and the small princess were going well. Mostly.

There had been that one episode where Desmean had tried to take a bite out of Monty. My little dog had taken it fairly well. He hadn't bitten her, so that was good. But I was keeping a very close eye on their interactions until I was sure Desmean understood he was a companion. Not a snack.

There were negatives, of course. I missed Wanda's presence in my home. Monty was sad.

Trish patted me on the knee. "I'm going back to Fairy. Nova has called a meeting of all the elders to discuss future and much-needed changes there."

"Thanks for making time for me," I told her, meaning it. To my surprise, tears filled my eyes as she hugged me goodbye.

"My pleasure." She got a funny look on her face.

"What?" I asked. Attuned to her and her moods as if we'd been friends all our lives.

"I was wondering. When I come back here for good. Do you think I could stay with you for a while? Luke has offered to buy my house, and it will take me a while to find a new place."

I kept my expression neutral. "You know Luke expects you to stay with him." Luke and Trish were good friends. Not in a romantic way, I didn't think. But close in a platonic way.

She made a face that made me smile. "I love Luke, but he lives like an ogre. If I lived there I'd spend all my time cleaning, gagging, and disinfecting."

I nodded, still grinning. "Well, you know dogs. They eat dirt and stuff. No concept of proper hygiene."

Trish barked out a laugh. "Exactly."

"I'd love to have you here. As long as you want. I'd honestly enjoy the company." I looked away as tears threatened, mentally slapping myself silly. I'd never been a crier, yet, since *Response* had ground itself into my bones, literally, I was always weeping about something. "The house is way too quiet these days. What will you do with your dogs?"

"Luke will keep them for me until I find a house with enough yard for them." Trish's expression softened with relief. "And, if you want noise, I can definitely take care of that."

I laughed with her. "What have I done?"

"Good question. I should probably tell you that I play loud rock music when I cook, or clean, or shower, or..."

"Got it. As long as it's rock music I like, I'm okay with that." Mostly.

Trish hadn't made it to the house before I heard the fluttering of small wings and the chirping of my friend in the belfry. To my shock, Batty settled onto a branch above my head, hanging upside down as her eyes glowed yellow through the dark. *The child is safe.*

Relief swept through me as my hopes were verified. I'd wanted to ask Bathilda about Wanda, knowing the two were strangely close, but I hadn't thought the magical bat would tell me anything. "That's a relief." I let silence fall between us for a beat. Batty honored the silence, an unmoving outline hanging from the branch. Finally, I said, softly so as not to disturb the bat if she was asleep, "I miss her so much."

The bat didn't respond. I sighed. A cool breeze sifted over me and I shivered. Regrettably, a cold front was supposed to come through Rome overnight and the weather gurus on the news were predicting snow.

Ugh. Even as I lamented the change of weather, I realized we'd already gotten more fall than was normal. Winter often came late in Indiana. Though it usually overstayed its welcome in the spring to make up for it.

I sighed, thinking about going inside.

The door to the house opened and closed softly, and a familiar tall form strode across the grass toward me, setting my heart to pounding and my stomach to fluttering with anticipation.

Gren stopped in front of me and leaned down, cupping my face with a large, deliciously warm hand. "Hello, lovely Aggy." His lips touched mine and heat flared between us, quickly turning to something I didn't want to ignore.

My body heated and melted toward his, which was awkward since I was still sitting and had an eighteen-pound cat on my lap. As if reading my thoughts, Wraith gave an irritated yowl and jumped down, trotting toward the grave-yard with her tail snapping angrily behind her.

Gren broke the kiss. His perfect lips curved upward in the corners. "Are you aware that Trish finished installing your clawfoot tub today?"

My eyes went wide with delight. "She did?"

He grabbed my hands and pulled me to my feet. "It's smaller than I expected, but I believe we could both fit in it if we press very close together."

My heart sang at the thought. "It would be a hardship..." I said, pretending to consider it.

He dropped an arm around my waist and led me back the way he'd come. "There's nobody here. Even your mother went home. I believe she had a date with the commendable Chief Marshal."

My pulse spiked at the feel of his hard muscles against my soft curves. "Good for her."

"I am very happy for her," Gren said. "But I am even happier for us." He pulled my hand to his lips and set the skin on fire with a lingering kiss. "It has been too long since we have been alone."

"It hasn't been that long," I said, a little coyly. Even though I knew it was a lie. "Only last week you helped me catch that bull snake and relocate it to the woods."

He arched a dark brow and I had to bite back a giggle. "That is not the kind of *alone* I was referring to, minx."

I loved when he called me that. He'd started using the term recently and the old-fashioned-ness of it reminded me that he'd lived a very long time and had many experiences I couldn't share. I was okay with that. Mostly. As long as any future experiences he had were with me. "I've decided," I said in a very serious tone.

"Do tell," he said as we stepped onto the patio stones.

"I will allow you to squash me into the tub with you if there are brownies and wine involved."

"You drive a hard bargain," he said on a laugh. "But I think that can be arranged."

Aggy?

I jolted to a stop and glanced back at the flying rodent hanging from the tree. I wasn't sure the bat had ever addressed me by name. It was a bit disconcerting. *Yes?*

Batty hesitated for a moment as if she wasn't sure she wanted to tell me what was on her mind. Finally, she said. *I miss her too.*

And I knew that was the goddesses honest truth.

I smiled.

Oh, and Aggy?

I nearly fell over from shock that she was still speaking to me. "Yes, Batty?"

Gren's dark eyebrows rose.

I'm totally making a ring out of this enormous red gem the angel gave me.

If she reacted to my bark of laughter, I wouldn't know. I was already headed inside with my favorite angel. And we had a clawfoot tub to christen.

The End

DON'T MISS OUT

Stay up on all Sam's news by joining her newsletter, and get a copy of a fun mystery just for signing up!

SIGN UP HERE!
https://samcheever.com/newsletter/

READ MORE MATURE MAGIC

If you enjoyed **What Spookery Is That?** you might want to check out the rest of the series: https://samcheever.com/books/#maturemagic

Enjoy this taste of Book 6 **What Treachery Is This?**:

Live ho the wicked old witch...the wicked old witch...the wicked old witch. Live hale the wicked old witch...Ye'll surely mourn her death.

The last person anybody ever expected to get into trouble was the crone. I'd believed she was pretty much bomb proof. I mean, who in their right mind would go after a two-thousand-year-old witch who was also a magical historian? The problem was, I didn't know what took her down. But something did. Whatever it was, it left her hovering on the razor edge of death.

If I don't kick it into gear and go after her attacker, the old witch's present condition could become permanent. And then I'd have a grieving teen to deal with. As well as an extremely irritated magical horse.

WHAT TREACHERY IS THIS?

A Messenger Both Fair and Fierce

Hooves thundered across hard, veiny earth, the sound echoing inside a broad white chest in overtaxed heartbeats, and the rhythm of enormous, straining lungs. Wild brown eyes rolled and flashed, foam flecking a silky nose, the nostrils flaring with effort. Overhead, an endless umbrella of ancient trees bent protectively over the messenger, their intent driven by an ancient magic whose dark portent flailed insistent urgings upon their rough skins as the messenger passed. The glossy leaves of the guardian trees were still and silent, despite a roiling pulse of rage and an even angrier wind.

My skin was clammy. My pillow damp and rumpled. Inside my chest the thunder of the creature's approaching hooves framed my own heartbeats. I twisted beneath the blankets, sweaty hands shoving at covers that felt more like a prison cell than protection against the cool early-fall night.

The sky I could barely see between the over-arching bulk of the protective trees was dark...dangerous...and fully embroiled in a rage-filled magic that tore through the midnight landscape.

Dark, reverberating screams ripped from a hoarse throat. Tear-filled eyes glossy with horror. A world ripped asunder by chaotic magic that recognized the loss of one of its own.

Tumultuous and frenzied with fear.

But it was the high-pitched scream of a single clear voice that reached me through the unruly, broken magic and wrenched me, drenched and frantic, from a fitful sleep.

Wanda!

I sat bolt upright in my bed, knowing I'd experienced a supernova of a *Response* vision.

Monty jerked to his feet as I cried out, frantically bathing my arm with kisses. I shoved shoulder-length black hair off my face with a shaky hand and gulped air as if I'd been suffocating a moment earlier. "I'm okay, buddy." I glanced over at Gren's side of the bed and found him missing. With a small sound of alarm, I wrenched the covers back and started to run.

As I ran, I determined the locations of each of my council members in the space of a single thought. In the next breath, I sent each of them a call to gather. I was vaguely aware of Monty flying through the house with me. When I opened the door, he squeezed past me into the darkness, running toward the tall form standing in the yard,

Gren's gaze was locked on the magical woods at the back of the property. He didn't turn as I let the mudroom door slam behind me. Even the oversized, yellow-eyed bat fluttering above his head didn't cause him to look up. My angel's stark, worried gaze was focused on the horizon. A horizon which roiled with black clouds, speared occasionally by the silver spurs of a waxing gibbous moon.

I lay a hand on his bare shoulder as I came up to him. To my surprise, his warm skin trembled slightly beneath my touch. "Gren?"

He finally looked at me. "What did you see?"

"The White Mare. She's coming with a message." I shivered as I remembered the dream vision. "I don't think the message is a good one." I chewed the inside of my bottom lip. "It's not Wanda. It can't be Wanda."

Gren looped a heavy arm around my shoulders and pulled me close, his lips touching my

forehead. "Let's not jump to conclusions."

A slight form burst from the woods and ran toward us. The man's leanly muscular frame moved effortlessly, bare feet forming moist footprints in the glistening grass.

I watched him come, my lips trying to curl with disgust.

When Bathos slowed to a walk twenty feet away, he wasn't even panting. "Is it the girl?"

The demon was only five feet eight inches tall, but he carried himself as if he were much larger. He had black eyes and glossy black hair and the face of an angel. A fallen angel. He was also Wanda's father, a man who didn't deserve to know what was going on with the teen, since it was his threat to take her away from me that had caused her to run.

Gren's arm tightened around my shoulders. He said, "We don't know yet. The Mare is coming."

The White Mare was a powerful magical creature. she was a loyal companion to the crone, but the old witch didn't own the stunning creature any more than I did. Though I'd felt a connection with the horse since the first time I'd laid eyes on her. The Mare was also a vessel. She could freely pass through the veil and transport her riders from one world to another. That trait made her both handy and dangerous...depending on your perspective.

It was the reason the crone had made it a habit to send the elegant creature to me when there was news I needed quickly.

A low, eerie howl split the night, followed by another, different kind of howl. A moment later, two long, muscular shapes, enormous in the fractured moonlight, loped across my lawn.

The giant moon hound shifted in a burst of silver light without losing a stride. Sir Ferral of the Guardian Assembly, otherwise known as my Advocate, strode up to Gren and me with the usual glower firmly affixed to his handsome face. Even freshly shifted from his moon hound form, Ferral's chin-length, wavy blond hair, square jaw, and piercing dark silver gaze still made him look like a character from the cover of a romance novel. "What's happened?"

"We don't know yet," Gren said, saving me from having to deal with Mister Happy when he was still feeling—shall we say—a bit growly. "We're waiting for the Mare." Ferral opened his mouth and Gren cut him off with a raised hand. "As far as we know, Wanda is fine."

Ferral's mouth snapped shut with a click of teeth and he nodded.

Behind him, the enormous wolf with the bright golden eyes lay down on the grass. Luke had chosen not to shift back, so he could snap and snarl at Bathos.

The demon simply rolled his eyes at the spectacle of enormous white teeth. It was no wonder. As the keeper of a prison for monsters, Bathos had likely seen and dealt with much worse than my intimidating but rational council member who was currently shaped like a wolf.

Behind me the door creaked open and closed with a quiet thump as the family of my heart, who were also two of my council members walked arm and arm toward our little group.

My sister's delicate features were tense, her thick mane of blonde hair, recently cut into a cute pageboy style, flew around her face with wild abandon, the glossy strands catching the moonlight and sparking with silver flame. "What's wrong? What happened? Are you okay? Monty?" She looked frantically around for my little man, finding him sitting at the base of the largest tombstone in our little graveyard, staring hopefully up at an annoyed black cat.

She relaxed as Wraith narrowed her round yellow eyes on him and swatted half-heartedly in his direction, hissing.

Mavis gave me a hug, looking up at me with worry etched in the corners of her pale gray eyes. I wrapped an arm around the mother of my heart, who'd recently turned sixty-three, but looked and acted twenty years younger with her peaches and cream complexion and strong constitution. "We're waiting for the Mare," I said responding to both of them.

Mavis patted my back and stepped away. "Good. As long as it's not Wanda."

Monty barked a greeting to someone, and we all turned to find Reverend Dodson rising from the ground beneath the tombstone. The sight of him made my shoulders soften, pleasure at knowing we had him back home again making me temporarily forget my worry.

He strode toward us instead of floating, his slender, six-foot-tall form looking as solid as I'd ever seen it. Something about his visit to the spectral plane had amped up his ghost mojo, until he was almost as corporeal a presence as any of my other council members.

He smiled when he saw my face, his hands coming out to clasp mine.

I noticed Wraith and Monty had followed him from the graveyard, something they never used to do.

"Aggy, my dear. How are you?"

I pulled him into a hug, noting the cold but no longer painfully icy aura surrounding him. It wasn't entirely unpleasant. "I'm better every time I see you here with us again."

His smile widened. He looked around and shared the smile with my council. "Is everyone here?"

I shook my head. "Trish is on king-training duty this week. She'll be late." The Unseelie Fairy court had recently lost its queen and Trish had found them a new one...well, actually a king...whom she'd been helping get up to speed for the last couple of months. It hadn't been easy. There had been many challenges, not the least of which was the fact that future King Nova had been a prince of the Seelie court, a distinction that didn't endear him to members of the Unseelie court. "And Niele is reading the roots," I added.

When everyone looked at me as if I had two heads, I shrugged. "Don't ask me what that means. He explained it but it made no sense." As a gnome, Niele spent much of his time beneath the soil, tending to things I only understood on the most basic, surface level. I knew that he and his many cousins and family members kept the very core of the earth's foundation solid and secure, but all I really understood was that he made my yard look spectacular in the spring and summer.

"Shall I tell you what I know now?" Reverend Dodson asked.

"Yes. I'll fill the others in when they get here."

"Well, it's good news," he said. "Of a sort. There are no new deaths reported in the crone's home world." He grimaced. "No humanoid deaths. It is my understanding that one of those nasty monsters of hers was killed. Grisly story."

I nodded, not inclined to feel bad about one of the crone's Leviathan being killed. The nasty creatures had nearly eaten all of us when we'd traveled to speak to the ancient witch the previous year.

The Rev's kind brown eyes found Bathos and the ghost twitched, the instinctive movement almost imperceptible. He'd had to fight a lot of demons when he'd been on the spectral plane. I figured he probably had a good case of demonic PTSD from the experience. But he forced himself to speak kindly. "Your daughter is well. The summons has nothing to do with her."

Bathos's cold black gaze narrowed slightly, and he inclined his head. "Thank you for telling me."

The Rev nodded.

"So, the crone is okay too?" I asked. I suddenly felt as if a shoe was in the midst of dropping even as I retrieved the one that had already hit the floor.

The Rev's smile wavered and died. His lean, heavily creased face folded into an unhappy mask. "Unfortunately, I cannot confirm that. I can only tell you that no one has entered the spectral plane from that world. And my spies can attest to the young historian's well-being."

His words pulled a weight from my shoulders and I took a deep breath, releasing it slowly. Some of the tension fell away from my neck and shoulders and I managed a small smile when I looked up at Gren. "She's okay."

He lowered his head and touched his lips to mine. "Yes, beautiful Aggy. That's great news."

Without warning, the ground between where we stood and the woods erupted in a geyser of dirt, rock, and vegetation and Niele flew out of the eruption. The gnome's small black eyes shone with an alarmed light and his thick features were formed into a frown. He shook himself slightly, clumps of dirt and rock sifting from his wild silver hair, and strode in my direction.

I'd like to think that I was past the shock of dealing with a naked gnome in my yard, but honesty compelled me to admit to myself that I wasn't. I kept my gaze determinedly on his face as he rushed toward us, stick and berries bouncing.

Okay, I tried to keep my gaze on his face, but peripheral vision is a witch.

"Madam Lares," Niele said, stopping in front of me and bowing—an annoying habit he'd picked up since I'd come fully into my guardianship. "The vessel is nearly here. She should emerge from the Mystical Wood in five..."

An equine scream rent the air and the sleek form of the White Mare burst from the trees, thundering toward us.

"Um...now," Niele finished with a grimace. Timing had never been one of his best things.

"Thanks, gnome," I said, grinning in an attempt to tease him out of the "ruler and subject" mentality that I hated more than cooked spinach.

He fell in behind the group, thankfully putting his dusty nakedness behind me, and I stepped forward. I held out a hand, palm up, to the now-trotting horse, hoping to soothe her fevered state. Heat and pale green light bathed my palm and, when it was gone, a fat, shiny apple rested there.

I glanced up as Trish buzzed toward me and popped into full size in another spray of magic. "Sorry I'm late."

I reached out and squeezed her arm. "Thanks for the apple. Is everything okay at court?"

She made a face. "Nova's great. Everything else sucks earthworms."

I grimaced at the thought. As it had a dozen times since we'd returned from the spectral plane, my curiosity flared about the two fairies. Was Trish falling for the handsome Nova, future king of Unseelie? Or were they just friends? I made a mental note to chat with Trish about it as soon as I had the chance.

The mare halted two feet away from me and stretched her glossy neck to snuffle my palm. She blew a couple of gusts of hot breath over my face to help her breathing return to normal. After a moment, the sleek animal began taking dainty bites from the apple as her sides rose and fell from her run. I smoothed my free hand over the mare's velvety nose. "Hello, beauty. It's good to see you again. Do you have news for me?"

"Caw!" The bird's call was louder than usual in the quiet of the night, and sounded strident even to me. I looked up at the big raven winging his way toward me and had a brief moment of déjà vu, remembering a time we'd been attacked in that very spot by hundreds of the birds, making it hard to choose friend from foe.

But the raven in front of me was definitely a friend. Ray came to a clumsy landing on my shoulder, one wing smacking me in the face as he fought for purchase and a claw slashing painfully across my skin.

"Pee!" the big black bird informed me as soon as he was settled.

Bev chuckled. "That never gets old, does it?"

Throwing my sister a glare, I wiped my slobbery, apple-juice-coated hand on my nightgown and stepped up to the mare. Leaning close, I pressed my forehead to her lowered head. I wasn't prepared for what happened next as the magic blasted into me, nearly sending me to my butt on the dewy grass.

Get What Treachery Is This?

ABOUT THE AUTHOR

USA Today and Wall Street Journal Bestselling Author Sam Cheever writes mystery and suspense, creating stories that draw you in and keep you eagerly turning pages. Known for writing great characters, snappy dialogue, and unique and exhilarating stories, Sam is the award-winning author of 100+ books.

To learn more about Sam and her work, visit her at one of her online hotspots:
www.samcheever.com
samcheever@samcheever.com

ALSO BY SAM CHEEVER

If you enjoyed **What Spookery is That?**, you might also enjoy these other fun series by Sam. To find out more, visit the **BOOKS** page at www.samcheever.com:

Mature Magic Paranormal Women's Fiction

(for more fun adventures with Aggy and Monty!)

Enchanting Inquiries Paranormal Cozy Mysteries

Yesterday's Paranormal Mysteries

Reluctant Familiar Paranormal Mysteries

Country Cousin Mysteries

Silver Hills Cozy Mysteries

Gainfully Employed Mysteries

Honeybun Heat Series